One

Sixteen-year-old Jessica Wakefield burst through the bathroom that connected her bedroom to her twin sister, Elizabeth's, room. "I've finally achieved it!" she announced dramatically.

Elizabeth stopped towel-drying her shoulder-length blond hair. Her blue-green eyes sparkled with curiosity. "Achieved what?"

Tossing her head, Jessica struck a glamorous, cover-girl pose in front of the full-length mirror on Elizabeth's door. "The perfect tan," she replied. She pirouetted, displaying her smooth, sun-bronzed skin from every angle; she was wearing a bikini, so there was lots of it showing.

Elizabeth burst out laughing. "What a breakthrough—it's bound to make the evening news," she joked. "Really, Jess. 'I've finally achieved it'—you made it sound so momentous, like you'd discovered a cure for cancer or climbed Mount Everest or something!"

"It just so happens that a perfect tan is *my* personal Mount Everest," Jessica informed her sister. She extended one slim leg so she could admire its even, golden tone. "Everyone sets a different goal."

"You can say that again!" Elizabeth agreed.

Jessica bounced back into the bathroom to take a shower. Facing the small mirror over her dresser, Elizabeth drew a comb through her damp hair. A smile played over her face. While Jessica dreamed of the perfect Southern California suntan, Elizabeth's own ambition was to become a famous writer someday: a journalist or a poet, or maybe both.

Elizabeth couldn't believe that some people—people who didn't know the twins well—actually had a hard time telling her and Jessica apart. True, the Wakefields were identical twins. They were the same height and shape—five foot six and slender—with silky, sun-streaked blond hair, eyes the color of the Pacific Ocean, and matching dimples in their left cheeks.

Elizabeth couldn't hold her tongue—she didn't even try. "Gee, Jess," she said sarcastically. "Did it ever occur to you that somebody else—*me*, for example—might want the Prom Queen title and the trip?"

"Liz, you're just *not* the Jungle Prom Queen type," Jessica stated, obviously feeling it wasn't open for debate. "Prom Queen is my kind of thing! *I* love being in the spotlight, and *you* love making things happen backstage."

"Well, for your information, you're dead wrong," Elizabeth shouted. "I'm sick of you and everybody else taking me for granted. You always get what you want, don't you, Jess? No matter how many people you have to trample over to get it!"

Jessica looked puzzled. "I get what I deserve," she told Elizabeth calmly. "It's not *my* fault everybody automatically thinks of me when it comes to things like picking a Prom Queen. You might as well give up any ridiculous idea you might have about becoming Prom Queen yourself."

"You mean *you* might as well give up the idea," Elizabeth countered. "It's my turn, Jessica. *I'm* going to be Prom Queen!"

Hands on their hips, the two sisters glared at each other, neither one willing to give an inch. It looked like they were in for an all-out, no-holds-barred battle for the Queen's crown—and the grand prize.

This is it, Elizabeth thought, gritting her teeth. *I'm not backing down and neither is she!*

Bantam Books in the Sweet Valley High series
Ask your bookseller for the books you have missed

#1 DOUBLE LOVE
#2 SECRETS
#3 PLAYING WITH FIRE
#4 POWER PLAY
#5 ALL NIGHT LONG
#6 DANGEROUS LOVE
#7 DEAR SISTER
#8 HEARTBREAKER
#9 RACING HEARTS
#10 WRONG KIND OF GIRL
#11 TOO GOOD TO BE TRUE
#12 WHEN LOVE DIES
#13 KIDNAPPED!
#14 DECEPTIONS
#15 PROMISES
#16 RAGS TO RICHES
#17 LOVE LETTERS
#18 HEAD OVER HEELS
#19 SHOWDOWN
#20 CRASH LANDING!
#21 RUNAWAY
#22 TOO MUCH IN LOVE
#23 SAY GOODBYE
#24 MEMORIES
#25 NOWHERE TO RUN
#26 HOSTAGE
#27 LOVESTRUCK
#28 ALONE IN THE CROWD
#29 BITTER RIVALS
#30 JEALOUS LIES
#31 TAKING SIDES
#32 THE NEW JESSICA
#33 STARTING OVER
#34 FORBIDDEN LOVE
#35 OUT OF CONTROL
#36 LAST CHANCE
#37 RUMORS
#38 LEAVING HOME
#39 SECRET ADMIRER
#40 ON THE EDGE
#41 OUTCAST
#42 CAUGHT IN THE MIDDLE
#43 HARD CHOICES
#44 PRETENSES
#45 FAMILY SECRETS
#46 DECISIONS
#47 TROUBLEMAKER
#48 SLAM BOOK FEVER
#49 PLAYING FOR KEEPS
#50 OUT OF REACH
#51 AGAINST THE ODDS
#52 WHITE LIES
#53 SECOND CHANCE
#54 TWO-BOY WEEKEND
#55 PERFECT SHOT
#56 LOST AT SEA
#57 TEACHER CRUSH
#58 BROKENHEARTED
#59 IN LOVE AGAIN
#60 THAT FATAL NIGHT
#61 BOY TROUBLE
#62 WHO'S WHO?
#63 THE NEW ELIZABETH
#64 THE GHOST OF TRICIA MARTIN
#65 TROUBLE AT HOME
#66 WHO'S TO BLAME?
#67 THE PARENT PLOT
#68 THE LOVE BET
#69 FRIEND AGAINST FRIEND
#70 MS. QUARTERBACK
#71 STARRING JESSICA!
#72 ROCK STAR'S GIRL
#73 REGINA'S LEGACY
#74 THE PERFECT GIRL
#75 AMY'S TRUE LOVE
#76 MISS TEEN SWEET VALLEY
#77 CHEATING TO WIN
#78 THE DATING GAME
#79 THE LONG-LOST BROTHER
#80 THE GIRL THEY BOTH LOVED
#81 ROSA'S LIE
#82 KIDNAPPED BY THE CULT!
#83 STEVEN'S BRIDE
#84 THE STOLEN DIARY
#85 SOAP STAR
#86 JESSICA AGAINST BRUCE
#87 MY BEST FRIEND'S BOYFRIEND
#88 LOVE LETTERS FOR SALE
#89 ELIZABETH BETRAYED
#90 DON'T GO HOME WITH JOHN
#91 IN LOVE WITH A PRINCE
#92 SHE'S NOT WHAT SHE SEEMS
#93 STEPSISTERS
#94 ARE WE IN LOVE?

Super Editions: PERFECT SUMMER
SPECIAL CHRISTMAS
SPRING BREAK
MALIBU SUMMER
WINTER CARNIVAL
SPRING FEVER

Super Stars: LILA'S STORY
BRUCE'S STORY
ENID'S STORY
OLIVIA'S STORY
TODD'S STORY

Super Thrillers: DOUBLE JEOPARDY
ON THE RUN
NO PLACE TO HIDE
DEADLY SUMMER
MURDER ON THE LINE

Magna Editions: THE WAKEFIELDS OF SWEET VALLEY
THE WAKEFIELD LEGACY: THE UNTOLD STORY
A NIGHT TO REMEMBER

Magna Edition

A NIGHT TO REMEMBER

Written by
Kate William

Created by
FRANCINE PASCAL

BANTAM BOOKS
NEW YORK • TORONTO • LONDON • SYDNEY • AUCKLAND

RL 6, age 12 and up

A NIGHT TO REMEMBER
A Bantam Book / June 1993

Sweet Valley High® is a registered trademark of Francine Pascal
Conceived by Francine Pascal
Produced by Daniel Weiss Associates, Inc.
33 West 17th Street
New York, NY 10011
Cover art by Keith Birdsong

ISBN: 0-553-29309-5

Published simultaneously in the United States and Canada

Bantam Books are published by Bantam Books, a division of Bantam Doubleday Dell Publishing Group, Inc. Its trademark, consisting of the words "Bantam Books" and the portrayal of a rooster, is Registered in U.S. Patent and Trademark Office and in other countries. Marca Registrada. Bantam Books, 1540 Broadway, New York, New York 10036.

PRINTED IN THE UNITED STATES OF AMERICA

OPM 0 9 8 7 6 5 4 3

But their styles, not to mention their personalities, were completely different. Jessica liked funky, racy clothes; she and her friends haunted the local mall, waiting breathlessly for the latest fashions to be unveiled. Elizabeth, meanwhile, preferred a more classic look; she simply couldn't be bothered with tracking the trends.

Although probably the reason Jessica needs to shop so much is that all her clothes end up on the floor! Elizabeth speculated. Jessica's room tended to resemble an earthquake zone. There was a pyramid of clothes on her bed and another on the floor; photo albums, CDs, and a duffel bag overflowing with cheerleading gear obscured the top of her desk, ensuring that she didn't get a lot of homework done there. According to the twins' older brother, Steven, a freshman at the local university, there was only one thing in Jessica's room that she was always able to put her hand on immediately: the telephone.

In contrast, Elizabeth's bedroom, with its off-white carpeting and cream-colored walls, was neat and inviting. A rectangular table held her computer, reference books, and school supplies—that was where she did her writing. Under the window was a secondhand chaise longue she'd re-covered in soft, pale velvet—that was where she did her reading.

But for all their differences, Elizabeth and Jessica shared an incredibly close bond. *Where would I be without Jessica?* Elizabeth wondered as she smoothed body lotion on her arms and legs. Who *would I be without Jessica?*

The water in the bathroom stopped running. A moment later, Jessica peeked into Elizabeth's room again. Her body was enveloped in a fluffy blue towel; another towel was wrapped around her head turban-style. "Hope you don't mind," Jessica said. "I borrowed some of your new honeysuckle shampoo."

Elizabeth rolled her eyes. "There's no point in my minding since you already used it, is there?"

Jessica grinned. "I can always count on you to be generous, Liz. Anyway, I knew you'd want me to be fragrant and beautiful for the big party tonight!"

"Your being fragrant and beautiful is my top concern," her sister said dryly.

"I'm so excited!" Jessica gave a little hop. Her turban unwrapped, the towel tumbling from her head to the floor. "This is going to be the biggest, best beach party that Sweet Valley, California, has ever seen!"

"You may be right," said Elizabeth. "It's the only thing anyone at school's talked about all week—the beach party Saturday night."

"Thank you, thank you." Jessica took a bow. "May I remind you that I was the one who talked the junior-class officers into funding the party with money from the class treasury?"

"You're a real wheeler-dealer," Elizabeth affirmed.

Jessica stepped back into the bathroom and plugged in the hair dryer. "Yep, it'll be the best party, and I have the best date," she concluded happily.

"Whoa, hold on!" Elizabeth exclaimed. "*I* have the best date."

"No, I do," Jessica argued.

"I do!"

"I do!"

The two sisters burst out laughing. "I guess it's like Mount Everest and suntans," Elizabeth reflected. "Boyfriends are a very personal thing."

"Sam's the best for me and Todd's the best for you," Jessica agreed.

"Speaking of dates, did Lila decide to go with Tony Alimenti?"

Jessica nodded. "But not until after Amy and I twisted her arm for hours and hours. You wouldn't believe the excuses that girl came up with! She wanted to do a home facial—she had some back issues of *Sweet Sixteen* magazine to read—she couldn't miss *Tarzan the Ape Man* at nine o'clock on channel seven."

"*Tarzan the Ape Man!*" Elizabeth giggled. "I didn't know he was Lila's type."

Jessica grinned and turned on the hair dryer. "Yeah, can you see Lila swinging from a vine with some guy in a loincloth?" she shouted.

As she dressed in a pair of black cotton jersey shorts and a jade-green tank top, Elizabeth tried to picture such an outrageous scene. Jessica's best friend, Lila, was one of the wealthiest girls in Sweet Valley, and a spoiled snob in Elizabeth's private opinion, which, tactfully, she usually kept to herself.

When Jessica was done drying her hair five minutes later, Elizabeth cut through the bathroom into her sister's room.

"You know, I didn't quite succeed in picturing Lila Fowler swinging from a vine," Elizabeth admitted. "But the Tarzan-movie thing gives me an idea," she went on. "Remember talking the other day about how it's been ages since Sweet Valley High put on a really big, really fun dance?"

"Yeah," said Jessica. "We need to dream up something—something original, with a theme."

"Well . . ." Elizabeth paused dramatically, "how about a Jungle Prom?"

Jessica tipped her head to one side, considering. "Hmm."

"We could decorate the gym with vines and palm trees," Elizabeth suggested. "The posters for it could say something like, 'Come Swing at the Jungle Prom.' Get it? Vines—swing. Like Tarzan the Ape Man." She wrinkled her nose. "Or maybe that sounds stupid. Maybe the whole *idea's* stupid."

Jessica shook her head. "No, hang on. Don't give up so fast. I think it's a *great* idea!"

"You do?" Elizabeth said, pleased.

"I do." Jessica's eyes lit up with inspiration. "And how about this? How about tying it in somehow with that new environmental group in town, the one you said you'd volunteer for if you had more spare time?"

"Environmental Alert. Jessica, you're a genius!" Elizabeth exclaimed.

"I've often thought so," Jessica said modestly. Elizabeth bounced onto Jessica's bed, shoving a pile of clean laundry out of the way. "We could recreate a rain forest in the gym and the prom could be a fund-raiser," she said, brainstorming. "Jessica, I think we've really hit on something!"

Jessica grinned. "Boy, when we Wakefields put our heads together, there's no stopping us."

It's a nice change, Elizabeth thought. She and

Jessica did *not* always see eye-to-eye on things!

"I mean, a Jungle Prom, with everybody dressed in Tarzan or Jane outfits," Jessica mused as she pulled from her dresser a pair of very short denim cutoffs and then started fumbling through a stack of brightly colored T-shirts. "Is that wacky and wild or what?"

Elizabeth frowned. "Well, that wasn't *really* what I had in mind. If we all came as Tarzan or Jane, it wouldn't be a *prom*—it would just be a costume party. I think the girls should wear dresses and the guys should wear tuxes."

"Dresses and tuxes? Please!" Jessica looked disgusted. "How boring and conservative can you get?"

"A prom is a special occasion, Jessica," argued Elizabeth. She gestured to her twin's cutoffs and T-shirt. "Do you really think it would feel special if you went dressed like that?"

"For a writer, you have very little imagination," Jessica observed scornfully, her hands on her hips. "Why do you always have to do everything by the book? What's wrong with bending the rules now and then? Geez, Liz, live a little!"

For a long moment, the two sisters glared hotly at each other. Then Elizabeth's face relaxed into a smile. Jessica's followed suit. "I can't believe we're picking a fight about what everybody's going to a wear to a prom that nobody but you and I even *knows* about yet," said Elizabeth.

"Yeah," agreed Jessica. "Especially since it really won't matter how people dress. Either way, our Jungle Prom is going to be the hottest, most happening event in the history of Sweet Valley High!"

Now, this *is what I call a party,* Jessica thought with approval.

She wrapped her arms tightly around Sam Woodruff's waist, her eyes drinking in the lively scene over his shoulder. The wide, sandy beach was swarming with bodies; it looked as if every student from Sweet Valley High was there. Some of the kids had constructed a huge bonfire, and as they fed it with pieces of driftwood, it burned ever more brightly, its flames leaping high into the dark night sky.

A dozen or so couples were already dancing to the music blasting from boom boxes set up on picnic tables. Elizabeth and Todd were slow-dancing, seeming blissfully unaware that everyone around them was going wild. Maria Santelli's long, dark hair whipped from side to side as her boyfriend, Winston Egbert, looking goofy as usual in baggy

Hawaiian-print shorts, spun her in crazy circles.

Meanwhile, DeeDee Gordon and Bill Chase, drama-club president and Sweet Valley High's top surfer, respectively, were doing the twist. Amy Sutton, whose knockout legs looked longer than ever thanks to a hot-pink Lycra micromini, shimmied up to her tennis-star boyfriend, Barry Rork. Tall, blond, well-built Ken Matthews, Sweet Valley High's hotshot quarterback, grasped his petite girlfriend, Terri Adams, by the waist; she squealed with laughter as he lifted her high over his head. April Dawson and Michael Harris were hopping around, clapping their hands and singing along to the music at the tops of their lungs. Annie Whitman, her stepsister, Cheryl Thomas, and Annie's boyfriend, Tony Esteban, were laughing over a shared joke.

Even stuffed-shirt Bruce Patman is getting down, Jessica noted with amusement. But that was probably only because he was at the party with Andrea Slade, the daughter of a famous rock star. Andrea wasn't the type to sit on the sidelines when tunes were cranking!

Jessica lifted her face, looking up at Sam. He gazed down at her, his smoky gray eyes warm with love and admiration. "Did I tell you yet that you're the prettiest girl in the state of California, and probably the whole world?" he asked.

Jessica smiled, her dimple deepening. "Do you really think so? Kiss me, then!"

He bent his head and she closed her eyes. Their lips touched, gently at first. Then Sam pulled her closer, pressing her body against his hard, broad chest.

As the kiss deepened, Jessica twined her fingers in Sam's thick, curly blond hair, surrendering to the delicious sensation of becoming one with him in the hot summer night. After an endless minute, they parted, laughing breathlessly.

"I'm not sure it's legal to kiss like that in a public place," Sam joked, his voice husky.

Jessica smiled, her cheeks flushed. "Lucky for us it's pretty dark."

He put an arm around her shoulders. "C'mon. I think we'd better join the crowd. We might get in trouble, left to our own devices!"

They strolled together toward the party. Some of the kids had taken a break from dancing in order to grab some food. Now Ken waved a can of soda in their direction. "Welcome to the greatest party ever thrown by the greatest school in the greatest town in the U.S. of A.," he boomed. "Glad you could make it, Woodruff."

Sam laughed. "You know I can't take a remark like that sitting down, Matthews. I'm honor-bound to speak up for Bridgewater High."

"No, you're not." Jessica gave her boyfriend a playful squeeze. "Tonight, you just *have* to acknowledge the superiority of my school."

"Sweet Valley High's the best, tonight and every night," Winston affirmed, grabbing a handful of tortilla chips.

"I guess I'm outnumbered," Sam conceded, sticking up a hand to field the can of icy-cold soda Ken tossed him.

"You'd better believe it," said Barry. "SVH has the best tennis team—"

"And the best cheerleaders," added Amy.

"The best swim team," contributed Bill.

"The best drama club," said DeeDee.

"The best football team," Ken said.

Elizabeth's boyfriend, tall, dark, and handsome Todd Wilkins, joined the group. "The best basketball team," he asserted.

"The best *everything*," Jessica exclaimed. "The best parties, the best proms . . ."

She caught her sister's eye. Elizabeth shook her head, but Jessica couldn't resist dropping a hint or two. It was a surefire way to make sure she would be the center of attention the entire night. "Speaking of which," she began in a tantalizing fashion, "we weren't going to say anything yet, but

Elizabeth and I have an idea for a fantastic all-school prom!"

"Really?" Terri said eagerly.

"What is it?" asked Maria.

"Spill the beans!" Winston demanded.

Jessica made excuses. It was so much fun to keep people in suspense! "We really haven't thought it all through. There are still a few details we need to get straight."

The gang turned to Elizabeth. "C'mon, Liz," urged DeeDee. "Give us a clue."

Elizabeth lifted her shoulders, smiling mysteriously. "I can only promise that it'll really *swing*!"

Jessica giggled. "And she's not *monkeying* around when she says that, either."

Avoiding any more questions, Elizabeth grabbed her boyfriend's hand. "C'mon, Todd. This is my favorite song. Let's dance!"

At the same moment, Jessica grabbed Amy. "Hey, Amy," she said. "Let's go see how Lila's doing."

Lila and her date, Tony Alimenti, were standing on the fringes of the party. Tony stood with his hands in his pockets, nervously rocking back and forth on his heels. *No wonder he's nervous!* Jessica thought, stifling a giggle. Lila had her arms tightly folded across her chest, as if the night breeze were cold instead of warm. She looked about as friendly as a prison guard.

"Hi, guys!" Jessica said brightly. "Having a good time?"

Tony grinned. "Having a *great* time," he replied heartily.

"Pretty convincing," Amy hissed under her breath to Jessica. "But then again, he's an actor."

"That's right," Jessica whispered. "I bet he had more fun playing Duncan in the school production of *Macbeth* than he's having playing Lila Fowler's would-be suitor!"

"Excuse me, what was that?" asked Lila, her slender dark eyebrows coming together in a scowl.

"I was just saying that you two make a really fun couple," Jessica lied smoothly. "Don't get too crazy, now!"

Lila glared. Laughing, Jessica and Amy headed back to the picnic tables. "I wish she'd lighten up," Amy remarked. "When is she going to get over what happened with John?"

Jessica shrugged. "It was a pretty traumatic experience for her," she reminded Amy. Weeks after nearly being date-raped by their classmate John Pfeifer, Lila was still attending private counseling sessions at Project Youth. "But I agree with you—she can't mope forever. One of these days, she's got to put it behind her and start over."

"I wouldn't mind starting over with Tony Alimenti," Amy reflected, her eyes sparkling mischievously. "He's cute."

"You don't need Tony—you've got Barry," Jessica said. "Hey, what's going on up there?" She pointed to the group gathered by the bonfire. Kids were shouting and waving their hands. "C'mon!"

Amy and Jessica sprinted toward the others. As they neared the group, they could hear one voice raised above the others. "Bruce Patman's arrived—and he sure knows how to make himself heard," Jessica commented to Amy.

Amy rolled her eyes. "Tell me about it. He's got an ego as big as the great outdoors, and vocal chords to match. And he's always extra loud when discussing his favorite subject: himself!"

They soon found out, however, that Bruce had something else to talk about tonight. His handsome face was tense and excited; his words had worked his audience up into a near frenzy.

"A raid!" Todd exclaimed. "Why didn't you say anything sooner? Why did you wait until now to tell us?"

Bruce sneered. "Take it easy, Wilkins. I didn't *know* until just about half an hour ago."

"Are you sure you're not just repeating a rumor?" Todd asked.

"It's more than a rumor," Bruce replied coldly.

"*What's* more than a rumor?" Jessica demanded, elbowing her way into the middle of the group.

"A raid," explained Elizabeth. "Big Mesa High is planning to raid our party!"

Jessica and Amy glanced at one another, their eyes wide. "Wow!" Jessica breathed.

The rest of the kids pressed Bruce for details. "Look, I don't know all that much," he admitted, raking a hand through his dark hair. "I don't know exactly when they're going to show up. I don't know how many of them there'll be, or what stunts they'll pull. I stopped in town on my way over here, and I ran into a buddy of mine who's got some connections at Big Mesa. According to him, Big Mesa heard about this party, that it was going to be big and exclusive, but also outdoors where they could get at us, and they've decided to try to crash it."

"What are we going to do?" asked Terri, casting an apprehensive glance over her shoulder.

"We've got to be ready for them," Ken declared, putting an arm firmly around her.

"That's right." Barry pounded a fist into his palm. "We need a defensive strategy."

A bunch of the boys put their heads together, football-huddle style. Jessica edged over to Sam, cuddling close to his side. "Are you going to save me from the big, bad, Big Mesa bullies?" she asked, fluttering her eyelashes at him.

Sam grinned down at her. "Don't play helpless female with me, Jessica Wakefield. If it comes to a fight, I'd pick you to come out on top any day!"

"OK, so I'm not so helpless. But I *am* a little scared." Jessica gave an exaggerated shiver. As she'd hoped, Sam wrapped his arms protectively around her. "That helps," she told him.

"How about this?" Bending his head, he brushed his lips against hers.

"Umm," Jessica murmured. "That helps a *lot*."

"I dare you!"

The words floated across the night air, somehow audible over the buzz of excited voices and the pulsing beat of dance music.

Elizabeth whirled to look at the speaker.

Standing apart from the groups of partygoers, his face gleaming in the flickering light of the bonfire, stood Bruce Patman, his hands on his hips, gazing down at someone with a taunting grin.

Jessica! What was she doing hanging around with Bruce? The last time Elizabeth had seen her sister, about a half hour earlier, Jessica had been wrapped tightly in Sam's arms, looking as if she would willingly stay there all night.

Lifting her chin now, Jessica tossed back her hair. "I accept the dare," she told Bruce, her eyes flashing boldly in response to his challenge.

Dare? Elizabeth thought, puzzled. *What's going on here?* Stepping away from Bruce, Jessica proceeded to pull her T-shirt off over her head, revealing a skimpy black bikini top. The boys standing nearby greeted this move with enthusiastic hoots and whistles.

Next, Jessica stepped out of her shorts. She kicked them aside, striptease-style. More hoots.

Now, wearing only her bathing suit, Jessica turned to face the dark ocean. Her head held high, she began to walk toward the water with long, confident strides.

Elizabeth chased after her. "Jessica, what are you doing?" she cried.

"Bruce dared me," Jessica explained without slowing her pace.

"Dared you to do what?"

Jessica pointed. "To swim out to the buoy," she replied. She flashed her sister a reckless grin. "And back again, of course!"

Elizabeth peered out at the water. The moon

hadn't risen yet. The sky and the sea below were pitch-black; Elizabeth knew the buoy was out there, but it was almost invisible.

A sudden, instinctive fear clutched her heart with ice-cold fingers. "Don't do it," she said. "It's late and it's dark. It's not safe."

Jessica laughed. "Duh. Of course it's not safe! Otherwise it wouldn't be a dare, right?"

Stepping forward, Elizabeth put a restraining hand on her sister's arm. "I thought you were through with Bruce's silly dare club," she said sternly. "Remember what happened with the freight train?"

Not long ago, Bruce had been restless and bored and looking to stir up some action in Sweet Valley. So he had started a secret, boys-only dare club. Eager to prove that a girl could do anything a guy could, Jessica had put herself forward for membership. Eventually, Bruce admitted her to Club X, meanwhile rigging the roulette wheel that was spun to determine who would perform each night's dare so that Jessica's name came up every time. Jessica caught on to him, but not until after she'd pulled off a number of dangerous stunts—the last being a near-fatal walk on a high, narrow train trestle.

Now Jessica laughed again, as if almost getting

hit by a train was no big deal. "Don't worry, Liz. I don't plan to run into any trains. A shark or two, maybe!"

A new, pleading note entered Elizabeth's voice. "Please, Jess," she begged. "Stay on shore—for me."

But there was no stopping Jessica. She had been swept up in the reckless, carefree mood of the evening—a mood that had grown even wilder with the anticipation of a raid by Big Mesa High.

Not heeding her twin, Jessica waded out into the still, dark water. "Don't you remember what I said earlier, Liz?" she called back. "You've got to live a little!"

With that, Jessica dove smoothly, her slim, straight body cutting the surface of the sea like a knife. Elizabeth held her breath until her sister reappeared and began stroking out to the distant buoy.

Jessica swam steadily; in just moments, Elizabeth was no longer certain she could see her sister's form. Was that Jessica, or was it the crest of a wave? *Or a shark's fin . . . ?*

Turning on her heel, Elizabeth dashed back across the sand toward the bonfire. The rest of the kids had gone on partying, apparently oblivious to—or unworried by—Jessica's venture out to the buoy.

"Todd!" Elizabeth called out. "Sam! We've got to do something!"

"What is it, Liz?" Todd asked.

"It's Jessica," Elizabeth panted. "Bruce dared her—she swam out—I can't see her anymore. . . ."

"She's just taking a little swim," Bruce scoffed, strolling by. "Get a grip, Liz."

"Yeah, Elizabeth, it's OK." Maria patted her reassuringly on the shoulder. "Jessica can handle it. She's a strong swimmer."

"And a *smart* swimmer," said Sam. "She won't get in any trouble."

"But it's dark," Elizabeth insisted. "There might be sharks, or riptides. . . ."

Bill Chase spoke up. "This is one of the safest beaches in Southern California," he told Elizabeth. "There's a very level shelf out there—no sudden drop-offs, no weird tidal stuff. And I've never heard of sharks feeding around here. They like the bay to the north."

For some reason, Elizabeth didn't find this particularly comforting. She turned to her best friend, Enid Rollins. "Am I the only one at this party who hasn't gone completely nuts?" Elizabeth asked Enid, who could usually be relied upon to be sensible. "Don't you think we should go after her?"

Before Enid could reply, her boyfriend, Hugh, seized her by the hand, pulling her in the direction of the dancers. "She'll be fine, Liz!" Enid shouted back.

Elizabeth turned away, frustrated now as well as anxious. "Just take a deep breath and count to ten," Todd advised lightly, slinging an arm around her shoulders. "Jessica swims a hundred laps a day in your pool at home. The buoy's a piece of cake for her."

Shrugging her shoulders impatiently, Elizabeth slipped out from underneath Todd's arm. Maybe everyone else, including Sam, could ignore Jessica's peril, but she couldn't.

She walked back to the water's edge to stand watch. Squinting, she combed the black water with her eyes. It was useless. As far as she could see, in all directions, the ocean was empty.

I can't just stand here and do nothing! Elizabeth thought desperately. Then inspiration struck. Bill Chase always had his surfboard stowed in the back of his car. She'd borrow it—she'd go out after her sister. . . .

At that instant, just as Elizabeth was about to race back to the others, a dripping figure emerged from the surf twenty yards down the beach.

"Jessica!" Elizabeth cried, tears of relief springing to her eyes. She hurried to her twin's side. "Are you all right?"

Jessica stared at her distraught sister. Then she burst out laughing. "Of course I'm all right! I just went for a dip. Geez, Liz, sometimes I don't know about you. Don't you have anything better to do besides worry?"

Pulling her hair over one shoulder, Jessica squeezed the water out of it. Then, without another glance at Elizabeth, she marched up the beach, where she was greeted with cheers by her friends.

Elizabeth was left alone, too stunned and angry to budge. *I thought you'd drowned,* she wanted to yell after her sister. *You ungrateful idiot!*

Just then, Elizabeth felt a hand on her arm. Penny Ayala, the editor of the school newspaper and a close friend of Elizabeth's, was strolling along the shore with her boyfriend, Neil Freemount, and had witnessed the whole scene. "Chill out, OK, Liz?" Penny said gently.

Penny and Neil moved on. Elizabeth stared after them, the tears that had sparkled in her eyes now spilling down her cheeks. Her anger increased, but now she was angry at herself rather than at Jessica.

I'm the idiot, Elizabeth thought, biting her lip.

It always happens like this. Jessica does something stupid, and I fret and fume, and it always ends up the same. She's fine, and I feel—and look—like a fool!

Elizabeth kicked at an abandoned sand castle. It was the story of her life, come to think of it. She might be only four minutes older than her twin, but she still spent all of her time playing "big sister." They each had fixed roles, which hardly ever varied: wild and crazy Jessica got into trouble, and mature, responsible Elizabeth got her out of it.

And where has my role as caretaker and peacemaker gotten me? Elizabeth asked herself. The answer was painfully clear: nowhere. She looked toward the beach party, of which her twin sister was now the triumphant center. Clearly Jessica and everybody else thought Elizabeth's concern over the midnight swim was wasted.

A waste . . . Yes, I've been wasting my time, Elizabeth realized. A new feeling of determination swept over her. Why *should* she squander her time and energy looking after Jessica if Jessica didn't even appreciate the effort?

From now on, I'm going to take care of myself, Elizabeth vowed, straightening her shoulders. *I'm going to put myself first. Jessica knows how to follow her desires—well, I can learn to do that, too.*

With long, purposeful strides, she hurried to rejoin the beach party. If she was going to live for herself instead of for other people, she might as well start right now!

SVH

Two

This is the worst party I've ever been to, Lila thought sourly. She shifted her position on the beach blanket, trying to find a comfortable way to sit that wasn't completely unfeminine and inelegant, given the fact that she was wearing a short, tight skirt. It was impossible.

"Don't you love this song?" Tony asked, bobbing his head to the tune currently blasting from the boom box. "WSVC plays the coolest music."

"It's kind of loud," Lila complained.

"Yeah, the Big Mesa kids won't have too hard a time finding us," Tony joked.

"Hmm."

"You're not nervous, are you, Lila?" he asked,

his tone suddenly protective and intimate.

Lila raised her eyebrows, surprised. Everyone at school knew what had happened to her, but they also knew better than to bring up the subject. The only person she ever talked about it with anymore was her counselor at Project Youth, Nathan Pritchard—and she tended to discourage even him from really going into it. Did Tony think that just because she had agreed to go on a date with him, it gave him the right to ask her personal questions?

Tony noticed Lila's startled expression; luckily, he misinterpreted it. "I mean, not to imply that *you're* the shrieking and swooning type. But some of the girls seem to be nervous about the raid. It won't amount to much, if you ask me," he assured her. "Big Mesa High is all talk and no action."

Lila yawned to show that she didn't really care about the Big Mesa raid. If it had to happen, she just hoped it happened sooner rather than later—so she'd have an excuse to go home!

"So . . ." Tony twiddled his thumbs, obviously trying to come up with another topic of conversation. *He does better when he has a script,* Lila thought scornfully.

"Are you comfortable sitting here? Because we could sit somewhere else if you want," he offered. "Or how about taking a walk down by the water?

It's probably nice and quiet a little farther along the beach."

Nice and quiet . . . Lila hunched her shoulders, as if to ward off a blow. Yeah, she bet it was nice and quiet down the beach, away from the party. *Guys are all alike,* she thought grimly. *They've got one thing and one thing only on their caveman minds.*

"I don't feel like taking a walk," she said, loading the sentence with extra meaning. *In other words, mister, don't try anything funny!*

"Then how about dancing?" Tony jumped to his feet and held out a hand. "I know you're a great dancer, Lila."

She shrugged. She *was* a great dancer; she couldn't deny it. But it had been a long time since she felt much like dancing.

Still . . . If she *danced* with Tony, she wouldn't have to *talk* to him. It was really the lesser of two evils. "OK," Lila agreed. She rose to her feet without touching Tony's hand. "Let's dance."

They joined the other couples. It was a fast song, and as she started dancing, Lila surprised herself—she actually started having fun. It felt good to move her arms and legs, to give her whole body a thorough shake. *I've been so stiff and tense,* she realized. *Like a statue made out of marble.*

Now, little by little, she found herself softening, relaxing. She couldn't help it—a smile flickered across her face. Tony spotted it and grinned back at her, his eyes bright with pleasure at the sight of her enjoyment.

The song ended and Lila paused to catch her breath. "One more?" asked Tony.

She nodded, almost eagerly. "Sure."

They waited for the music to continue. There was a short delay while Ken fiddled with the boom box, switching off the radio in order to slip in a cassette.

When the music started up again, the mood of the party altered instantly. Instead of a fast dance beat, the song was melodic, caressing, and slow.

Slow. Lila gulped. A slow dance. The kind of dance where the guy put his arms around the girl's shoulders and the girl put her arms around the guy's waist. The less space in between the two bodies, the better. An occasional kiss was optional.

Lila's eyes darted around. She saw Sam wrap Jessica in a warm embrace; Jessica melted against him like butter on a piece of toast. Todd pulled Elizabeth close; she rested her head against his chest. Everywhere, couples were coming together, their shuffling feet in sync, their bodies swaying to the music as one.

Panicked, she turned back to Tony. He took a tentative step in her direction. Lila stepped backward so abruptly, she lost her balance. She teetered, then caught herself.

"Are you OK?" Tony asked.

Lila bent, massaging her ankle. "I twisted my foot," she lied. It was as good an excuse as any. "I think I'll sit this one out."

Solicitously, Tony got her settled again on the blanket, which he'd moved closer to the bonfire. He sat down next to her. In silence, they watched the other couples slow-dancing.

Why did I come here tonight? Lila asked herself unhappily. She used to think there was nothing worse than staying home alone on a Saturday night, but now she knew better. A date wasn't always a dream come true; in fact, most dates were disappointing in one way or another. They could be downright boring like this one; the guy could be cute and nice but basically uninteresting. *Or the guy could be not so nice. . . .*

Lila stared at her friends, so cozy and romantic with their boyfriends. Sam was a big guy—tall. Did Jessica ever worry that he'd try to overpower her, force her to do something she didn't want to do? And Barry had biceps like Popeye—on his right arm anyway—from playing tennis. If he wanted to, he could probably pin Amy to the ground with the other hand tied behind his back. . . .

Lila squeezed her eyes shut against the unwelcome images and made an effort to keep her breathing deep and regular. *What was it Nathan said to me at our session last week?* She tried to remember. *Something about staying in control. That's what's scary, not being in control. So, if I don't feel like I'm in control of a situation, I should just walk away. I'm in charge of me—nobody else is.*

She opened her eyes. Was it her imagination or had Tony edged closer to her on the blanket?

He was gazing at her, his eyes dark and soft in the flickering light of the bonfire. "I'm really glad you came to the party with me tonight," he said.

"Hmm," Lila mumbled.

"Ever since we acted in the play together, I've been hoping for an opportunity to get to know you better. I just wanted to thank you for giving me a chance."

"Yeah, well . . ." Lila stared at the flames. She didn't look at Tony; she didn't want to encourage him.

A gust of wind stirred across the dark sand. The bonfire crackled. Lila shivered, suddenly cold. Tony glanced at her profile. Then, gingerly lifting one arm, he placed it lightly around her shoulders.

The touch of his hand on her bare skin caused Lila to jump as if she'd been electrocuted. "What do you think you're doing?" she squeaked, squirming away from him.

Tony flushed, embarrassed. "I was just . . . I thought maybe you . . . I wasn't going to . . ." He cleared his throat and started over. "I'm sorry, Lila. I really didn't mean—"

Don't make a scene, Lila said to herself. *I don't want a scene—I can't handle it. Just act normal.*

She waved a hand with a high-pitched laugh. "Oh, forget about it. C'mon." She jumped to her feet. A bemused Tony followed suit. "Let's go get some food before it's all gone."

"You're a great dancer, Bruce," Andrea Slade murmured into Bruce Patman's ear. "I love the way your arms feel around me. So strong . . ."

Bruce pulled Andrea even closer. "You feel good to me, too," he whispered into her silky hair.

Andrea sighed and rested her head contentedly against Bruce's chest. Bruce sighed, too, but for a different reason.

His eyes wandered restlessly around the party, which in his opinion had gotten totally dull since everyone started slow-dancing and making out.

We could really use some action, Bruce thought as he ran a hand idly up and down Andrea's back. *Hope those Big Mesa guys don't wimp out and blow off the raid!*

Andrea was saying something to him. "Huh? What?" asked Bruce.

"Do you want to sit down for a while?" she repeated.

"Sure." Bruce gave her a squeeze. "Let's go find a secluded place where we can sit and . . . talk."

Pausing to grab their beach blanket, Bruce steered Andrea away from the bonfire. A few yards off from the party, he spread the blanket out in the shelter of a low sand dune. "Looks like a good spot," he grunted.

Andrea smiled at him, her eyes glowing. "Yeah, it does," she said softly.

They sat down side by side. Without preamble, Bruce leaned back on one elbow and pulled Andrea to him for a long, hard kiss. He rated the kiss in his mind: good, but not great. Then he drew away from Andrea so he could look over his shoulder to see if any Big Mesa High students were skulking in the shadows—he didn't want to miss out on anything.

Unaware of his disinterest, Andrea snuggled against him, her head tucked under his chin. "I hope Big Mesa doesn't come and spoil our party," she breathed. "It's such a perfect night, just the way it is."

Bruce yawned. "Right."

Andrea played with the top button of his polo shirt. "I guess you know how I feel about you," she said shyly. "You're really special, Bruce."

"You, too," Bruce said, figuring it was what she wanted to hear. He stifled a snicker, thinking that she probably wouldn't be thrilled with his true feelings about her: he considered her good-looking, fairly sophisticated, and a decent doubles tennis partner. She was a way to pass the time.

Andrea raised her face to his for another kiss. Bruce pressed his lips on hers, trying without success to muster up some passion. With a girl like Andrea, who couldn't hide the fact that she had a crush on you, it was really too easy, not to mention boring, Bruce thought disdainfully. Where was the challenge? In his opinion, the only fun in dating was the sport of it. The more it was like a tennis match, where he had to wear down his opponent through expertise and sheer force of will, the better he liked it. Taking out Andrea was like wading in a baby pool. Sure, you got your feet wet right away, but it didn't get any more exciting than that. There was no deep end.

"I was just thinking," Andrea murmured, tracing her finger along Bruce's chiseled jawline, "about next weekend. Wouldn't it be fun to—"

Bruce brushed her hand aside. "Why are you worrying about next weekend? It's still *this* weekend."

"Of course it is!" Andrea gave him a winning smile. "But there's a great outdoor concert in L.A. next Saturday afternoon. We could take a picnic, make a day of it. It'd be a blast."

"I don't make plans that far in advance," Bruce reminded her.

"Maybe not usually, but, well . . ." She blushed slightly. "We've gone out a bunch of times now, and I thought —"

"Look, Andrea," Bruce snapped. "I'm not into commitment—I told you that."

She hung her head. "I remember. But I thought—I hoped—after all the time we've spent together lately . . ."

There was a tremor in her voice. For some reason, knowing that he'd hurt and embarrassed her only made Bruce more irritated. "Get with the program, Andrea," he advised coldly. "That's the way I operate. You can take it or leave it—I really don't care which."

Andrea put a hand to her eye and wiped at

something. *Geez, she's not crying, is she?* Bruce thought, disgusted. *I swear, some girls bawl at the drop of a hat.*

"Sorry," Andrea said, her voice small. "I didn't mean to put pressure on you."

"Let's just forget about it," said Bruce. "I'm kind of hungry. Why don't we check out the—"

At that instant, the night was broken by a strange, wild cry. "What was that?" yelped Andrea, her eyes wide.

From the other end of the beach, the war whoop was repeated, growing louder and louder as dozens of hollering voices joined in.

"It's them!" Bruce heard someone shout. "Big Mesa!"

Bruce leaped to his feet, a surge of electricity coursing through his body. The raid!

Andrea put a restraining hand on his arm. "Let's stay here, out of the way," she pleaded.

Bruce shook her off. "You can do whatever you want." He broke into a run. "But I'm not going to sit back and let my school get dumped on!"

It happened so fast, Elizabeth didn't even have time to slip her feet back into her sandals.

The beach party had started to simmer down. The music was softer, allowing the sounds of talking and laughter to dominate. As the bonfire burned lower, kids were pairing off.

She and Todd danced, holding each other close and talking quietly. "I guess the Big Mesa raid was just a rumor," Elizabeth said.

"Looks like it," Todd agreed. He nuzzled her neck. "Too bad. I was looking forward to a chance to be your knight in shining armor and save you from the dragon."

Elizabeth laughed. "Do I strike you as the damsel-in-distress type?"

He smiled. "Hardly. But I still like the part where I sweep you up in my arms and carry you off."

"Umm," Elizabeth murmured. "That *does* sound like fun."

"So, what do you say?" Todd kissed her forehead, her temple, her mouth. "Can I carry you off?"

"You can do whatever—"

A piercing yell shattered the magical moment. Instinctively, Elizabeth clutched Todd's arm. "What . . . ?"

Before she had time to phrase the question, she had her answer. A flood of dark shapes swarmed over the nearest sand dune and charged toward the Sweet Valley High beach party. It was people—dozens of people. "Big Mesa!" Elizabeth cried.

"Hide the food!" Winston shouted, sprinting for the picnic tables.

"Get the radios!" someone else commanded.

But there wasn't time. The rampaging group was upon them.

There was a chaos of noise and shadow and light. All the Big Mesa students—mostly boys but some girls, too—were dressed in red and black, their school colors. T-shirts and varsity jackets proclaimed the prowess of the Big Mesa Bulls. Some of the kids wore bull masks with horns; the faces of others were streaked with red and black war paint—to Elizabeth, they looked like characters from a dream, a nightmare.

The Big Mesa raiders burst upon the party, waving high-powered flashlights and chanting. "It's the running of the Bulls—we trample all before us—we conquer all our foes—so bow down and adore us."

They pointed shaving-cream cannisters at the shouting Sweet Valley students, spraying them with foam. A Big Mesa student tossed something onto the bonfire and suddenly it roared, flames rocketing high into the sky. With one arm, a huge boy in a bull mask flung over a table piled with food; someone else ripped the cassette out of the boom box and threw it toward the water.

"Stop!" Elizabeth yelled. "Why don't you just leave us alone!"

At that moment, someone grabbed her from behind. Elizabeth gasped. Laughing harshly, a Big Mesa guy dragged her along with him for a few yards, then flung her aside.

Elizabeth fell to her knees in the soft sand. Scrambling to her feet, she saw another boy pulling Jessica with him. Jessica slapped him and he let her go. When a boy grabbed Lila, Lila screamed at the top of her lungs.

The Sweet Valley High students were running in all directions at once, confused and overwhelmed by the random tactics of the Big Mesa raiders. Winston and Barry tried to salvage some of the food; Terri and Maria quickly gathered up armfuls of beach blankets and shoes.

"Forget that stuff!" Elizabeth heard Bruce holler.

"C'mon, guys. Let's go after those low-life scum!"

His face purple with fury, Bruce was about to chase after the Big Mesa gang. His cousin Roger grasped his arms, restraining him. "There's no point, Bruce," Roger shouted. "There are too many of them. Just let them go."

"Roger's right," affirmed Todd. "Our best bet is to form a solid wall of people instead of scattering all over the place. C'mon, everybody!" he yelled. "Gather together for strength!"

Not everyone could hear Todd's command, but those who did clustered together in a tight, impenetrable knot of bodies. It worked; the last Big Mesa people ran around the Sweet Valley group rather than charging through them.

And as suddenly as it started, the raid was over. The triumphant shouts of the Big Mesa students faded into the distance. Far away, Elizabeth heard car engines roar to life, and the squealing of rubber tires on pavement. Then there was complete silence, broken only by the muffled thud of the ocean waves.

Slowly, the Sweet Valley students separated and looked around themselves at the damage.

Beach towels, shoes, and articles of clothing were scattered far and wide. Cookies, fruit, potato chips, and popcorn had been dumped onto the sand. Everything was covered with white shaving cream.

"Ugh," said Bill.

"What a mess," moaned DeeDee.

Elizabeth was still breathing fast. As she put a hand to her forehead to wipe away the perspiration, she glanced at her watch. "Five minutes!" she exclaimed. "That only lasted five minutes."

"It felt like an eternity," declared Penny.

"I can't believe we let them get away with it," Bruce raged. He pounded a fist into the open palm of his other hand. "Like total fools, we didn't even go after them." He narrowed his eyes, glaring at Enid's boyfriend, Hugh Grayson. "I don't suppose *you* knew anything about this," he said, his tone accusing and sarcastic. "I don't suppose you were the one who tipped off your Big Mesa friends about our party. Are you enjoying Sweet Valley High's humiliation?"

Next to her, Elizabeth felt Enid stiffen.

"Bruce!" Andrea exclaimed.

"Cool it, Bruce," advised Roger.

Hugh folded his arms across his broad chest. "I *didn't* know anything about this," he told Bruce calmly. "And I *didn't* tip anyone off. Believe me, I'm as bummed about it as you are."

"I'll bet," Bruce sneered.

"Hey, the damage is done," Todd pointed out. "There's no sense blaming anybody for it. The thing to do now is clean up."

"And start planning our revenge," added Jessica.

Her proposal was met by nods and exclamations of support. "That's right!" Bruce declared, his eyes flashing with anger. "An eye for an eye, a tooth for a tooth."

"We can't take this lying down," Ken agreed.

"Big Mesa is *not* the top school in Southern California," declared Amy. "Sweet Valley High is!"

Elizabeth shivered, suddenly cold. In just five minutes, the entire tone of the evening had changed. Happiness, high spirits, and camaraderie had given way to anger and a thirst for revenge against their archrivals from Big Mesa. The party was over.

SVH

Three

"When the going gets tough, head for the Dairi Burger," Todd joked half an hour later as he, Elizabeth, Jessica, Sam, and most of the other kids who had been at the beach party piled out of their cars into the parking lot of Sweet Valley's most popular teen hangout.

"Do you think any of the Big Mesa kids followed us here?" asked Jessica, looking over her shoulder, almost hoping she'd glimpse one of the red-and-black-garbed raiders. The sneak attack had happened so fast, she hadn't gotten a chance to fight back—except for the slap she'd delivered to that one guy—and she was itching to teach someone a lesson.

"Nah." Sam hugged her. "They wouldn't make trouble in a public place. Besides, I think they accomplished their goal."

"Which was to ruin our party," Amy said glumly.

"Well, hey—the night isn't over yet." Barry held open the door to the restaurant. "In my experience, there's absolutely no disaster that a double-thick chocolate milk shake can't make up for!"

Within minutes, the Dairi Burger was packed with Sweet Valley High students, eating burgers and fries and talking fast and loud about the Big Mesa beach-party raid.

The twins, Todd, Sam, Amy, and Barry squeezed into a booth next to the jukebox and ordered a couple of burgers and a round of shakes. Jessica gulped down half of her milk shake in one long, angry slurp. "I'm still just so *steamed*!" she exclaimed. "What gave Big Mesa the right to invade our party and trash our stuff?"

Amy examined a strand of her blond hair. "I'll never get the shaving cream out of my hair," she complained. "It's disgusting."

"The rivalry between us and them is a pretty long-standing one," Barry observed. "It's been heating up lately and I guess now it's just ready to explode."

"They exploded, all right," Todd said grimly.

"They hit us like an atom bomb. Now we have to get revenge on *two* counts."

"You really got robbed at the last basketball game," Sam commented as he polished off his burger. "If the ref hadn't made that bad call, you'd have beaten them by two points instead of the other way around."

Todd, high scorer for the Sweet Valley High varsity basketball team, drummed his fingers on the table. "Tell me about it. I've played the last minute and a half of that game over in my mind about a thousand times."

"Big Mesa is just so underhanded," Jessica fumed. "The girls are as bad as the boys. Their cheerleaders played the nastiest trick on us at that game!"

"They vandalized our pom-poms," Amy recalled.

"When we weren't looking, they put Super Glue on the handles," Jessica elaborated. "So there we were with our stupid pom-poms glued to our hands for the whole game!"

Elizabeth put a hand to her mouth, smothering a giggle. Jessica frowned. "It *wasn't* amusing, Liz," she huffed. "It took *hours* to get that junk off our fingers!"

"I'm sorry." Elizabeth's eyes twinkled. "It just makes a funny picture."

"You wouldn't've been laughing if *you'd* had pom-poms Super-Glued to your hands," Jessica wagered. "And I guarantee those Big Mesa cheerleaders won't laugh when we give them a taste of their own medicine."

"You're going to retaliate?" asked Sam.

Amy nodded emphatically. "Next chance we get," she confirmed. "There's another bunch of athletic matches against Big Mesa in a couple of weeks."

"We'll nail them," Jessica stated. "They'll be sorry they tangled with us!"

Elizabeth sipped her milk shake. "You know, Big Mesa High took a shot at *The Oracle,* too."

"How?" asked Jessica. "What did they do?"

"The other day someone sent me a copy of the *Bull's Eye,* the Big Mesa paper," Elizabeth explained. "Anonymously, of course. There was a cartoon in it about *The Oracle,* basically dumping on us and saying we're a crummy paper with lousy writers and editors and photographers."

"So, what are you guys going to do about it?" Jessica demanded.

Elizabeth laughed. "Are you kidding? Nothing! *The Oracle*'s not going to stoop to their level. It wouldn't be good journalism."

"Who cares about good journalism? Our school

pride is at stake!" Jessica declared. "You can't let Big Mesa get away with an insult like that."

Elizabeth shrugged. "I guess it just didn't seem that serious to me."

"I'd think you'd change your attitude after tonight," Jessica remarked. She glanced at a nearby table where Enid and Hugh were sitting with two other couples. That was another thing she felt like challenging her sister about. How could Elizabeth be best friends with someone who not only was a total drip, but also dated a guy from Big Mesa?

"You've got to fight back!" Jessica commanded Elizabeth, pounding the table for emphasis. "Tell the staff of the *Bull's Eye* and the whole Big Mesa student body to—"

"OK, stop right there." Sam held up a hand. "Big Mesa has spoiled our evening enough already. Can we talk about something else for a change?"

Jessica stuck out her tongue. "I was just trying to help my sister and her nerdy, pencil-necked friends figure out how to show some backbone," she mumbled.

Elizabeth folded her arms across her chest, narrowing her eyes. "Excuse me, Jessica, what did you say? I didn't quite catch that."

Now Todd intervened. "I agree with Sam. Hey,

let's hear the scoop on this prom idea you two Wakefields have been hinting about all night."

For a minute, Jessica and Elizabeth remained stubbornly silent. Then Jessica gave in. It *was* a great idea—they might as well tell people so everyone could start getting psyched for the prom of the century. "Oh, all right, if you insist," said Jessica. "This is it: We're going to put on a *Jungle* Prom!"

"We'll decorate the gym to look like a tropical rain forest," explained Elizabeth.

"With vines, like in Tarzan," added Jessica.

"We'll ask an environmental organization to sponsor us," Elizabeth went on. "You've heard of Environmental Alert, right? Any money we have left over from selling tickets, we can donate to them."

"It'll be totally hot!" Jessica concluded. She glanced slyly at her sister. "Which is why I think we should dress *down* and wear jungle outfits." She turned to Sam. "I'm thinking of a leopard-print mini."

"I like the sound of that," he said approvingly.

Across the table, Elizabeth frowned. "But it's a *prom*. Don't you think it's more fun to dress *up*?"

"Hey, that's a minor point," Sam said quickly, forestalling another disagreement.

"Right," agreed Todd. "What matters is that

you've dreamed up a fantastic prom theme."

Jessica was mollified. She smiled at her twin. "We know."

"I bet you two'll have a lot of fun working on this project together," Sam predicted.

It will *be fun,* Jessica reflected. Seeing as how in general, she and Elizabeth had completely different hobbies and extracurricular activities.

The twins smiled at each other and raised their milk-shake glasses. "Here's to the Jungle Prom," Elizabeth toasted.

Jessica couldn't resist one final dig. "And here's to getting back at *Big* Mesa in a *big* way!" she added.

Bruce leaned back against the black Porsche with the "1BRUCE1" plates. He had ditched Andrea inside the Dairi Burger and returned to the dimly lit parking lot, where a bunch of Sweet Valley guys were hanging out, rehashing the beach-party raid and arguing about what, if any, retaliatory action to take.

With satisfaction, his dark eyes roved around the loose circle that had gathered near his car. Bruce was where he liked to be: in the center, at the helm.

"So, what are we going to do about this insult?"

he challenged the others. "How are we going to punish those losers?"

"We have to win our next tennis match against them, that's for sure," said Michael Harris, a tennis teammate of Bruce's and a former member of the disbanded Club X.

Bruce glowered. He didn't like being reminded of Sweet Valley High's recent loss to the Big Mesa squad. Bruce, the team's top-seeded player, had defeated his own singles opponent easily; he always did. But Big Mesa had racked up more total victories to take the match.

"We'll win the next match, but we need to do more than that," Bruce told Michael. "This isn't just an athletic rivalry anymore. This is *war*."

"I say we raid *their* next big party," said Ronnie Edwards, a malicious gleam in his light-blue eyes.

"Why wait for a party?" asked Jim Sturbridge, another former Club X member.

"Yeah," said unofficial junior-class bully Charlie Cashman. "Why not go after individual kids' houses? The school president, the captains of the football and basketball teams, people like that."

"Or we could just trash the school," suggested beefy Tad Johnson, Sweet Valley High's 240-pound linebacker.

Roger Barrett Patman laughed at these suggestions. "Don't you think you guys are overreacting a little? I mean, the raid tonight was really pretty harmless." He shrugged. "They didn't hurt anybody."

"Yeah," said Winston. "They spilled our popcorn and got us with some shaving cream, so what?" He grinned, stroking his jaw. "I, for one, had a five o'clock shadow."

"You wish you needed to shave, Egbert," Bruce scoffed. "Look, if you don't have the stomach for revenge, no one's making you stick around. Go on inside and sit with the girls."

Winston guffawed. "Ooh, Bruce, that really hurts."

"The point is, Bruce," Roger insisted, "we don't need to go overboard. We could just let it slide, let the whole thing drop. The rivalry will probably cool off on its own. Why do something that'll make the situation even worse?"

"Because only wimps and cowards let themselves get slapped around without taking a swing in return," Bruce retorted. He turned his back on his cousin, sending an explicit message: Roger and Winston were total geeks; who needed their help, anyway?

Club X can handle it, Bruce thought, eyeing the guys who remained after Roger, Winston, and a few other pacifist types wandered back into the restaurant.

Of course, technically, Club X didn't exist anymore. But Bruce knew the need for it was still there. His lips twisted as he remembered the dares, the danger. For a while, Club X had really spiced up life in this boring town! His big mistake was letting Jessica Wakefield stick her nose into it, demanding her equal right as a girl to try out for membership. It had all been downhill from there.

"So, are you with *those* guys"—Bruce jerked his head toward the Dairi Burger—"or are you with me?"

Charlie, Michael, Ronnie, Tad, and Jim took a step closer to Bruce, closing the circle. "We're with you," they swore.

"Excellent." Bruce rubbed his hands together. It felt good to have a mission, a purpose. "Because I, for one, don't believe in turning the other cheek. I say we answer insult with injury."

"It's been kind of a long, strange evening," Tony said, peering into Lila's face. "Don't take this the wrong way, Lila. You look beautiful . . . but you also look tired."

Lila tilted her head, hiding behind a curtain of glossy brown hair. She really didn't like it when people looked at her that closely. "I *am* tired," she admitted.

They were sitting in Tony's car in the Dairi Burger parking lot. Now he gestured at the brightly lit restaurant. "We don't have to go in, you know," he told her. "Why don't I just take you home?"

A wave of relief washed over Lila. *Thank heavens this horrible date, this horrible night, is almost over. If I can just hold on a little longer . . .* "That's probably a good idea," she said, barely able to mask her eagerness.

Tony started the engine and flicked the headlights back on. As the car pulled out of the parking space and headed toward the exit, a group of people were momentarily illuminated in the bright arc cast by the headlights. *Bruce,* Lila noted with mild interest. *Bruce and his committee of jerks and bullies. I wonder what they're up to?*

She didn't say much to Tony as they drove through town on the way to her neighborhood, but then again, she hadn't said much to him all night. *I wonder if he'll ask me out again.* Lila almost burst out laughing. He'd have to be a real glutton for punishment!

Tony fiddled with the radio. Then he cleared his throat. "Uh-hum. Um, Lila . . ." He stole a quick glance at her impassive profile. "I just wanted to say . . . I had a good time tonight."

She lifted her eyebrows in her best look of ironic disbelief. "Even though the beach party was a total bust?" she asked dryly.

"It wasn't all bad." He smiled. "We got a chance to talk, and I enjoyed that a lot."

"Yeah." Lila left it at that. She wasn't about to bother lying to him, telling him she had a good time too, when she *didn't* have a good time—she'd had a rotten time.

"I'm sorry about the raid, mostly because I think it upset you," Tony ventured as he turned onto Country Club Drive.

"It didn't upset me." Lila clenched her fists, her fingernails digging into her palms, as she recalled the moment when that brute from Big Mesa had grabbed her. He'd acted as if he had a right to put his hands on anyone he wanted! *I'll probably have bruises on my arms,* she thought. *Maybe I'm lucky it was no worse than that.* "It didn't upset me," she repeated, a shade too loudly.

A minute later, they coasted down the long driveway of Fowler Crest. Tony braked in front of the white, Spanish-style mansion. Walking around to Lila's side of the car, he opened the door for her.

Lila stepped out. It took an effort to stroll casually up the flagstone path, keeping pace with Tony, rather than to give in to the urge to sprint and leave him far behind.

Lila had her key ready. She inserted it into the lock, then turned to say good-bye to Tony. "Thanks," she mumbled, not meeting his eyes.

"Thank *you*," Tony said sincerely.

She thought he would turn and walk away. But instead, suddenly he was leaning toward her, his face getting closer and closer to hers. His hand hovered above her shoulder; his lips nearly brushed her cheek.

Lila's heart leaped into her throat. A strangled cry escaped her. With a jerk of her wrist, she flung the heavy door open behind her.

Tony stepped back, a startled expression on his face. "I'm sorry, Lila. I was only—I would never—please. Don't be afraid of—"

Lila stumbled backward, practically falling into the front hall. Regaining her balance, she slammed the door shut in Tony's face.

She crumpled, her back braced against the door. Her heart was pounding like a jackhammer and her eyes were smarting with tears. She stood for a moment trying to catch her breath. What a narrow escape! Guys like Tony were so sneaky, acting like gentlemen, pretending to be concerned about you, walking you to the door, and then *bam*: they moved in for the kill.

Lila took a few steps, the heels of her sandals echoing on the marble floor of the high-ceilinged foyer. Fowler Crest was empty, as usual. Her father was off on a business trip; Eva and Lucinda, the housekeeper and the maid, had weekends off. She was alone.

There was a telephone and answering machine on the mahogany table near the foot of the wide staircase. The light on the answering machine was blinking. Lila hit the "play" button to listen to the messages.

There was just one—from her father. "Hi, honey, it's Daddy," the recorded voice said. "Just checking in. Hope you're having a nice weekend. I'll see you tomorrow night in time for dinner."

Lila stared at the answering machine and the telephone, her only link to the only family she had in the whole wide world. *I could call him,* she thought. He'd left a phone number. But what would she say? Where would she start?

He didn't know she was supposedly having "problems," that she went to Project Youth for counseling; she'd never told him about what had happened with John Pfeifer.

Lila pressed her hands to her eyes, rubbing them. *I'm just tired,* she told herself, explaining away her momentary weakness. *I can take care of my own life. I don't* need *to talk to Daddy. I'm grown up. I can be my own parent now.*

Suddenly, a dim, misty memory fluttered into Lila's consciousness, elusive and unwelcome; a memory so vague, it almost seemed it must belong to someone else's life; a memory that might not even be a memory at all, but a story told to her over and over through the years until it had become a part of her. A young mother abandoning her husband and baby, running off to Europe and never once seeking to contact, to know, to love the little girl she'd left behind. . . .

A wave of loneliness as black and bottomless as the ocean washed over Lila. She pressed her hands even harder against her face, but she couldn't stop the tears that coursed down her cheeks.

"What a night!" Elizabeth said as the BMW coasted to a stop at the edge of Miller's Point.

The dead-end road on a hilltop overlooking Sweet Valley was a popular late-night parking spot for Sweet Valley High students. Tonight, though, she and Todd were the only people there.

Todd killed the engine. Immediately, the soft,

fragrant silence of the Southern California night blanketed the car. A breeze wafted through the open windows, stirring Elizabeth's hair.

She turned to Todd and he wrapped his arms tightly around her. "You still feel a little tense," he told her, rubbing her back.

Elizabeth rested her head against Todd's chest, thinking about the Big Mesa raid and the scare Jessica had given her earlier in the evening, when she swam out to the buoy. She remembered the important promise she had made to herself. *I'm just not the same person I was six hours ago!* she thought.

Aloud to Todd, she said, "It's weird, that's all. It feels like *years* have passed since the beginning of the night, when Jessica and I were hanging out at home, getting ready for the party and talking about the Jungle Prom."

Todd stroked her hair. "It turned out to be a party people will remember for a long time, that's for sure!" Elizabeth sighed. Slowly, she relaxed in Todd's arms, hypnotized by the lights of the town twinkling far below. "Sweet Valley looks so tiny from up here," she mused. "So peaceful."

"It *is* peaceful," said Todd.

"That raid tonight was just a bunch of rowdy kids out for a little fun, wasn't it?"

Todd brushed the top of her head with his lips.

"That's all it was," he confirmed, his voice deep and soothing. "The guys, especially Bruce, just like to talk—it's not going to lead to anything except maybe an extra-intense matchup at the next basketball game. Anyway, where would Sweet Valley High be without an archrival?"

As usual, Todd's common sense reassured her completely. The last measure of tension melted out of Elizabeth's body and a feeling of utter well-being and security took its place. It was a beautiful night and Sweet Valley was a perfect place; she and her sister were going to organize the greatest prom their school had ever seen; she was safe in the arms of the boy she loved. Elizabeth knew she really couldn't be happier. *Who could dream of a better life than this?*

SVH

Four

"So, what's the word on the Jungle Prom?" asked Olivia Davidson, *The Oracle*'s arts editor and a good friend of Elizabeth's, as they settled down at a corner table in the cafeteria on Tuesday.

"Yeah, did Chrome Dome Cooper give it the official A-OK?" Penny asked.

Elizabeth grinned at this irreverent reference to Mr. Cooper, Sweet Valley High's bald-as-an-egg principal. "When I first approached him with the idea yesterday *morning,* he said it sounded promising," she related. "But he wanted me to get a definite commitment from the environmental group before he made a final decision. So yesterday *afternoon* I met with some people at the

Southern California chapter of Environmental Alert—they recently opened an office downtown."

Enid popped the top on a can of diet soda. "They're an international organization, right?"

"Right," said Elizabeth. "One of their big projects is trying to raise public awareness—and money—for their rain-forest preservation program. So, the timing of this Jungle Prom idea is really perfect. We struck a deal on the spot!"

Elizabeth's eyes lit up with excitement. "Environmental Alert will provide us with all sorts of stuff," she continued. "Some really cool posters, informational literature, T-shirts to raffle off. And in turn, we'll donate the money we make from holding the prom to their rain-forest program!"

"It sounds like you've been incredibly busy and organized, as usual," remarked Cheryl Thomas, the Wakefields' new neighbor and Annie Whitman's new stepsister.

Elizabeth shrugged modestly. "It's the only way to make sure this prom gets off the ground. Anyway, when I told Mr. Cooper about Environmental Alert just now, he gave me the green light. The prom is scheduled for two weeks from Saturday!"

"All right!" cheered Rosa Jameson.

"Way to go, Liz," said DeeDee.

Elizabeth pulled a sandwich and an apple out of her lunch bag. "It's not all my doing," she reminded her friends. "This is Jessica's project, too."

Penny laughed. "Typical Elizabeth. You always want to give somebody else the credit."

"No, I don't!" Elizabeth protested. "In this case, I just want to *share* the credit, and that's only fair because we *did* come up with the idea together."

Penny looked at Olivia, who exchanged a knowing smile with DeeDee. DeeDee looked at Elizabeth. "Who got Chrome Dome's permission to hold a dance?" she asked.

"Well, I did, but—"

"And who arranged everything with Environmental Alert?" pressed Olivia, her hazel eyes crinkling in a smile.

"Me," admitted Elizabeth. "But—"

Penny grinned. "We rest our case!"

Elizabeth chuckled. "OK, so Jessica hasn't done a whole lot—yet. When the time really comes to get down to work, though, she'll pull through." Elizabeth said this as much to convince herself as to convince the others. "She has to," she added. "She's co-chair of the Prom Committee!"

"Who else is on the committee?" asked Cheryl.

"Anyone who wants to be," Elizabeth replied. "I'm planning to make an announcement at the end of lunch period, inviting everybody who wants to get involved to come to the committee's first meeting today after school."

"I'll be there," promised Enid.

"Me, too," said Olivia.

DeeDee ran a hand through her glossy dark bangs. "I'd love to help, and I know Bill would too."

"The more, the merrier," Elizabeth said cheerfully. "It's a big job, putting on a prom!"

"A prom . . ." Rosa's dark eyes grew dreamy. "Will there be a Prom King and Queen?"

Elizabeth looked at the others. "I don't know. What does everybody think?"

"Definitely," said Enid. "A prom just isn't a prom without a queen and king."

There were nods all around. "Then it's decided." Elizabeth smiled. "That was easy!"

"We didn't have proms at my old school in Manhattan," said Cheryl, who'd recently moved to Sweet Valley High from New York City. "How do you decide who gets to be King and Queen?"

"Usually you vote," answered Olivia. "Sometimes you nominate four people, say four girls for Queen. Then, on the night of the prom, you pick one. She'd be Queen, and the runners-up would be her court."

"You can also skip the whole nomination business and just hand out ballots the night of the dance," said Penny. "Then people can vote for absolutely anyone they want. The girl who racks up the most votes is crowned Queen, and the boy with the most votes is King."

"Which way do you think is better?" asked Rosa.

"Who do you think would get the most votes?" wondered Cheryl.

The girls launched into an animated discussion on the subject. Elizabeth crunched into her apple, listening idly. *Prom King and Queen . . .*

Her gaze traveled to the plate-glass windows looking out over the outdoor eating area. Slowly, Elizabeth's eyes grew hazy and she drifted off into a daydream. It was the night of the Jungle Prom and the dance was an unprecedented success. Ballots were collected and the name of the Prom Queen was announced to the sound of thunderous applause. *"Elizabeth Wakefield!"*

Elizabeth snapped out of her daydream. Her cheeks grew pink. It was so unlike her to fantasize like that! *Really*, she lectured herself sternly. *Why on earth would* you *be chosen over every other girl in school?* It would be far better, not to mention more unselfish, to promote one of her friends or maybe even Jessica for Queen.

Elizabeth frowned. *No, wait a minute. What happened to the resolution I made just a couple of nights ago?* Hadn't she decided to assert herself, to be an Elizabeth Wakefield who nurtured all sides of her personality, even the part that dared to be self-centered and ambitious?

"Well, how about it, Liz?" Olivia's question startled Elizabeth from her reverie. "Wouldn't you like to be Queen of the Jungle Prom?"

Elizabeth shook her head, blushing profusely. Were her innermost thoughts being broadcast over the P.A. system? "Me? Well, I don't know . . ."

"You're the logical choice, Liz," Cheryl declared. "This prom was your idea."

"And Jessica's," insisted Elizabeth.

"But you're the better candidate," DeeDee argued. "You've already done so much for the cause!"

"Not to mention everything you do for Sweet Valley High in general," added Enid.

"Everybody loves you," said Rosa.

Smiling, Elizabeth continued to shake her head. "Stop flattering me, you guys," she joked.

But inside, Elizabeth couldn't help wondering. *Would I be the best Prom Queen? Could I really win more votes than any other girl at Sweet Valley High?*

Lila heaved a sigh of annoyance as she nosed

her lime-green Triumph into a parking space in front of the Sweet Valley youth center on Tuesday afternoon. *I could be at the beach with Jessica and Robin and Amy,* she thought, disgruntled. Instead, she had to spend an hour talking to Nathan Pritchard, part-time guidance counselor at Sweet Valley High and her self-righteous, goody-two-shoes counselor at Project Youth.

Well, to be accurate, she didn't *have* to talk to him. The counseling sessions were completely voluntary. *I'm just doing it to please people, to shut them up,* Lila reminded herself as she entered the center. Her friends, the administrators at school—everyone had urged her to get some professional support, as if talking about her life to a total stranger was going to help her forget the night John Pfeifer drove her up to Miller's Point and attacked her.

Lila shoved the horrible memory from her mind. "I'm meeting with Nathan at three," she told the receptionist. "Am I early?"

The receptionist smiled brightly. Everyone at the center was nauseatingly cheerful. "You're right on time," she chirped. "Go on in."

Lila shuffled into Nathan's office. It was a mess, as usual. His desk was piled with books and potted plants; he'd taped a couple of new postcards to the wall, which was already plastered with posters and magazine clippings; the sofa and both easy chairs were the repository for throw pillows, jackets and extra shoes, a tennis racket, a Frisbee, and more books. *What a sty,* Lila thought. *If this is what his office looks like, imagine the shape his house is in!*

"Hey, Lila, good to see you," Nathan greeted her. "Sit anywhere you want."

Lila looked at the chairs, raising her eyebrows with eloquent disdain.

Nathan caught her expression and laughed. "Sorry. Let me clear those off." Scooping up an armful of junk from the chairs, he tossed it onto the sofa. "There." He dropped into one of the chairs. Lila had noticed that he always sat in a chair during their sessions, never behind his desk. "We're all set."

Lila perched stiffly on the edge of the other chair. She crossed her legs and smoothed the hem of her linen skirt over her knees. "So," she said, her voice cool and slightly disdainful. "What soul-searching questions are you going to ask me today?"

Nathan laughed again. "I was just going to ask how your weekend was."

"Fine," she replied. "How was yours?"

He grinned. "Very relaxing. I went for a five-mile sprint on the beach with my crazy black labrador, J.D., on Friday night, and I spent the rest of the weekend recovering."

"J.D.?" asked Lila.

"As in Salinger," Nathan explained. "You know, *The Catcher in the Rye*."

"Oh, I loved that book!" Lila exclaimed, leaning forward. "The part where—" She caught herself. "Well, we had to read it in my English class last year. It wasn't *quite* as boring as most of the stuff on the syllabus."

"It was one of my favorites when I was your age," Nathan remarked lightly. He raked a hand through his shaggy, sun-streaked brown hair. "Back to the weekend. Was your dad around?"

"No, he was out of town." Lila thought she saw a frown flicker across Nathan's face. "He has to travel a lot for business," she added quickly. "He owns his own computer-chip company, you know."

"I know." Now Nathan had that concerned, thoughtful look on his face—the same look he'd gotten during their first session when he'd said something about her "parents" and she'd had to correct him, informing him that she only had one parent.

For some reason, that look really got under Lila's skin. "He's a very important man," she went on. "He has better things to do with his time than just sit around stupid old Sweet Valley." *And go jogging with his dog,* she added silently, her tone snide. "Anyway, it's not like *my* idea of a good time is hanging out with my father. I have a life of my own."

"That's right," Nathan confirmed. "Speaking of which, did you decide to go with that Tony person to the big beach party on Saturday?"

Lila bit her lip. Dropping her eyes, she fidgeted with the ruby ring on her right hand. "Yeah, I went to the party with him," she said, her voice shaky with anger. "My stupid friends Amy and Jessica talked me into it. 'You need to start getting out more. It'll be good for you,'" Lila mimicked Amy's encouraging tone. "'Give Tony a chance—he's a nice guy.'"

"Well, is he?" inquired Nathan.

"No," Lila stated flatly. Her hands curled into tight fists. "I don't think there *is* such a thing as a 'nice guy.' He came on way too strong. He just kept *pushing* to get close to me when it wasn't what I wanted." The words spilled out fast, swept from her by a wave of emotion. "At the beach, he tried to put his arm around me, and at the door—at the door—"

Lila hid her face in her hands, a sob escaping her. "It's OK," Nathan said. He didn't touch her, but somehow his low, gentle voice was like a comforting, fatherly hand on her shoulder. "Ssh. You're all right. Just take a deep breath."

Lila sniffled. Fumbling in her pocketbook, she found a tissue and blew her nose loudly. Inhaling, she filled her lungs, then let the air out in a sigh. She smiled tentatively at Nathan. She felt a little better already.

"I understand you're upset by what happened on Saturday night," Nathan said. "You'd probably rather not talk about it, but I think it'll help to go over it—it'll put you back in control."

Lila nodded. That was what she wanted, what she needed: to be in control.

"So, just elaborate a little for me," Nathan suggested. "What kinds of things did the two of you talk about?"

"Oh . . ." Lila tried to remember. "Ordinary boring stuff. School, the play we acted in together a while back, whether or not Big Mesa High would raid the party—that kind of thing."

"Did he get personal with you? Bring up the subject of dating, or sex?"

Lila blushed. "Well, he told me he wanted to get to know me better. He told me he thought I was beautiful."

"Those are kind of nice things to say," Nathan commented.

Lila bristled. "Sure, if he didn't have an ulterior motive. Obviously he was just trying to butter me up so he could make a move on me!"

"Unfortunately, some guys do that," Nathan conceded. "But not *all* guys."

"So, how are you supposed to tell the difference?" Lila demanded, pounding her fist in frustration on the arm of the chair. "How do you tell which guys are *really* nice and which ones are just *acting* nice because they think it's going to get them somewhere?"

Nathan rubbed his jaw thoughtfully. "There's probably no foolproof technique. Your best bet is to get to know a person as well as possible before you actually go on a date. Take time to forge a friendship first. Study together, play tennis, just *talk*. And if you're ever uncomfortable in a certain situation, if it's too intimate too soon, get out of it."

"Maybe I wasn't ready for the party," Lila admitted.

"What didn't you enjoy about it?"

"Well, it was OK at first," Lila told him. "When people were dancing and talking. Later, though, everybody started pairing off, getting romantic and all that. Tony and I were sitting by the bonfire and he just sort of slipped his arm around me."

"What did you say?"

Lila smiled wryly. "I don't remember what I *said*. I just swatted him away from me."

"Did he persist in trying to put his arm around you?"

Lila shook her head. "No, he apologized. He knows about . . . what happened with . . ."

Nathan nodded; he understood. "So, then what happened?"

"Big Mesa raided us, and that was basically the end of the beach party. Most people went to the Dairi Burger, but I was tired, so Tony took me home."

"That was nice of him," Nathan observed. "Unless, of course, he tried to coerce you into going parking somewhere on the way home."

"He didn't," said Lila. "He took me straight to Fowler Crest. He—he was pretty polite, I guess."

"But he pulled a fast one at the door."

Lila fidgeted with the strap of her purse. "He went to grab me, to kiss me. I ran inside and slammed the door in his face."

"He grabbed you?"

"Well, he didn't actually *grab* me. He was about to—I didn't give him the chance." Remembering the moment, Lila felt her skin crawl. "I didn't want him to touch me!"

"At any point during the evening did you tell

him that you wanted to keep things strictly platonic between you?"

"I shouldn't *have* to tell him!" Lila declared.

"You're right." Nathan's tone was soothing and supportive. "But communication between two people of the opposite sex can be a tricky thing." He smiled wryly. "I'd say we understand each other about fifty percent of the time. The more you actually articulate your feelings and wishes, the better you'll make out."

"Or not make out, as the case may be," Lila added dryly.

Nathan laughed. "Right."

Lila stared straight at him, a wistful look in her shadowed eyes. "I don't *want* to be scared of every boy in the world," she said quietly.

"You don't need to be," Nathan assured her. "Right now, you're still recovering from what happened with John. You're very sensitive, maybe oversensitive. That's *not* a bad thing. It's instinctive—you're protecting yourself."

"Oversensitive," Lila repeated. "So you think I made up all this stuff about Tony," she accused.

"I didn't say that," Nathan insisted. "I'm only suggesting that his intentions might not have been so bad."

Lila sighed deeply. She wanted to believe Nathan; she really did. But when it came right down to it, what could Nathan Pritchard know about Tony Alimenti's intentions?

She looked at her watch. Thank goodness—the hour was over. "You're probably right about Tony," she mumbled, rising to her feet. "Well, I have to go."

Nathan walked her to the door. "You're doing great, Lila," he told her, his hazel eyes warm with encouragement. "Keep it up."

"Yeah." She turned her back on him.

"I'll see you next week."

"It's a date," Lila called over her shoulder. As she strode out of the center, she smiled to herself. *It's a date,* she thought ironically. *At least that's* one *date I won't be afraid to keep!*

Elizabeth paused as she was crossing the Sweet Valley High student parking lot on her way to meet Todd. Her boyfriend was leaning against his car, his profile turned toward her, unaware of her approach. It was too tempting—she had to stand still for a moment and just look at him.

Todd's glossy brown hair was still wet from a post-basketball-practice shower; a faded indigo-blue T-shirt made the most of his tan—and his biceps. Elizabeth's heart skipped a beat. Suddenly, she felt as giddy and love-struck as when she had first started dating tall, strong, wonderful Todd Wilkins.

Just then, Todd turned in her direction. His handsome face creased in a smile. "Hey, good-looking," he called. "Need some help with those heavy books?"

Elizabeth laughed. "How many girls have you tried that line on?"

"Only a dozen or so this afternoon," he kidded. "You're the first one who responded."

"I'll tell you what." Elizabeth walked over to stand right in front of Todd. "I can manage the books myself. But how about a kiss?"

"Your wish is my command." Todd wrapped his arms around Elizabeth, books and all. Their lips met in a deep, satisfying kiss. "Umm," he murmured. "How come every time I kiss you feels like the first time?"

A delicious shiver ran up Elizabeth's spine. "I don't know," she replied. "But it's great, isn't it?"

Todd kissed her cheek, then her neck. "I could do this all day. Why don't we get in the car?"

Elizabeth laughed. "It's a little early for a drive to Miller's Point."

Todd grinned. "You're probably right. Would you settle for Casey's Ice Cream Parlor?"

Five minutes later, they were seated at Casey's, digging into a hot-fudge sundae piled high with walnuts and whipped cream. "I can't believe I'm eating this," Elizabeth said. She spooned up a big bite of ice cream and fudge. "You earned it—you played basketball all afternoon. All I did was sit around at a Prom Committee meeting!"

"That's right," said Todd. "How'd it go?"

"Really well," Elizabeth answered. "A lot of people showed up." She listed off the names. "Enid, Penny, Olivia, Winston, DeeDee and Bill, Andrea, Roger, Annie Whitman and Tony Esteban, Jade Wu, David Prentiss, and Melanie Forman. It's a great committee."

"How about Jessica?"

"She blew off the meeting. She went to cheerleading practice, then took off for the beach with her friends."

Todd shook his head. "I thought she was co-chair of the Prom Committee."

"She is." Elizabeth smiled. "She just has a different management style than me, that's all."

"Well, I'd join the committee, but practice is going to take up more of my time than usual," Todd told her. "We're determined to revenge that loss against Big Mesa, no matter what it takes."

Elizabeth squeezed his hand. "I know you'll get 'em."

"You bet," he said. "They're going to wish they'd taken up ballet."

They each took another bite of the sundae. "It's OK that you're not on the committee," Elizabeth remarked. "Since the basketball game is the night before the Prom, you can help set up in the gym the day of the dance. You should be pumped from your big victory!"

Todd grinned. "It's a deal. So, what great ideas did you all come up with?"

"We basically talked about organization today," Elizabeth said. "We split up into subcommittees: refreshments, decorations, music, tickets and raffle, that sort of thing. Oh, and we agreed that there should be a Prom Queen and King. We decided to pass out ballots the night of the dance. First, people will vote for the King. Then, an hour or so after he's crowned, we'll count the ballots for the Queen. That way, the suspense will be drawn out for as long as possible," Elizabeth explained.

"Prom King and Queen, eh?" Todd nudged her foot under the table. "I know who'd be the *perfect* Queen of the Jungle Prom."

Elizabeth reddened. "You do?"

"I'm looking at her." Todd smiled. "The beautiful, talented, dedicated girl who's making this prom happen!"

"Well . . ." Elizabeth remembered her conversation at lunch with her friends. They'd repeated their suggestion at the Prom Committee meeting. "Enid, Penny, Olivia, and some of the rest of the gang *did* tell me that I should consider campaigning for Queen," she admitted shyly.

"They're right," Todd said with enthusiasm. "You should!"

"I'm not so sure." Elizabeth shrugged. "It's really not my style, campaigning and all that."

Todd looked deep into her eyes. "You wouldn't even have to campaign," he pointed out, clasping her hand firmly. "All you'd have to do would be to let people know you wouldn't turn down the crown if they offered it to you. You'd be a shoo-in!"

Elizabeth smiled. "Well, when you put it that way . . . I did decide recently—the night of the beach party, actually—that it's time I started asserting myself more," she confided. "You know, taking a page or two from Jessica's book instead of always being satisfied with a place in the background—good ol' reliable, she's-always-there-when-you-need-her Elizabeth. I want to be a different person—a more complete person."

"Give it some thought, then," Todd urged her. "If you ask me, you'd be the best Prom Queen this school has ever seen."

Elizabeth nodded. "OK." Suddenly, she was filled with excitement and self-confidence. *Todd's right*, she thought. *I don't necessarily have to* campaign. *All I have to do is not take myself out of the running, for once.* Wasn't that what her vow was all about: making the effort to see herself in new roles?

"I'll give it some thought," she declared. "Why not?"

"So, how'd your counseling session go today?" Jessica asked Lila late Tuesday afternoon.

Lila had met Jessica, Robin Wilson, and Amy at Guido's Pizza Palace for dinner. Now the four girls slid into a booth.

Lila picked up a menu. She ducked her head and started reading it. Jessica couldn't see the expression in Lila's eyes. "Mediocre," Lila said.

"How come just mediocre?" Amy wanted to know.

Lila shrugged, still not lifting her eyes. "Nathan doesn't take me seriously. I told him about how Tony acted Saturday night, and he thought I was exaggerating."

"Really? He said that?" Jessica glanced at Robin. As far as she'd been able to see, Tony had personified gentlemanly restraint. "Well . . . how *did* Tony act?"

"Look, I don't want to talk about it, OK?" Lila

slapped the menu down on the table. "Can we just order?"

The girls ordered a large deluxe vegetarian pizza and a pitcher of ginger ale. "I wonder how the Prom Committee meeting went this afternoon?" Robin said after the waitress left their table.

Amy turned to Jessica. "That's right. Wasn't it the very first meeting, Jess? Shouldn't you have gone to it instead of going to the beach?"

Jessica waved a hand nonchalantly. "I've already been appointed co-chair of the committee. I'm not really into that organizational stuff. Elizabeth is better at that. I'll leave it to her." She smiled mischievously. "That's why there's two of us, haven't you figured that out? She's good at some things and I'm good at others. We make a perfect team!"

Her friends laughed; even Lila's lips pursed in a tiny smile. "There *is* one thing I feel strongly about, though," Jessica added. "No Big Mesa High students will be allowed at *this* prom!"

"What about people who go out with Big Mesa students, like Enid?" asked Amy. "What'll they do?"

Jessica wrinkled her nose as if a bad smell had wafted by. Frankly, she didn't give a darn what drippy Enid Rollins and her drippy boyfriend were going to do. "There will be absolutely no exceptions," she stated firmly. "The Prom Committee co-chair has spoken."

The pizza arrived and they all reached for a slice.

"So, who do you think will be the Queen?" Robin asked before taking a bite.

Jessica paused in the act of raising her slice of pizza to her lips. Word had gotten around quickly that the Prom Committee would probably vote to have a Jungle Prom King and Queen. Jessica had immediately envisioned herself crowned and enthroned. "I know *exactly* who's going to be Queen," she replied, slightly peeved that Robin even had to ask. "Me!"

"Of course," said Amy. "You're a natural."

"Right." Robin darted a look at Lila. Ordinarily, they'd all wait for Lila to announce that she, too, planned to campaign for Queen. But the old Lila was missing in action these days. "You'd be a perfect Jungle Prom Queen, Jessica."

"I think so, too," Jessica declared. She laughed, but her laughter couldn't disguise the fact that she was dead serious about what she said. "I expect to be named Queen on the night of the prom. And anyone who tries to stand in my way is going to regret it!"

Five

The phone started ringing just as Elizabeth walked through the door on Wednesday afternoon. Dropping her book bag, she sprinted across the kitchen to pick it up. "Hello?"

"May I speak to Elizabeth Wakefield, please?" a deep male voice requested.

"This is she."

"Elizabeth, this is Larry Logan at Environmental Alert. We met the other day."

"Sure. Hi, Larry!" Elizabeth said brightly. "You're probably calling to find out what progress we're making on the prom," she guessed.

I've got to make it sound good, Elizabeth realized. *Environmental Alert has to be glad they've decided to sponsor us!* "Well, the principal gave us the green light," she began before Larry could reply. "And we had our first Prom Committee organizational meeting yesterday. We didn't get *all* the details worked out, but we decided to elect a Prom King and Queen. Lots of kids are getting involved, and we're all really excited about helping your rain-forest preservation program. In fact, we're looking for more ways to make money at the dance—besides selling tickets and holding a raffle—so we'll have more to donate to Environmental Alert!"

Elizabeth held her breath, waiting for Larry's response. To her surprise, he laughed. "To tell you the truth, Elizabeth, I wasn't calling for a progress report," he said. "Though now that I've heard one, I'm even more sure that it was a good idea—no, a great idea—to team up with you on this prom."

Elizabeth dropped onto a stool at the counter, relieved. "I'm glad you think so."

"We're impressed by your dedication, Elizabeth," Larry went on. "In fact, when I presented your prom proposal to the rest of the staff at the regional office, everyone agreed that Environmental Alert should do more for you than just provide pamphlets and posters and T-shirts."

"Really?" said Elizabeth, sitting up straight.

"Really," Larry confirmed. "So we've gotten together with a local travel agent, Dream Destinations. As a promotion, Dream Destinations and Environmental Alert are going to fund a grand prize—an all-expenses-paid trip to Brazil for a student from Sweet Valley High."

A trip to Brazil! "Wow," Elizabeth breathed.

"And that's not all." Elizabeth thought she could hear a smile in Larry's voice. "In addition, that person will become an honorary Environmental Alert student staff member, and have the opportunity of representing the group at various high-profile events in and around California. You know, giving speeches and helping with presentations—that sort of thing."

Elizabeth came close to falling off her stool. "Larry, that's fantastic!" she exclaimed. "But who's the lucky student?"

"That's what we didn't completely work out," said Larry. "Some of us—including me—thought we should simply offer the prize to you, Elizabeth. But a few others felt the process should be more democratic. We talked about making it part of the raffle—the grand prize. But since you mentioned that you're going to elect a Prom Queen and King . . ."

"Yes?" Elizabeth prompted.

"Back when I was in high school, the Prom Queen was always the girl who had the most school spirit—the head cheerleader, the president of the student body, what have you. It wasn't just a popularity or beauty contest."

"It's the same way at Sweet Valley High," Elizabeth told him.

"Good," Larry said. "We've been hoping to find a young woman to become the new honorary staff member; last month we had a young man from one of the local private high schools join our team. A student from Sweet Valley High will round it out nicely. Then I think the Prom Queen should get the trip and be the spokesperson. And I think her classmates will be happy to know the prize will go to someone they've recognized as a concerned leader—it won't be just the random luck of a raffle."

Elizabeth's heart was galloping with excitement. "I can't wait to tell everybody at school," she gushed. "This is *really* going to get people psyched for the Jungle Prom!"

"That's what we're hoping," Larry declared. "Tell you what, Elizabeth. Next time you're downtown, stop by the office. I'll give you all the information about the Dream Destinations trip to Brazil and the events the winner will appear at."

"Sounds great. 'Bye, Larry."

Hanging up the phone, Elizabeth spun around the kitchen in a dizzy circle. *Brazil! If I'm chosen Queen, I'll get to go to Brazil!* she thought, thrilled from the top of her head to the tips of her toes. She'd get to see a real rain forest and really learn about another culture. And to act as an honorary spokesperson for Environmental Alert . . . What an incredible opportunity!

Elizabeth glimpsed somebody through the sliding glass door that opened onto the patio behind the house. Jessica and Lila were lounging by the swimming pool.

She dashed outside to tell her sister the latest news. "You'll never believe this, Jess," she exclaimed breathlessly. "Larry Logan from Environmental Alert just called."

Jessica peered over the rim of her dark sunglasses. "And he wants to come to the prom dressed as a member of an endangered species," she said dryly.

"No, silly. Listen." Elizabeth perched on a deck chair. "They're getting together with the Dream Destinations travel agency in town and offering a prize to the student selected as Prom Queen. She's going to win an all-expenses-paid trip to Brazil *and*, more important, she's going to be one of the honorary student spokespersons for Environmental Alert!"

Jessica's sunglasses slipped all the way down her nose. Her eyes grew as round as saucers. "Awesome!"

Lila was less impressed. "Whoop-de-do," she drawled.

Lila's lack of enthusiasm didn't dampen Elizabeth's spirit one bit. "Isn't this going to be great publicity for our prom?" Elizabeth raved to Jessica. "I can't *wait* to tell everybody about it at school tomorrow!"

Springing to her feet, she bounded back inside and up the stairs to her bedroom. She couldn't wait a whole day—she wanted to talk about it now. As she dialed Enid's phone number, Elizabeth smiled to herself. *Now I* really *have a good reason to want the Prom Queen title!*

"Brazil," said Jessica after Elizabeth disappeared back inside the house. She drew out the word, savoring its exotic and glamorous flavor. "Boy, wouldn't I love to go there! The sun, the fun . . ."

Tipping her face skyward, Jessica closed her eyes. In her imagination, she saw herself on a white, sandy Brazilian beach, wearing an impossibly brief bikini. *Red,* she thought. *No, white. No, turquoise—to match the color of the ocean.* Jessica didn't know a lot about Brazil, but she pictured it sort of as one big Club Med. During the day, she'd probably go windsurfing and water skiing and snorkeling, and at night she'd dance under the tropical stars with a sun-bronzed South American hunk. . . .

Lila twisted in her lounge chair, reaching for a bottle of suntan lotion. "Brazil isn't so great," she said with a sniff. "In *my* opinion, the beaches are nicer here in California. And who said anything about sun and fun? Elizabeth said the winner was going to have to act as spokesperson for that stupid environmental group."

Jessica brushed this consideration aside. There was simply no way she intended to waste her time on such boring stuff. "I'll find a way to get out of that part of it," she said carelessly. "All I want is the trip." She sat up in her chair, suddenly galvanized. "Hey, maybe we should go shopping. I'll need a couple of new bathing suits and a beach cover-up or two, and maybe a new dress and a pair of sandals—"

"Don't forget a jungle-proof khaki safari suit and one of those pith helmets with the netting hanging off it," Lila interjected, her voice dripping with sarcasm.

"You're just jealous because it's highly unlikely that *you'll* be elected Prom Queen."

"I have absolutely no interest in being Prom

Queen," Lila claimed. "Who wants to tramp around a muddy, smelly old rain forest?"

Jessica frowned. "Brazil has *rain forests*?" That was news to her!

"Duh." Lila shook her head, apparently amazed at her friend's ignorance. "Why else would Environmental Alert send a spokesperson there?"

"I'll just have to tell them I'm allergic to jungles," Jessica decided. A broad smile replaced the frown. "Anyway, the *beach* is an ecosystem, isn't it?"

Lila reclined the back of her chair and rolled over onto her stomach without replying.

Her silence didn't discourage Jessica. "Brazil . . . Oh, I'll have so much fun!" Jessica's eyes sparkled with anticipation. "I wonder if they'll let me bring a friend. Wouldn't it be great if Sam could come, too? Of course, Environmental Alert will probably make me bring one of my parents as a chaperone . . . but maybe I could tell Mom and Dad the trip would be chaperoned by the organization, you know, like on those dating games where the couple goes on a cruise or something."

Lila didn't comment. Jessica peered at her friend. Lila's eyes were closed and her breathing was deep and even. *She's asleep,* Jessica concluded.

Jessica went on fantasizing, but in a lower voice, out of respect to Lila's snoozing. "This will be the biggest, best prom ever held at Sweet Valley High," she reflected. "And the Prom Queen is going to be the most important person in Sweet Valley!"

She tried out the words—"Jessica Wakefield, Queen of the Jungle Prom"—and liked the way they sounded. Jessica smiled, looking as satisfied as the cat that swallowed the canary. The title of Prom Queen was turning out to be even more desirable than she could ever have dreamed. And it went without saying, she had absolutely *no* competition. The crown was hers for the asking!

Lila opened one eye and peeked at Jessica, who was now sunbathing peacefully. *Thank heavens she finally shut up,* Lila thought, raising her chair to a sitting position. All that "Hi, I'm Jessica, Queen of the Jungle Prom" stuff was just too much—completely immature, not to mention just plain nauseating.

Lila reached for a fashion magazine lying nearby. As she flipped idly through the pages, she glanced at her watch. The afternoon was winding down; it was probably time to head home.

Home. Lila came close to laughing aloud. It was really a stretch, calling Fowler Crest a home. There sure wasn't any point in hurrying over there. No one would be around: her father usually worked late at the office, then ate out with clients or colleagues. No cozy apple-pie mom would be standing at the stove in a gingham apron, baking a casserole, ready to fix Lila a snack of homemade cookies and lemonade.

"Hey, girls!"

Lila and Jessica both turned in their chairs at the sound of the bright, musical voice.

Alice Wakefield walked around the pool toward them. She wore an emerald-green linen coatdress that flattered the curves of her slender figure, and carried a brown leather briefcase. Chunky gold jewelry finished off the elegant look.

Wow, she looks smashing, Lila marveled. Jessica said that people sometimes mistook her and Elizabeth's mother for their older sister, and Lila believed it. *I sure hope I hold up that well when I'm her age!*

"Hi, Mom." Jessica jumped up to greet Mrs. Wakefield with a kiss. "How was your day?"

"*Very* exciting." Mrs. Wakefield deposited her briefcase and pulled up a chair. "Doug and I met with an accountant over lunch. We're seriously thinking about expanding the firm by taking on a third partner!"

"Mom, that's great!" Jessica exclaimed. "Lila, isn't that great?"

Lila managed a polite smile. She didn't want to rain on anyone's parade . . . *But let's face it,* she thought. *The expansion of a two-person interior design firm isn't exactly going to make the front page of* The Wall Street Journal*!* "Congratulations, Mrs. Wakefield."

Mrs. Wakefield gave Lila a warm smile. "Thanks, honey. But enough about me—I want to hear about you two. How were *your* days?"

Lila didn't have much to say about herself; she just shrugged. Jessica, however, launched into a detailed and animated recital of every little thing she'd done all day long.

"I got an *A* on the last French quiz," she told her mother. "Ms. Dalton actually told me after class that she thinks I should join the French Club, can you believe it? It's way too geeky for me, but it's kind of nice to be told I'm smart enough to be in it. Oh, the *best* thing—Mr. Russo decided to give us an extra week for our science project."

"Lucky for you, Jess." Mrs. Wakefield winked at Lila. "Because as far as I can tell, you haven't done a stitch of work yet on that project."

Jessica smiled impishly. "It wasn't luck at all. I made an educated guess that he'd relent and give us extra time, and he did!"

As Jessica chattered on about cheerleading

practice, Lila felt herself withdrawing from the conversation, from the whole scene. She watched Jessica and Mrs. Wakefield talk, studying them dispassionately, as if the mother and daughter were part of a quaint museum exhibit or characters in a TV documentary.

They're really too cute to be true, she decided. They were the same size and had the same coloring; they wore each other's *clothes,* for heaven's sake. And Mrs. Wakefield was just so *interested* in everything her daughter said! You'd think Jessica was telling her that she'd just qualified for the Olympics, instead of mastering a handspring-back-crunch-split combination.

"I don't know how you do it," Mrs. Wakefield said to Jessica. "I play a little tennis myself," she confided to Lila, "but I'm pooped after one set. All those jumps and splits . . . !" She laughed ruefully. "I never even learned how to do a cartwheel."

"That's OK, Mom." Jessica gave Mrs. Wakefield a hug. "Moms aren't supposed to be able to do cartwheels. It wouldn't be dignified."

"And that's me, always the personification of dignity," Mrs. Wakefield kidded. She got to her feet. "Well, I'm off to the kitchen. I thought since I got home early tonight for a change, I'd cook. I'm going to make your favorite dinner, Jess."

"Stir-fried Chinese chicken!" Jessica said happily.

"And Elizabeth's favorite side dish," Mrs. Wakefield continued.

"Cold rice and vegetable salad," Jessica guessed.

"And your dad's favorite dessert."

"Peach cobbler! Yum." Jessica licked her lips. "I can't wait!"

Mrs. Wakefield turned to Lila, a welcoming smile on her face. "Will you stay for dinner, Lila? There'll be plenty of food, and we'd love to have you."

Lila clenched her jaw. She *could* stay. She could pretend that she was part of this absurdly perfect, adorable family. . . . "Uh, thanks, Mrs. Wakefield," she said, straining to keep her voice level and polite. "But I have other plans."

"Well, stop in and grab a piece of fruit or some cookies on your way out." Mrs. Wakefield picked up her briefcase and headed across the patio. "Don't get too much sun, girls," she called over her shoulder.

Alice Wakefield disappeared into the house. Jessica sank back in her chaise longue with a contented sigh. "Stir-fried Chinese chicken," she said, oblivious to the shadow that had darkened her friend's face. "Moms are great, aren't they, Li?"

Lila stiffened. There was a long pause before she answered her friend's thoughtless question. Her tone cold and bitter, she said, "I wouldn't know."

Elizabeth glanced around the outdoor eating area at school, then checked her watch one more time. It was Friday, twelve noon, and everybody on the Prom Committee had gathered promptly for their second meeting . . . everyone but Jessica, that is. She was still nowhere in sight.

I scheduled this during lunch just to make sure she could be here! Elizabeth thought, frustrated. Plus she had reminded Jessica about the meeting at breakfast that morning, and again on the way to school, and during homeroom. . . . *Well, it looks like we'll just have to start without her.*

"Today the different subcommittees are going to report on their ideas and let Roger, our brilliant financial manager, know how much money they think they'll need for their particular project," Elizabeth announced as she removed the lid from a carton of yogurt.

Roger grinned. "And I'm a tightwad, folks. Thrift is my middle name. The goal of this prom is economical extravagance." He considered for a moment. "Or extravagant economy. One or the other!"

"But first," Elizabeth interrupted, "wait'll you guys hear the latest proposal from Environmental Alert!"

Quickly, she told the rest of the committee about her conservation with Larry Logan two days before.

"An all-expenses-paid trip to Brazil!" Winston exclaimed. "Wow! Don't they have beaches there where the girls don't wear any—ouch!" His question was cut short by an elbow in the side from Olivia.

Penny's hazel eyes sparkled. "And to get to be a spokesperson for Environmental Alert—that would be an incredible experience."

"The Prom Queen is going to have to be *way* more than just a pretty face, that's for sure," commented Bill, ripping open a bag of potato chips.

Olivia pulled a bunch of grapes from her lunch bag. "She will be—don't worry."

Everyone looked knowingly at Elizabeth. Elizabeth dropped her eyes, trying very hard not to smile. She wasn't going to discourage her friends from supporting her for Prom Queen; at the same time, she didn't want to come across as vain and presumptuous. She wouldn't want people to think she took it for granted that she was a shoo-in for the title. Even though the more she thought about it, the more confident she was that she would do a great job of representing Sweet Valley High and Environmental Alert. . . .

"Anyway," Elizabeth said, steering the meeting back to its original direction, "how about hearing from the music subcommittee?"

Bill raised his hand. "That's me, Melanie, and Jade."

"We thought about hiring the Droids," sophomore Melanie Forman said. "After all, they're the most popular band at Sweet Valley High."

"But somehow, rock music didn't seem right for a Jungle Prom," said Melanie's best friend, Jade Wu. "We decided we needed something more *tropical*."

Elizabeth and the others nodded in agreement. "So, instead," Melanie continued, "we're thinking about booking that great reggae band, Island Sunsplash."

"Oh, I've heard them!" Andrea said eagerly. "They're fantastic."

"Out of this world," Bill confirmed. "*And* their fee is reasonable."

"How reasonable?" Roger wanted to know.

Bill told him.

Roger pretended to gasp and cough. "Just kidding," he said. "We can afford that."

"Great!" Elizabeth made a check next to an item on her agenda. Then she looked at DeeDee. "Any ideas yet for decorating the gym?"

DeeDee nodded. "David, Olivia, and I are bursting with ideas—we have way too many for just one dance." She smiled. "I guess that's what happens when arty people get together."

"We decided to go with the most obvious scheme," said Jade's boyfriend, David Prentiss, a talented sophomore who'd designed sets for a number of school productions. "We'll transform the gym into a jungle."

"The walls and ceiling will be covered with huge, glossy green leaves and big exotic flowers and trailing vines," Olivia elaborated. "All artificial, of course."

"And we'll create life-size cardboard cutouts of jungle animals and birds," said DeeDee. "Gorillas and monkeys, snakes, parrots . . ."

"We'll also have some posters from Environmental Alert," Elizabeth reminded them.

"Right." DeeDee stuck a straw in her bottle of grapefruit juice. "Oh, and I almost forgot. The thrones and crowns for the Prom Queen and King!"

"We're not going to do the usual jeweled-velvet and gold routine," said David.

"We thought the thrones could be more rustic," explained Olivia. "Fake bamboo or something like that, all covered with vines."

"The crowns will be simple, too." DeeDee sketched an imaginary crown in the air with her hands. "The Prom Queen's will be made of fresh flowers, and the King's will be a wreath of green vines. Doesn't that sound nice?"

It did sound nice, Elizabeth thought. Half closing her eyes, she pictured herself, a crown of flowers on her hair, presiding over a leafy gymnasium packed with kids dancing to the rhythms of Island Sunsplash. . . .

With an effort, Elizabeth brought herself back down to earth. "There was one more thing I wanted us to make a decision about today," she told the others. "I was hoping Jessica would be here for it, though. . . ."

"Yeah, why isn't she here?" asked Winston. "I thought this prom was her idea, too."

Elizabeth opened her mouth, ready to make excuses for Jessica. Just in time, she caught herself. *Remember your vow. You've been covering for her all your life. From now on, Jessica has to take responsibility for her own actions—or lack thereof!*

"I don't know why she isn't here," Elizabeth told Winston. "You'll have to ask her that yourself."

"I'll do that," he said. "Meanwhile, what's the thing we need to decide?"

"Whether or not the prom should be traditional and formal, or more casual with a jungle-wear theme," Elizabeth replied. She smiled. "So, what'll it be? Gowns, jackets, and ties, or Tarzan and Jane outfits?"

"Tarzan and Jane outfits, definitely," Bill declared enthusiastically. "I've got a pair of bright orange surf trunks—I'll paint them with black tiger stripes and I'll be all set!"

DeeDee laughed. "Very creative, but don't expect me to dance with you. I think we should dress up. It's a prom, not a pool party!"

"Why don't we vote on it?" suggested Andrea.

Elizabeth nodded. "Good idea. Let's have a secret ballot so there won't be pressure one way or the other." She tore off a scrap of paper and the others did the same. "Write down . . ." she grinned, "'Tuxedo' or 'loincloth,' then pass your votes this way."

A minute later, there was a pile of slips in front of Elizabeth. One by one, she unfolded them, then recorded the vote with a mark in the appropriate column.

"Eleven votes for formal clothes, and four votes for jungle outfits," she pronounced after a moment. "A clear majority."

"Rats," said Bill ruefully.

"That leaves one more thing," Elizabeth said, scanning her list. She had saved the best for last; she knew her friends were going to love this one.

"Tell me what you think of this idea—it came to me just this morning, when I was going through some old Sweet Valley High yearbooks in the newspaper office, looking for some photographs to use for an article I'm writing. How about . . ."

All eyes were on her, so she drew out the suspense. "How about putting together a special Jungle Prom miniyearbook? With pictures, quotations, and places to collect autographs and store keepsakes like tickets and stuff. We'd solicit contributions from local businesses in order to finance the publishing costs—they'd pay for ad space. Any funds we had left over could be a further donation to Environmental Alert."

The proposal met with immediate and unanimous approval. "It will be so much fun to have a souvenir of the dance!" exclaimed Patty.

"Somewhere to press your wilted old corsage," said DeeDee.

"I'll help you with it," Penny offered Elizabeth.

"Great." Elizabeth beamed. "Does everybody else know what they have to do? Enid, Tony, and Annie will handle the refreshments, and Winston, Patty, and Andrea are in charge of ticket sales, the raffle, and ballots for Prom King and Queen."

"Not that we'll even need to *count* the votes for Prom Queen," Patty predicted. "It's going to be a landslide."

"No doubt about it." Penny smiled at Elizabeth. "I mean, I'd love to win a Dream Destinations trip to Brazil—who wouldn't? But none of us can compete with you, Liz."

"You deserve it, Elizabeth," Annie Whitman agreed. "The title, the trip, the whole shebang!"

"Hey, I haven't won yet!" Elizabeth protested. "Don't take yourselves out of the running, girls."

"The point is, we don't *want* to run against you," Enid explained. "We all want you to win. No one would be a better Prom Queen!"

"What about Prom King?" Winston put in. "Doesn't anybody want to speculate about my excellent chances at being crowned as Elizabeth's royal escort?"

With everyone laughing, the meeting broke up. As she and Enid headed back into the cafeteria, Elizabeth's imagination ran away with her . . . as it had been doing on a regular basis lately.

I'd take the speaking duties seriously, she reflected. *And I can't deny it—I sure wouldn't mind the trip to Brazil!* It looked like none of her girlfriends were interested in being considered for Prom Queen. Come to think of it, Elizabeth hadn't heard of anyone who was openly vying for the title. That meant she was the only unofficial "candidate" so far. *And maybe I* am *the best candidate. What's to stop* me *from wearing the crown?*

SVH

Six

"We missed you at lunch today," Elizabeth said as she stopped by her sister's locker after the final bell.

Jessica straightened up, a book in each hand. "Lunch . . . ? Oh, right—the meeting. I completely forgot about it," she admitted nonchalantly. "How'd it go?"

"Really well." Elizabeth leaned against a neighboring locker. "We're pretty well organized. The different subcommittees made reports and I told everybody about my idea for a prom miniyearbook."

Jessica dropped the books into her book bag and put her hands on her hips. "*Your* idea for a prom miniyearbook? That was *my* idea!"

Jessica saw her twin's face and body tense. "No way!" Elizabeth said, her eyes flashing. "It came to me just today—I never even talked to you about it!"

Jessica laughed at Elizabeth's overreaction. "Get a grip, Liz. I was just kidding."

"Oh." Elizabeth's shoulders relaxed. After a moment, she laughed, too. "Sorry. Don't know why I was so defensive."

"It doesn't matter," Jessica said breezily. She slammed her locker door shut. "A prom miniyearbook sounds like fun. Is there anything else I should know about?" She figured it didn't hurt to be up to date, in case any of her schoolmates came to her, as Prom Committee co-chair, for information.

"As a matter of fact . . ." Elizabeth's gaze shifted off to the side. "We voted on a dress code for the prom."

Now it was Jessica's turn to stiffen slightly. "What do you mean, a dress code?"

"You know, what you and I talked about the very first night that we came up with the Jungle Prom theme," Elizabeth replied. "Whether or not to dress up or wear costumes. The majority of people at the meeting wanted the prom to be formal, so I guess that matter's settled."

"You voted, even though I wasn't there," Jessica stated in disbelief.

Elizabeth raised her hands in a gesture of helpless innocence. "It wasn't like a conspiracy or anything, Jess. The committee needs to make a lot of decisions, and if you don't happen to be there when things come up . . ."

Now it was Jessica's turn to overreact. "I can't believe you'd be that sneaky!" she burst out. "You purposely pushed through your little dress code while I wasn't around, didn't you? I bet you didn't speak up at all for my side of it. Don't forget, this prom was my idea, too, Liz!"

"If you want to speak up for your ideas, why don't you come to the meetings?" Elizabeth countered.

Jessica bit her lip, trying to come up with a biting retort. It was tough; Elizabeth had made a good point. "I *meant* to go to the meeting," she said somewhat lamely.

"Well, if it makes you feel any better, the vote wasn't even close," Elizabeth told her, "so it probably wouldn't have made a difference if you *were* there. But in general, Jess, we could really use your help with stuff. Everyone asked where you were. You don't need to worry—nobody, including me, has forgotten that this was half your idea."

"That's good," said Jessica, her ruffled feathers

smoothed by her sister's conciliatory tone. "Just see it stays that way," she teased.

"Just see it stays that way yourself," Elizabeth rejoined good-naturedly. "I'm off to the newspaper office. See you later."

Elizabeth merged with the crowd of students streaming down the corridor. For a moment, Jessica stood at her locker, looking after her sister. *Elizabeth was pretty protective of her dumb old prom-yearbook idea,* she mused. *Like I really would want to take credit for something so nerdy!*

Well, Jessica decided, Elizabeth could be as protective as she wanted. Running meetings and putting together yearbooks was the kind of thing she did best, after all. *Good ol' behind-the-scenes Liz.* Jessica smiled to herself. *I really should be more grateful. Thanks to her, I'm going to Brazil!*

"Hey, Bruce. I'm glad I caught you."

Bruce kicked his locker shut and turned around. Andrea stood before him, wearing tight faded jeans, a boxy, pink, raw-silk jacket, white tank top, and a hopeful smile.

"How're you doing?" he grunted.

Her smile brightened at this acknowledgment of her existence. "Great," she said cheerfully. "Aren't you psyched it's the weekend?"

Bruce shrugged his broad shoulders. "Sure. I'm always ready for a break from this dump."

"Well, how about getting out of Sweet Valley altogether?" Andrea hooked an arm through his as they strolled down the hall together. "There's a little restaurant my dad told me about, up near Marpa Heights, and I've been dying to check it out. How would you like to drive up there tomorrow night and—"

Bruce put on the brakes, planting his tennis shoes firmly. With a subtle but sharp jerk of his arm, he shook Andrea off. "I'm not sure I'll be free," he told her, relishing the way her smile faded and a look of disappointment shadowed her big bright eyes. "*Maybe* I'll call you tomorrow . . . if nothing better comes up."

It was about the most obnoxious thing he could think of to say, short of telling her he never wanted to see her again, anywhere or anytime. Bruce waited. This had to be it—this time, she'd tell him to take a hike. How much abuse could a person tolerate?

Andrea's lower lip trembled slightly; she took a step backward. But she didn't yell, lecture, or curse. "OK," she said, her voice small. "Call me, if you get the chance. I'll probably be around."

Bruce walked away without bothering to reply.

Pathetic, he thought. *That girl gives new meaning to the word "doormat."* Still, he'd probably call her. It was kind of fun, stringing her along. It had turned into a very interesting game, trying to find out just how far he could push her, just how badly he could use her.

Bruce pushed his way through the main lobby and out the front door of the school, heading for the student parking lot. As he approached his Porsche, he pulled his key ring from the front pocket of his khakis and jingled it idly. Still thinking about Andrea, he didn't focus on his car until he was only a few yards away from it. Then he stopped abruptly, his eyes snapping wide open with surprise . . . then fury.

The glossy black body of the Porsche made a perfect backdrop for the words written on it in white shaving cream. "SVH WIMP," someone had scrawled in huge block letters. Also in shaving cream, right smack on the front windshield, was a crude sketch of a bull. The Big Mesa logo!

Bruce whirled, his eyes raking the parking lot for signs of the perpetrator. Instead, what he saw were more cars, similarly trashed.

The windows of the Wakefield twins' Jeep were completely obscured by a snowfall of shaving cream. Lila's Triumph declared itself the property of an "SVH BIMBO." Todd's BMW proclaimed "SVH LOSER—BIG MESA RULES!" Not a car in the lot had been spared!

Bruce clenched his fists, nearly blind with impotent anger. "When I find out who did this . . . !" he roared.

"My car!" a girl's voice cried.

"What the . . . ?" someone else yelped.

Suddenly, Bruce was surrounded by a dozen other Sweet Valley High students, all shocked by the act of vandalism.

"Are any windows broken?" Ken asked, running to his Toyota. "Any tires slashed?"

Jessica and Lila dashed over to their cars to investigate. "No broken windows or slashed tires," Jessica announced, disgusted. "Just tons of shaving cream."

"Who do you suppose did it?" Terri asked her boyfriend.

"Who do you think?" Ken pointed to the shaving cream bull decorating his driver's-side window. "Big Mesa, who else?"

"Ugh. What a mess!" Lila complained. Digging in her pocketbook, she pulled out a tissue and started to wipe her car clean. "I can't believe they'd go to all this trouble just to antagonize us."

Whipping off his T-shirt, Bruce used it to rub

the shaving cream from the Porsche's windshield. If he had to look at that bull for a second longer, he'd explode. "They're asking for it," he growled. "Boy, are they asking for it."

"And they're going to get it," Todd grunted, applying a beach towel to his BMW. "At the next basketball game, we're going to—"

His words were lost in the sound of screeching tires. People jumped back as a dark blue pickup truck, seeming to come out of nowhere, tore at top speed through the parking lot. There was a boy at the wheel and another boy hanging out the passenger-side window, a bullhorn held to his mouth.

"Big Mesa rules and Sweet Valley High cowers!" the passenger taunted. "We're going to beat the shorts off you—*again*—at the next basketball game. So long, losers!" Brakes squealing, the pickup swung out of the lot and onto the street.

Bruce stared after it, his eyes black with hatred as they fixed on the Big Mesa High sticker on the truck's rear bumper. "They got us again," he hissed, seething at the humiliation.

The pickup roared off, leaving the Sweet Valley High students speechless with fury . . . and possessed by a desire for revenge.

"I just need to stop at the *Oracle* office for a

minute," Elizabeth told Enid as they headed toward the library, where they planned to spend a few hours studying for a history exam. "I left a notebook there."

"No problem." Enid smiled ruefully. "Make as many pit stops as you want. I'm in no hurry to hit the books!"

Elizabeth laughed. "Tell me about it," she commiserated. "Mr. Jaworski's tests are killers. I always feel like I've run a marathon by the time they're over."

They found the door to the newspaper office open. A few staff members had already settled in front of typewriters and computer screens to rattle off their latest stories. Tina Ayala, Penny's younger sister, was sorting through a pile of black-and-white pictures with Allen Walters and Jeffrey French, staff photographers. Meanwhile, Abbie Richardson, creator of the newspaper's humor cartoon "Jenny," was discussing layout problems with Eddie Strong.

"Hi, Mr. Collins," Elizabeth said. "Hi, everybody."

The Oracle's adviser and Elizabeth's favorite English teacher greeted Elizabeth with a broad smile. "Hey, Liz," he responded, his bright blue eyes crinkling. "I just read your latest 'Personal

Profiles.' It's a solid, exciting piece of writing—one of your best columns so far."

There was no one whose praise meant more to Elizabeth. She couldn't help beaming. "Thanks. I'm glad you like it."

"Hey, Liz," Penny called out. "You got some mail."

Enid trailed Elizabeth over to the big rectangular desk she shared with Olivia. Lying on top of it was a manila envelope with her name scrawled in Magic Marker. Something about the handwriting, messy as it was, seemed vaguely familiar.

Elizabeth picked up the package, turning it over in her hands. There was no return address.

Suddenly, she had a hunch she knew who—or rather, where—it was from. Tearing the envelope open, she saw in a flash that her hunch had been correct. Inside was a copy of Big Mesa High's school paper, the *Bull's Eye*.

"What is it?" Enid asked curiously.

Elizabeth held up the paper for her friend to see. "This is the second time someone's sent me a copy of the *Bull's Eye*," she said, her expression grim. "Last time, there was a mean cartoon about *The Oracle*. I wonder what's in it this time."

It didn't take long to locate the article that the package's anonymous sender obviously had intended for her to see. The headline was splashed across the lower half of the front page: "'Bulls Prepare to Bulldoze Gladiators in Upcoming Series of Sports Competitions,'" Elizabeth read out loud.

"They're pretty cocky," Enid commented.

"They're more than cocky," Elizabeth told her. "Listen to this! 'Big Mesa varsity and junior-varsity squads are honing their athletic skills in preparation for a series of games and matches against the Sweet Valley High Gladiators. Easy victories are expected across the board as we confront some of the weakest SVH teams in recent memory.'"

"What garbage!" Enid exclaimed indignantly.

"'Especially pathetic this year is the boys' varsity basketball team,'" Elizabeth continued, an angry flush staining her cheeks. "'Despite his height, SVH team captain Todd Wilkins came up short in our last matchup. His teammates call him "Whizzer"; we suggest "Whimper" might be a more appropriate sobriquet.'"

Enid shook her head in disgust. "They call that journalism?"

Elizabeth scanned the rest of the article. "That's just the beginning," she informed Enid. "They go on to trash every guy on the SVH basketball team, one by one. They even take a stab at the cheerleaders!" Elizabeth could just imagine how irate Jessica would be if she read this description of herself. "'Jessica Wakefield and Robin Wilson are co-captains of the collection of klutzes and cows who deserve credit for contributing to the lackluster performance of the hapless SVH hoopsters.'"

Enid whistled. "Talk about harsh!"

"Who are you calling klutzes and cows?" asked Olivia, coming up behind Elizabeth.

Elizabeth handed the paper to Olivia, pointing to the offensive article. The other *Oracle* staffers and Mr. Collins gathered around Olivia as she read it aloud.

Elizabeth watched their expressions. Curiosity gave way to shock and then outrage.

"What garbage!" Penny cried, her eyes flashing. "I can't believe they'd print this, and on the front page!"

Mr. Collins ran a hand through his strawberry-blond hair, frowning. "I'm surprised their faculty adviser didn't encourage them to tone it down."

"It's all a bunch of lies," declared Jeffrey, a star of the Sweet Valley High boys' soccer team. An uncharacteristic scowl darkened his usually friendly face. "We can't let them get away with this. We've got to hit them right back—and hard!"

"I'll write a retaliatory editorial," Penny proposed.

"I can do a cartoon," offered Abbie.

"Wait a minute!" Elizabeth held up a hand. She

knew how Jeffrey and the others felt. On behalf of her sister, Todd, and her other schoolmates, Elizabeth was as furious as Jeffrey. But in her opinion, "an eye for an eye" wasn't the answer. "I think we're getting carried away by the heat of the moment," she said. "Do you really want to dignify this junk by responding to it?"

"If we don't, we'll look like the wimps they say we are," Jeffrey pointed out.

"I disagree," Allen said mildly. "Elizabeth is right. We should just ignore it."

Penny bit her lip. "You mean, you think we should just let them get away with this kind of trash?"

"If we rise to the challenge, we're *really* sinking to their level," Elizabeth reasoned. She glanced in distaste at the *Bull's Eye*. "And that's pretty darned low."

Penny looked at Jeffrey and Abbie. Jeffrey shrugged. "It's up to you, Penny," Abbie said. She looked at Mr. Collins. "And you, Mr. Collins."

All the *Oracle* staffers turned to their adviser. Mr. Collins reflected for a moment. "I've always trusted you folks to make your own policies and set your own standards," he said at last. "The decision on how to respond to this—or how not to—lies with you."

Penny sighed. Her eyes met Elizabeth's. "For now, I guess . . . I guess we should do what Liz suggests. Nothing." She tossed the Big Mesa paper aside. "But it burns me. It really burns me."

"We'll get back at them by destroying them in the games and matches next week," said Eddie, striking a more positive note.

"Right," agreed Elizabeth, relieved that fellow staffers seemed to be calming down. "This kind of stuff will only get people fired up to play their hardest. Big Mesa will be sorry they have such big mouths."

One by one, the *Oracle* staffers drifted back to work. Retrieving the notebook she had come for, Elizabeth beckoned to Enid. "C'mon. Let's go."

Both girls were quiet as they continued on their way to the library. Finally, Enid broke the silence. "This feud is really getting out of hand," she reflected. "I'm starting to get a little nervous, Liz. What if people give me a hard time—I mean, more than just kidding around—because I go out with a guy from Big Mesa?"

"No one would do that," Elizabeth assured her. But even as she spoke, she knew she couldn't promise Enid that she wouldn't be criticized for dating Hugh. A lot of kids at Sweet Valley High were pretty mad—and tempers were getting hotter all the time. "No one who counts," Elizabeth amended. "Your friends will stick by you. Don't worry."

Lila stomped into the youth center. Her heels clattering loudly on the tile floor, she stomped past the Project Youth receptionist and through the open door of Nathan's office.

He looked up from the book he was reading, his eyebrows arched in surprise. "Hello, Lila. Looks like you're in an exceptionally sunny mood today."

Lila flopped into a chair, glowering. "I'm in a crummy mood," she grouched. "Some clown sprayed shaving cream over all the cars in the school parking lot, including mine." She wiped at a greasy smudge on her rayon tank top. "I managed to get the crud off my car, but I got it all over myself in the process."

"What's the deal?" Nathan asked. "It's not Halloween."

"It's this stupid school rivalry," Lila muttered. "The cars were trashed by some of the same Big Mesa creeps who wrecked our party last week-end."

"Hmm." Nathan bent sideways in his chair. Reaching into a backpack lying on the floor, he pulled out a six-pack of candy bars and extended them in her direction. "Nestlé's Crunch?" he offered.

Lila waved them away.

Nathan unwrapped a chocolate bar. "So, Li," he said, taking a bite.

Lila was surprised to hear him use her nickname, as her friends often did. And she was also surprised that, for some reason, his easy familiarity didn't bother her.

"You know," Nathan continued, "I can't help noticing that whenever I run into you around school, you take off in the opposite direction."

Lila wrinkled her nose. It was true; when she spotted Nathan in the halls of Sweet Valley High, she always pulled an abrupt about-face.

Nathan hadn't asked a direct question, but clearly he expected some sort of response. "I—I just don't feel comfortable talking to you at school," Lila mumbled, focusing on a San Diego Zoo poster on the wall so she wouldn't have to meet Nathan's eyes.

"Hmm." Nathan finished the candy bar. "Li, I've been thinking. If you don't feel all that comfortable around me . . . Maybe you'd be happier, more relaxed, working with another counselor. There are a lot of great people at Project Youth—including a couple of young women who aren't that much older than you. What do you think? I wouldn't take it personally, so don't worry about that."

Nathan's voice was mild; still, his words hit Lila with the crushing impact of a freight train at full speed. Her fingers clutched convulsively at the chair arms; she felt as if she had been tossed over the side of a boat into a stormy sea without a life preserver. *He's deserting me, abandoning me,* Lila thought, her eyes blurring with tears. *How come the people I rely on never stay around?*

Her panic must have shown on her face. Nathan leaned toward her, concerned. "Hey, Li. It's OK. That was just a suggestion. I'll stick with you if you'll stick with me."

Lila dabbed quickly at her eyes, ashamed of her momentary weakness. "Sure, I'll stick with you," she said, trying to sound as if she didn't really care. "I guess you're not so bad."

Nathan grinned. "High praise, coming from Lila Fowler."

She smiled despite herself. "You got that right, bud."

Nathan tipped his head to one side, contemplating her. "One more question, Lila. If I'm not so bad, why are you holding back? Why do you feel you can't trust me?"

Lila shrugged. "I trust you, I suppose," she said. "As much as I trust anyone."

"But you don't talk with me as freely as you do, say, when you're with Amy and Jessica."

Lila considered this. Now that she thought about it, she realized she didn't really open up that much to Amy and Jessica either. With her girlfriends, she talked about superficial things: clothes and parties and what movies they wanted to see and what CDs they wanted to buy. Did she talk to anyone about how she *felt,* about what was going on *inside*?

"It's not that I don't trust them," she said, pursuing this line of thought aloud. "I just don't think that in general other people are all that interested in your problems, you know what I mean? People want to be around you when you're *fun*. They don't want to hear sob stories."

"I guess I have the opposite view of what friends are for," said Nathan. "The way I see it, friends and family stand apart from the rest of the world, from strangers, because you *can* talk to them about personal things. You can really be yourself with them, let it all hang out."

Lila rolled her eyes. *Let it all hang out? Where does he get this garbage?* "Face it, Nathan," she snapped. "We're all on our own. You can't count on other people to take care of you. Everybody's looking out for number one. People don't *really* care about each other."

"I care about you," Nathan argued.

"The only reason you care about me is because you get paid to listen to me whine about my problems," Lila countered.

Nathan shook his head, smiling sadly. "Are you really as hard-boiled and cynical as you make yourself out to be, Lila?"

She checked her watch and got to her feet. "It works for me," she said blandly.

Nathan walked her to the door. "See you next week, Lila."

"Take *care*," she said, her tone laden with irony.

With his left hand, Bruce tossed the tennis ball high and straight into the air. With a smooth, powerful, lightning-quick stroke, he swung his racket over his head, nailing the ball. It rocketed across the net into the service court.

"Ace!" Bruce grunted to himself.

With satisfaction, he viewed the dozens of bright yellow balls carpeting the far side of the tennis court that was cut into the slope below his family's hilltop mansion. He must have hit a hundred consecutive serves; the muscles in his right shoulder felt as limp and loose as spaghetti. But he knew it would pay off; he'd be ready for Big Mesa.

Bruce leaned his tennis racket against the

fence. He left the tennis balls—someone else would pick them up—and walked toward the swimming pool.

At the same time, he saw his cousin Roger trotting toward the pool from the opposite direction. Roger's T-shirt was soaked with sweat; in the rosy light of the setting sun, his thin face looked as red as a beet. *He probably just ran ten miles on top of what he did at track practice,* Bruce guessed, feeling a momentary flicker of respect for his cousin. *Ol' Rog is fine-tuning the machine, too.*

Reaching poolside, Bruce stripped down to his shorts, using his tennis shirt to blot the sweat from his neck and forehead.

Roger bent over, his hands on his knees. "How's your serve coming along?" he panted.

"It's lethal," replied Bruce. He dove into the pool, relishing the cool slap of water against his overheated skin. Surfacing, he shook the drops from his hair, then stroked back to the edge of the pool and pulled himself out. "I'm ready to kick butt in the match against Big Mesa next week."

Bruce's face darkened as he remembered the scene that afternoon in the parking lot at Sweet Valley High. His cousin noticed his expression. "Did you get the Porsche cleaned up?" Roger asked, kicking off his running shoes.

Bruce lay back on the pavement. "I had them put it through the wash at Jansen's Imported Auto Service," he snarled through clenched teeth, clearly still simmering over the incident. "Man, I sure wish I knew who to send the bill to."

"A good tennis serve is the best revenge," Roger joked. "Go for the aces."

"I'm going to go for the jugular," Bruce promised.

Roger sat down on a chair, stretching his long legs out in front of him. "So, are you taking Andrea out tonight?" he asked conversationally.

"Maybe tomorrow night." Bruce closed his eyes. "If she's lucky."

"You know, Andrea's on the Prom Committee with me," he remarked. "She's a pretty nice girl."

"Huh," Bruce grunted.

"After the meeting the other day, she and I got to talking . . ." Roger paused.

Here it comes, Bruce thought sardonically. *The cousinly-bonding routine. "Is there anything on your mind, Bruce? Anything you want to talk about?"*

Roger's tone was mild, but his question was blunter than Bruce expected. "She really likes you, Bruce. Why do you treat her so badly?"

Bruce sat up. "What is this, the new-age male-sensitivity patrol?" he scoffed. "I really can't believe she went crying to *you*. If she doesn't like the way I treat her, why does she keep hanging around?"

As far as Bruce was concerned, the conversation was over. He jumped to his feet and grabbed his shirt and his shoes.

Roger looked at him. "I don't know why she keeps hanging around you, Bruce," he said quietly. "She probably doesn't know herself. Do you always know why *you* do what you do?"

Bruce stared back at his cousin. For once, he didn't have a ready answer.

I don't owe him an explanation of my behavior, Bruce thought angrily. *I don't have to put up with Mr. Sensitivity's nosy scrutiny.*

Without another word, Bruce stomped off across the emerald-green lawn toward the house. But even though he'd turned his back on his cousin, Bruce couldn't escape Roger's words; they echoed in his brain.

Why I do what I do . . . No, I don't always know, Bruce reluctantly admitted to himself. He thought about his recent near-violent outbursts, the urge that would come over him to hit somebody, to hurt somebody. In one way, it was exhilarating, that feeling of abandoning all self-control, of allowing his mind to sail above his body. Exhilarating . . . but also scary.

Because Bruce knew he *wasn't* always in control. Something had turned him into a human time-bomb. He could explode any day.

SVH

Seven

Elizabeth picked up a crisp copy of *The Oracle* from the stack in the main lobby at school. Even though she had been working on the newspaper staff for a long time, it still gave her a thrill to see the finished product. After hours and hours of investigating stories, writing and rewriting, editing and layout, the staff finally handed over the pasted-up version to the printer. And it came back a real live newspaper!

All the hard work was worth it—*The Oracle* was an important part of life at Sweet Valley High. It was Monday morning, and Elizabeth guessed that by the time homeroom started, just about every student would be carrying a copy of the paper, looking for articles about his or her sports team or club, reading the editorials, laughing at the cartoons.

Continuing on, Elizabeth unlocked the door to the newspaper office and sat down at a desk. She ran a hand lightly over the front page of the paper. *I'm glad we're not stooping to dirty tricks like the Big Mesa High journalists,* she thought, remembering the staff's heated argument the other day. *I just couldn't be proud of* The Oracle *if we did.*

As was her habit, Elizabeth flipped open the paper and started skimming the articles, half looking for missed typos. The staff was pretty careful about proofreading; still, there was always at least *one* that slipped by.

Basketball . . . honor-society volunteers . . . science-club field trip . . . choral concert . . . tennis team . . . Jessica Wakefield. Elizabeth stopped as her sister's name caught her eye. She checked the headline of the story in which it appeared: "Get Ready to Go Wild at the Jungle Prom!" by Caroline Pearce.

"That's right," Elizabeth said out loud to the empty room. "Caroline's article about the prom. But what . . . ?"

Elizabeth started reading the piece from the beginning. She expected a no-frills, informational article; that was what she herself had requested

Caroline to write. She had provided Caroline with all the necessary details and intentionally kept them basic; she wanted the story to promote the prom, not the people behind the scenes. In fact, if she remembered correctly, she had made a point of asking Caroline not to use any names at all in the article, including Elizabeth's own.

As for the basic details, they were there all right, Elizabeth saw, her jaw dropping as she read. The basic details . . . and a whole lot more!

Unbelievably, Jessica's name appeared in every other sentence. "Jessica Wakefield reports that the committee has decided. . ." "According to Jessica, Environmental Alert has promised . . ." "Jessica plans . . ." "Jessica hopes . . ."

Elizabeth blinked. She had to be seeing things! "*Jessica* reports?" she said indignantly. "*Jessica* plans?"

The article's final sentence was the crowning glory. "'Without a doubt,'" Caroline gushed, "'the Jungle Prom is the best idea Jessica Wakefield, the reigning queen of extracurricular fun, has had so far this year!'"

So Jessica was the reigning *queen* of extracurricular fun . . . ! Elizabeth rubbed her forehead, which had started to throb. She hadn't wanted to take all the credit for the prom; that was why she had presented the information to Caroline the way she had. But not to get *any* credit—not to be mentioned even *once* in the story while Jessica's name was all over the place! Jessica, who had yet to do a single ounce of work!

Where on earth did Caroline come up with this stuff? Elizabeth wondered, suddenly suspicious.

At that moment, the door to the *Oracle* office sprang open. Penny strode in, a cheerful smile on her face. "Doesn't the paper look great?"

"Actually . . ." Elizabeth tried to sound casual, but she couldn't totally suppress the note of anger in her voice. "Penny, can I talk to you for a minute?"

As she sliced a cucumber and tossed it into the big wooden salad bowl, Elizabeth checked the clock on the kitchen wall. She knew the cheerleaders had scheduled an extra-long practice that afternoon to prepare for the anti–Big–Mesa pep rally the next day. Still, Jessica should be home any minute now.

Maybe she doesn't know anything about Caroline's piece in The Oracle, Elizabeth thought, half hoping that would be the case. *Then again . . .*

Penny, who as editor-in-chief was always the final eye on the newspaper, had offered Elizabeth a simple explanation for Caroline's article.

Apparently, just as the paper was about to be pasted up, Caroline had dashed into the office with some "updated" prom information.

"We had some time, so I told her to go ahead and add it to her story," Penny had told Elizabeth that morning. "Why? Is there a mistake?"

Elizabeth had shaken her head—and bitten her tongue. "No . . . no mistake," she'd murmured.

Now she cut into a sweet red pepper. Scraping out the seeds, she carved the pepper into thin slivers. At this point, only one question remained in Elizabeth's mind: just how did Caroline happen upon this "updated information"? Obviously Caroline didn't invent it—someone fed it to her. And Elizabeth had a hunch she knew Caroline's source.

"Hey, Liz." Jessica entered the kitchen, her cheerleading bag tossed jauntily over one shoulder. "Need any help fixing dinner?"

"You could set the table," Elizabeth suggested.

Elizabeth studied her sister out of the corner of her eye as Jessica scattered place mats around the butcher-block table. *She doesn't* look *like she feels guilty about anything,* Elizabeth thought. But then, who knew better than Elizabeth what a good con artist Jessica could be?

I don't want to pick a fight, Elizabeth reminded herself, doing her best to swallow the resentment that had been brewing inside her all day long. *I don't want to make any accusations. I just want an explanation.*

Jessica joined Elizabeth at the counter. Opening a drawer, she started counting out knives, forks, and spoons, all the while humming an irritatingly cheerful tune.

"I suppose you saw the article in *The Oracle* today, about the Jungle Prom," Elizabeth began tactfully. "Do you happen to know—"

Jessica whirled on Elizabeth, her eyes lighting up. "Yeah, wasn't it *great*?" she exclaimed. "When Caroline told me she was writing something about the prom, I just sat her right down and gave her the interview of her life!"

"You sure did," said Elizabeth dryly.

Jessica didn't pick up on her twin's irony. "I thought you'd appreciate it." She leaned her elbows on the counter. "She showed me what she'd put together so far and it was so *boring*. I wanted to make sure people got excited about the prom, you know? So I talked it up for all I was worth."

Elizabeth looked at her sister. Jessica gazed up at her, her expression so open, so sincere. Obviously she had no idea her actions had rubbed Elizabeth the wrong way.

She wasn't trying to upstage me, Elizabeth recognized with a stab of remorse. *She's not trying to hog all the credit. I can't believe I was so suspicious! How oversensitive can you get?*

She decided not to ask her question. She would just drop the subject; there was no point making a fuss. Anyway, hadn't she vowed to be less concerned with Jessica and more self-assertive? It was silly to let herself get sidetracked from the main project of planning a great prom. She would have plenty of chances to get her own name in the paper if she wanted to.

With a quiet sigh, Elizabeth resumed chopping vegetables. Jessica picked a piece of carrot out of the salad bowl and popped it into her mouth. "It really *is* going to be the best prom ever held at Sweet Valley High," she chattered on. "The best prom *ever* held at *any* school anywhere! The best theme, the best decorations, the best prize for Prom Queen . . . I can't *wait* to go to Brazil!"

Elizabeth was about to slice into a tomato. Jessica's last words hit her like a brick; the knife slipped and she nearly cut her finger. "*What* did you just say?" Elizabeth asked her sister.

"I said, I can't wait to go to Brazil," Jessica repeated glibly.

Elizabeth stared at her twin, stunned. *So Jessica wants to go to Brazil!* she thought, her resentment bubbling back up to the surface like hot lava. *As usual, Jessica just* assumes *she'll be Queen! How outrageously, disgustingly typical!*

This time, Elizabeth couldn't hold her tongue—she didn't even try. "Gee, Jess," she said sarcastically. "Did it ever occur to you that somebody else—*me*, for example—might want the Prom Queen title and the trip?"

Jessica gaped at Elizabeth. Then she burst out laughing as if she had just heard the funniest joke in the world. "*You,* Queen of the Jungle Prom?" More giggles erupted from her. "Oh, Liz, please!"

Elizabeth frowned. "What's so hilarious about that idea, if you don't mind my asking?"

"Liz, you're just *not* the Jungle Prom Queen type," Jessica stated, obviously feeling it wasn't a matter open for debate. "Prom Queen is my kind of thing! I *love* being in the spotlight, and *you* love making things happen backstage."

"Oh, I do?" said Elizabeth, her voice dangerously cold.

"Of course. And Brazil—you'd hate it!" Jessica proclaimed. "You really don't want to go there, take my word for it. It's just beaches and nightclubs and stuff. *You* like museums and monuments and *that* sort of thing."

Elizabeth's eyes flashed. "What makes you such an expert on what I like?" she challenged.

"Because I'm your twin sister," Jessica replied with supreme self-confidence.

"Well, for your information, you're dead wrong," Elizabeth shouted. "I do *not* always like making things happen backstage—I want to be in the spotlight for a change. And I do *so* want to go to Brazil!"

Jessica blinked, startled by her sister's uncharacteristic vehemence. "What's with you, Liz?"

"I'm sick of you and everybody else taking me for granted, that's what's with me," Elizabeth snapped. "You always get what you want, don't you, Jess? No matter how many people you have to trample over to get it!"

Jessica still looked puzzled. "I get what I deserve," she told Elizabeth calmly. "It's not *my* fault everybody automatically thinks of me when it comes to things like picking a Prom Queen."

"They don't *automatically* think of you. Don't you think you help them along just a little bit?" Elizabeth accused. "Little Miss Innocent, giving Caroline an interview to promote the prom—yeah, right. You were promoting yourself and you know it!"

"I was *not* promoting myself!" Jessica cried. "I don't need to. You might as well face it, Liz. I'm going to be Prom Queen and there's absolutely nothing you or anyone can do or say to change that. So you might as well give up any ridiculous idea you might have about becoming Prom Queen yourself."

"You mean *you* might as well give up the idea," Elizabeth countered. "It's my turn, Jessica. *I'm* going to be Prom Queen!"

Hands on their hips, the two sisters glared at each other, neither one willing to give an inch. It looked as if they were in for an all-out, no-holds-barred battle for the Queen's crown—and the grand prize.

This is it, Elizabeth thought, gritting her teeth. *I'm not backing down and neither is she!*

"It was just so *weird,*" Jessica related to Sam later that night.

She had driven over to his house in Bridgewater so they could study together. He had a math test on Friday; she had a French test. They had gotten comfortable on the den sofa with their books—and with each other. As a result, so far they had done far more kissing and talking than studying.

"I mean, it was like she was possessed," Jessica went on. "She didn't even *look* like herself. We're standing around in the kitchen talking about the prom and all of a sudden, *completely* out of the blue, she starts ranting and raving about how she wants to be Prom Queen."

"I don't blame her." Sam grinned. "An all-expenses-paid trip to Brazil, the chance to be a spokesperson for Environmental Alert . . . Hey, how do you get nominated? I'd like to be Prom Queen myself!"

Jessica punched him lightly. "Then *I'd* have to run for Prom *King*," she kidded. "But seriously. Don't you think it's strange?"

"Maybe a little," he conceded. "I know what you're getting at—it's usually not her style to go for the high-profile position. But she's really into this environmental stuff, just like I am. And it's her prom, too, you know."

"Yeah." Jessica sighed, still troubled. "It's her prom, too. Oh, let's just forget about it!"

She really didn't want to dwell on her spat with Elizabeth. Chances were, it would blow over; by morning, everything would be back to normal between the two of them. Elizabeth would realize she could never win and would content herself with the none-too-shabby honor of being the Prom Queen's twin sister. "Let's talk about *you*," Jessica suggested. She nuzzled her boyfriend's neck. "How was *your* day?"

"Pretty good," said Sam. "I spent a couple of hours at the track. I posted some hot times."

"So, did you decide to enter that big dirt-bike

race in a couple of weeks?" Jessica asked.

"You bet," he confirmed. "And get this—I just found out there's a lot of prize money involved. If I win—and I'm planning to win," he added with determination, "I'll add a big chunk to my college savings account."

Jessica hugged him. She knew that Sam had very focused career goals, especially after spending a month at Colorado State University, participating in a special program for high-school seniors interested in studying environmental science. "That's great!" she exclaimed. "Although . . ." She pretended to pout. "I suppose you'll be so busy training for the big race that I'll hardly ever see you."

"Are you kidding?" Sam wrapped his arms tightly around her, holding her close as if he would never let her go. "Winning that race is important to me, but nothing—I repeat, *nothing*—is more important to me than spending time with you."

Jessica raised her face to his, smiling. "That's what I like to hear," she murmured.

Their lips met and they lost themselves in a long, passionate kiss. "I meant what I said, you know," Sam remarked after a while. "Being with you is my top priority, Jess. I have two main goals for the future—to go to college and study environmental science, and to keep on dating you."

Jessica looked into Sam's eyes. She'd never gone out with a boy who had been this serious about her . . . or about whom *she'd* been this serious. "I want that, too," she said softly. "I want us to stay together, even if we end up at different colleges. I just can't imagine not having you in my life."

They kissed again, and this time the kiss was like a pledge. "I could stay with you forever, Jess," Sam whispered into her hair.

Jessica pressed her face against his neck. The moment was so perfect. . . .

Maybe it was *too* perfect. *Can this kind of happiness really last?* she wondered, suddenly uncertain. "I wish we could always be this happy," she said, her voice tinged with melancholy.

"Hey." Sam put a finger under her chin, tilting her face to his. "Why so sad all of a sudden?"

Jessica shook off the vague, gloomy premonition. "I'm not sad," she protested, forcing a bright smile for his benefit. "Hey, we should probably hit the books one of these days if we don't want to fail our tests. I know how we can make it fun—let's make a bet!"

"A bet?"

"Yes. I bet . . . I bet I'll score higher on my French exam than you will on your math exam.

The loser has to take the winner out to breakfast the morning after the prom."

"Hmm . . . breakfast the morning after." Sam's eyes twinkled. "Does that mean we get to stay out all night long?"

Jessica smiled provocatively, her dimple deepening. "We very well might."

"Then you're on!"

Elizabeth pushed her sandwich aside to make room for the pile of advertising information she had received from local businesses. Mentally, she tried to calculate how many pages the prom miniyearbook would need to be. She multiplied numbers in her head, but they kept coming out wrong. *Why am I so distracted?* she wondered, rubbing her eyes.

There was a knock on the door. Todd stuck his head into the newspaper office. "Thought I'd find you here," he greeted her.

Elizabeth smiled at him. "I figured I'd use my lunch hour to work on the prom yearbook," she explained. "I won't have time after school because of the pep rally."

Todd crossed the room and pulled up a chair next to Elizabeth's. "How's it going?"

"Not all that well," she admitted. "I just can't seem to focus."

"Too much going on these days?" he guessed.

Elizabeth hesitated. She *could* just nod. It was a plausible enough explanation for her stress. But she knew it wasn't the truth. She'd always been good at juggling things. No, something else was bothering her.

Quickly, she told Todd about the confrontation she had had with Jessica the previous night. Todd whistled. "Sounds like some major fireworks!"

"It was pretty hairy," Elizabeth agreed. "Jessica really wants the title. But I want it, too!" She pounded her fist on the desktop, her eyes blazing with sudden fire. "It would *mean* something to me, Todd. Getting to travel and speak on behalf of Environmental Alert—I really care about their work and their cause. All Jessica wants is to sit on a stage and wear a crown and get her picture in the paper for the zillionth time."

"Her goals are different from yours, that's for sure," Todd said lightly.

But Elizabeth couldn't just laugh it off; not this time. Her expression remained intense. "So, what do we do?" she questioned Todd. "If she wants it, and I want it . . ." Elizabeth bit her lip. "I hate fighting with her, and I don't much like the prospect of competing with her, either."

Reaching over, Todd pulled Elizabeth to him

for a hug. "Hey, don't worry." He mussed her hair playfully. "We're talking about Prom Queen here. So what if you compete with each other for once? Something that trivial could never come between you two."

Elizabeth pulled away from him. "I don't know, Todd. I've got a bad feeling about this whole thing."

He shook his head, puzzled. "What do you mean?"

"Remember how I told you I'm not going to be the caretaker and peacemaker anymore, not going to just sit back and let things happen to other people?" Elizabeth asked him. "Well, the Prom Queen title may only be the beginning—the tip of the iceberg."

She looked at him, a prophetic shadow darkening her eyes. "I'm starting to worry that if I try to be myself, my *whole* self, there's going to be trouble between me and Jess. I just don't know if there's *room* for both of us on center stage!"

SVH

Eight

The Sweet Valley High gymnasium was already packed and rocking when Elizabeth walked in later that afternoon. She stopped dead in her tracks, amazed. Pep rallies were always pretty rowdy occasions, but this was out of control. *What a madhouse!* she thought as she took in the scene. *How am I ever going to find my friends?*

The bleachers were crammed full of bodies; the overflow of students milled about on the floor next to the basketball court. Music blasted from the P.A. system; people had to shout to be heard over it, and as a result the noise level was deafening. And the rally hadn't even started yet!

Elizabeth looked around, searching for someone she knew. Suddenly, she spotted someone waving at her. It was Enid, sitting with Olivia and Penny.

Relieved, Elizabeth made her way in their direction. It didn't take her long to get where she was going; she felt as if she was on a raft shooting the rapids as the excited crowd swept her along.

"Is there room for me?" she called up to her friends when she neared the bleachers.

"Sure, we can squeeze you in," Enid responded. Elizabeth wedged herself in between Enid and Penny. "Lucky you have a small butt," Penny teased her.

Elizabeth laughed. "Small enough, anyway. Can you *believe* this turnout?"

The pep rally's purpose was to launch the upcoming series of competitions against Big Mesa High. "Everybody really wants to beat Big Mesa," Olivia said. "And the Bulls are good at just about everything. We've *got* to be totally psyched if we want to come out on top."

Suddenly, the loud hum of voices crescendoed into a roar. Coach Schultz, the Sweet Valley High Athletic Director, had walked onto the court.

"We all know why we're here," Coach Schultz boomed into the microphone. Elizabeth cheered and whistled along with the others. "So without further ado, I'm going to stand aside and let our athletes take the stage."

To the sound of wild clapping, the Sweet Valley High cheerleading squad cartwheeled onto the court. As Jessica and Robin, the two co-captains, waved their pom-poms to lead the audience in a rousing school cheer, Elizabeth felt a surge of pride. Instantly, she forgot the conflict that was brewing between her and her twin.

Jessica was in her element at moments like this: beautiful, vibrant, magnetic. *Nobody at Sweet Valley High has more school spirit than she does,* Elizabeth thought. *Nobody.*

"And now," Robin yelled through her megaphone, "give a hand to the boys' and girls' track and field teams!"

The crowd responded with an enthusiastic whoop. The members of the track team trotted forward, waving and punching their fists in the air.

Next, Jessica raised her megaphone. "Also ready to march to victory, the girls' and boys' tennis teams!" Dressed in whites and carrying his racket, Bruce Patman strutted onto the court at the head of the teams. "Boo," Elizabeth whispered into Enid's ear.

Enid giggled. "Now, Liz, he's our schoolmate. We have to support him—when he's on the tennis court, anyway!"

"And last but not least," Robin shouted, "gearing up for the biggest game of the year, a week from Friday night, getting ready to out-dribble, out-shoot, and out-*class* the Big Mesa Bulls . . ." Even with the megaphone, her voice was almost drowned out by the cheers. "The one, the only, Sweet Valley High boys' basketball team!"

Elizabeth jumped to her feet, clapping wildly. "Go, Todd!" she screamed as Todd and his teammates ran onto the court.

Each player dribbled a ball, and as they sank baskets one after another—swish, swish, swish—the students in the bleachers howled for more.

"Go Paul, go Keith, go A.J.!" Olivia yelled.

"Go Jason, go Jim, go Tom!" shrieked Penny.

Elizabeth had eyes only for Todd. In his crisp sleeveless Gladiators jersey, his biceps rippling as he lifted his arms to take a shot at the basket from midcourt, he looked like an Olympian, a Greek god. She held her breath as the basketball sailed from Todd's hands; everyone held their breath.

Swish. The ball dropped through the net without touching the rim. The crowd went wild. Elizabeth hopped up and down, hugging Enid.

The teams that were going to compete against Big Mesa lined up along the boundaries of the basketball court and began clapping rhythmically.

Their hands on their hips, the cheerleaders fanned out in front of them, forming a big "V" for victory.

"They choreographed this cheer specially for the pep rally," Elizabeth told her friends.

The cheerleaders dropped their pom-poms at their feet. Stomping and clapping, they started chanting. "Sweet Valley, Sweet Valley, Sweet Valley High. We're the best and do you know why?"

"Why?" the crowd shouted back at them.

"Because we've got Todd!" the cheerleaders answered. "Shelley! Bruce! Roger!" One by one, they named each and every basketball, tennis, and track athlete. As punctuation, after every name one of the girls would perform a dazzling jump. There were handsprings, spread eagles, and splits galore.

Elizabeth's hands were numb from clapping so much. "I guess that's it," she said to Enid as the last name was called out and Amy executed a round-off, back-handspring combination.

She had spoken prematurely. Suddenly, a figure dashed across the court. It was Jessica.

Holding her pom-poms against her hips, Jessica flung herself into a spectacular no-hands cartwheel. As the gym full of students shouted their appreciation, she bounced straight into a lightning-quick series of handsprings, culminating in a back flip. Without skipping a beat, she leaped skyward into a perfect spread eagle, then dropped into a Chinese split.

The crowd roared. Elizabeth's jaw dropped.

"What a finale!" Penny exclaimed breathlessly.

What a finale, all right, Elizabeth thought. *What an opportunity for Jessica to show off!* As Jessica grinned up at the enthusiastic crowd, Elizabeth couldn't help wondering: Did the cheerleaders plan that solo for Jessica, or was it Jessica's own little improvisation?

Bouncing to her feet, Jessica trotted over to the microphone. "Thank you," she yelled to the audience. "Thanks, guys, for your enthusiasm and support."

She waved her hand and the students quieted somewhat. "Save a little of that energy," Jessica advised, "so you can cheer on your schoolmates at the track, tennis, and basketball matches this week. *And,*" she added momentously, "so you can dance up a storm at the Jungle Prom a week from Saturday!"

Elizabeth stiffened as cheers and whistles broke out all around her. Jessica had succeeded in getting everybody's attention . . . now just what was she going to do with it?

"A big part of our prom celebration will be selecting a Prom Queen," Jessica continued. "We all know that the Queen of the Jungle Prom must show an *enormous* amount of school spirit. She'll be someone who goes out of her way for Sweet Valley High—someone who sacrifices her own interests to the interests of her fellow students—someone who gives her school all she's got, all the time."

All around the gym, there were murmurs of assent. Enid elbowed Elizabeth in the side. "That's you!" she hissed.

"Yes," Jessica concluded, "I think we all know who that person is . . . the girl behind the most fantastic prom theme Sweet Valley High's ever had!"

As people applauded wildly, Elizabeth sat stunned and frozen. She couldn't believe what she had just witnessed: Jessica, blatantly campaigning for the title of Prom Queen!

She did that extra cheer just to win popular support for herself by proving that she has more school spirit than anyone else! Elizabeth realized. It was just like the newspaper interview with Caroline; it wasn't an accident. Jessica had actually *announced* to the whole gymnasium that *she* was the one who had come up with the idea for the prom and so *she* was the one who deserved to be Queen!

Did she . . . or didn't she? Elizabeth turned to Enid, Penny, and Olivia, expecting them to look shocked and outraged. But instead, they were cheering enthusiastically along with everybody else.

At that instant, Elizabeth saw just how clever Jessica had been. She hadn't come right out and named herself; she hadn't said "I." Her laudatory speech might just as well have been referring to Elizabeth.

As for the applause, *it* could mean just about anything too. *Are people clapping for Jessica,* Elizabeth wondered, *or for me?*

Only one thing was for certain, Elizabeth realized grimly. Jessica didn't intend to change her mind about competing for the Prom Queen title. And she wasn't leaving anything to chance—she was playing to win.

"Don't you just *love* shopping for prom dresses?" Jessica gushed on Wednesday afternoon as she and Lila riffled through the racks at Lisette's, an exclusive boutique in the Valley Mall.

"Humph," Lila grunted. She was committed to pretending to be not that interested; she had told her friends she wasn't even sure she would go to the prom. But she couldn't help getting just a *little* excited, seeing all the exquisite dresses. Lisette's *did* have the best selection of hot new fashions around.

Lila held a dress up to herself and looked at her reflection in the mirror. *And I've always been the most gorgeous and fashionable girl at every single Sweet Valley High dance,* she reminisced.

Jessica bent to examine the price tag on a strapless red dress. "You *are* going, aren't you?" she said. "You don't have to go with Tony, you know, or anyone, for that matter. A lot of people are going stag."

"Nathan thinks I should go," Lila told Jessica. "He's positively bullying me. At our last session, he tried to feed me a bunch of psychoanalytic baloney about how I'm being negative about the prom to cover up my mixed feelings about socializing and stuff like that."

"Well . . . maybe he's right," Jessica suggested, turning to the next rack.

"He thinks he is, anyway," Lila said disparagingly. "He thinks he's Sigmund Freud's grandson or something."

Jessica giggled.

Lila grinned. "Maybe I *will* go," she said, pulling a short flounced dress from the rack. As she examined the dress, imagining how terrific she would look in it, her spirits lifted. Shopping was fun; it always cheered her up. *That's one thing I can say for Daddy,* Lila thought. *He's not around much, but he's always there when it's time to pay the charge-card bills!*

"You definitely should," Jessica encouraged

Lila. "After all, don't you want to be there to see me crowned Prom Queen?"

Lila rolled her eyes. Sometimes Jessica's totally unsubtle, ultra-peppy self-confidence made her want to vomit. *Doesn't it ever occur to her that she might* not *get everything she sets her mind on?* Lila wondered. *That things might not always go her way?*

It was very tempting to rain on Jessica's parade—too tempting. Lila gave in to the urge to sprinkle a few drops. "I wouldn't take this Prom Queen thing for granted if I were you," she advised Jessica. "The whole school is buzzing with the rumor that Elizabeth is an absolute *shoo-in* for the title of Queen."

Jessica stared at Lila. Then she laughed and shook her head. "Elizabeth, a shoo-in? I don't think so, Li. Sure, she told me she wants to go to Brazil, but as far as I can tell she's not actually campaigning. I haven't seen her trying to win support or anything, have you? You must have gotten the story wrong," Jessica concluded breezily. "After the pep rally yesterday . . ."

Lila snorted. "You think you've got it all sewn up just because of your pitch at the stupid pep rally? All the cartwheels in the world can't change facts, Jessica. Elizabeth doesn't have to *try* to win support. Everyone loves her!"

Jessica wrinkled her nose. "Yeah, but who'll vote for her if she doesn't campaign for it, if she doesn't get out there and let the whole school know she wants to be Queen?"

"I wouldn't be so sure she's not campaigning. It's the quiet ones you've got to watch out for," Lila said knowingly. "Don't you think she's making the most of the fact that you haven't made time for a single Prom Committee meeting? And don't you suppose she's taking advantage of your not being around to take over all the arrangements for the prom so it'll end up being totally her own creation?"

Jessica frowned, her upbeat mood sullied. "Sure, I've missed all the meetings. But why should I have to worry about all that boring organizational stuff? I thought up the thing," she insisted. "I did my part."

Lila smiled smugly. "All I'm saying is, if you're smart, Jess, you'll keep your eye on your sister from now on. You know what they say—still waters run deep. There might be a dangerous current underneath there that you don't know about."

It was easy for Lila to see that she'd given Jessica something to think about. Her friend stood stock-still, an unhappy look on her face.

Then suddenly Jessica's eyes focused on something. Putting out a hand, she pulled a dress from the rack and held it up for Lila to see.

The dress was beautiful—midnight-blue taffeta with a low-cut neck and back. "It's perfect!" Jessica raved. "And it's a six—my size!"

Lila contemplated the dress. "It *is* pretty," she agreed. "But if you ask me, Jess, it really doesn't look like *you*."

Jessica laughed. "You're just saying that because you wish you'd found it first!" she accused playfully.

Lila shrugged. "If you say so."

Jessica grabbed Lila's arm and pulled her toward a dressing room. "C'mon. I've just got to try it on!"

"I just don't see anything I really, really like," Elizabeth said to Enid as they wandered through the dress department at Lytton and Brown. "Maybe I should save my money. I could wear something I already have, or borrow something from you."

"No way." Enid shook her head emphatically. "You've *got* to have a new dress. The Prom Queen can't show up in just any old rag! Let's try Lisette's—their stuff is really special."

"And really expensive," said Elizabeth.

"Some of it's outrageous," Enid admitted. "But

they usually have a few reasonably priced things. You just have to hunt for them."

Full of purpose, Enid marched off with Elizabeth trailing reluctantly after her. For some reason, she couldn't muster a lot of enthusiasm for dress shopping—maybe because she didn't share Enid's conviction that she was going to be crowned Prom Queen. Did she even have a chance, now that Jessica had proclaimed herself a candidate for the title and was willing to lie to get it?

"The very dressy, very expensive things are over there," Enid whispered to Elizabeth as they entered Lisette's. She pointed. "But over *there*"—she pointed again—"they have some less fancy but still really pretty dresses. Let's look at those, OK?"

"Sure."

Enid took one rack and Elizabeth took another. Enid flipped expertly through the dresses, stopping at a simple, flowing, rose-pink dress with a lace collar and a dropped waist. "What do you think of this?" she asked, showing the dress to Elizabeth.

Elizabeth studied the dress. "It's lovely, but . . ." She shook her head. "I'm not *exactly* sure what I have in mind, but that's not it."

Enid laughed. "OK. We'll keep looking."

Elizabeth riffled through the size sixes. There were a number of pretty dresses—one white, one pale green, one a soft floral print. But somehow, none of them was quite right. They were dresses she would have chosen in the old days, but now . . . Somehow, none of them seemed appropriate for the Prom Queen.

Elizabeth was about to give up when suddenly she spotted an incredible dress. A thrill chased up her spine. She'd found it!

"This must have been misplaced," Elizabeth said, eagerly pulling the dress from the rack. "It belongs over with the evening gowns. But, oh, Enid—it's perfect! What do you think?"

Enid's eyes widened. "It's gorgeous, Liz, no doubt about it," she replied. "But . . . I don't know. It just doesn't look like *you*."

Elizabeth held the dress against her body, reveling in the rich, sensuous feel of the stiff, glossy taffeta. "Well, maybe I want to be someone *other* than me the night of the prom," she declared. "Maybe I want to surprise everyone! C'mon, let's go try it on."

There were two large dressing rooms, and one of them was vacant. Elizabeth and Enid hurried into it, locking the door behind them.

Quickly, Elizabeth pulled off her polo shirt and stepped out of her Bermuda shorts. Enid unzipped the dress and carefully removed it from the hanger. Then she helped Elizabeth slip it over her head.

As Enid zipped up the back, Elizabeth turned to face the mirror. She caught her breath. The dress transformed her; she *looked* like a different person already.

The bodice was tightly fitted; the open neckline left her shoulders bare. When she moved, the dress's full skirt made a satisfying rustling sound. Elizabeth stared at her reflection, observing that the deep, midnight-blue fabric brought out the blue of her eyes, making them flash like sapphires.

"You look . . . incredible," Enid breathed. "That's a pretty racy neckline, though!"

"I like it," Elizabeth declared rebelliously.

"Well, there's a bigger mirror outside," said Enid. "You can get a better look at yourself."

Elizabeth pulled open the door and stepped from the dressing room. As she did, someone emerged from the dressing room next door.

For a moment, Elizabeth thought she was facing the mirror. But no, the mirror was behind her. . . .

It was Jessica, her twin sister, standing in front of her. And Jessica was wearing the exact same dress that Elizabeth had on!

"Elizabeth!" Jessica exclaimed, her eyes as round as saucers.

"Jessica!" Elizabeth cried at the same instant. "What . . . ?"

Enid clapped a hand over her mouth. Meanwhile, Lila drank in the scene with hooded eyes, her lips curved in a knowing smile.

Standing as still as statues, the two sisters stared at each other in dead silence, for a moment that seemed to last an eternity.

SVH

Nine

Jessica leaned back against Lila's car, tilting her face to the warm afternoon sun. She figured she might as well make the most of her time while she waited for Lila, who seemed to travel everywhere at a snail's pace these days.

"Hey, Jess, need a ride to Big Mesa?" someone called out.

Jessica opened her eyes. Dressed in their cheerleading uniforms and carrying their pom-poms, Amy and Maria walked toward her across the student parking lot.

"I'm getting a ride with Lila," Jessica told them.

"*Lila* wants to watch the Sweet Valley High–Big Mesa track meet?" asked Amy in disbelief.

"I'm making her go," Jessica explained. "My theory is that she needs to get out and do more stuff—if she keeps busy, she won't have time to mope. Besides," Jessica's lips curved in an evil smile. "I told her she'd see a great show when we get our revenge on the Big Mesa cheerleaders!"

Maria grinned. "I can't wait."

Amy rubbed her hands together gleefully. "Me either."

"So, Jess." Maria lounged against the Triumph. "Speaking of Lila, she told me you guys went prom-dress shopping yesterday. She said you found a dress at Lisette's you really liked."

Jessica stiffened, remembering the encounter outside the dressing room at Lisette's. For a moment, she felt a pang. She really didn't like being mad at Elizabeth—and she *hated* having Elizabeth mad at her. They were twin sisters, two halves of the same coin; it just wasn't natural for them to be at odds with one another.

Two halves of the same coin . . . Suddenly, Jessica's anger reignited. *Who picked this fight, anyway?* she reminded herself. *Elizabeth did, that's who. She's not satisfied with being her half of the coin—she's trying to be the whole coin!*

Jessica pictured her sister in the low-cut, midnight-blue dress and her outrage mounted. *Ob-*

viously Elizabeth is trying her hardest to look less like herself . . . and more like me. As Jessica saw it, Elizabeth could have only one motive for wanting to look more like her sister—in order to be chosen Prom Queen. And conversely, she could have only one motive for wanting to be Prom Queen: to deprive Jessica of her inherent right.

"Did Lila also tell you I decided not to buy that dress?" Jessica asked Maria. She lifted her chin haughtily, an expression of supreme distaste on her face. "I wouldn't be caught dead in it. It was way too conservative—like something my *sister* would wear. I don't know what attracted me to it in the first place!"

Elizabeth drummed her pencil distractedly on the desktop, unable to concentrate on the newspaper column she was trying to edit. Instead of words typed on a page, she kept envisioning . . . a crown. The Prom Queen's crown.

This is ridiculous, she berated herself. *What am I, a little girl dreaming of winning a beauty pageant?* She'd never been the type to entertain those kinds of dopey fantasies. But lately, being crowned Prom Queen seemed to be all she could think about.

Elizabeth tipped back in her chair, her eyes

roving restlessly around the empty *Oracle* office. Another voice joined in the internal debate. *Well, why* shouldn't *I want to win the title?* she challenged herself. *For once, why shouldn't* I *enjoy the kind of fame and attention that Jessica's always basking in?*

Besides, it wasn't just a question of vanity, of a crown and a title. If she were named Prom Queen, she would win the trip to Brazil: a matchless educational opportunity and a fantastic vacation wrapped into one. *Plus I'd be really good at the spokesperson job,* Elizabeth thought. *Really good. I know a lot about environmental issues, and I* care *a lot about them, unlike some people I know, who think recycling means wearing the same outfit twice.*

She looked at the fat folder on the corner of her desk, and the big cardboard box on the floor. The folder was bulging with notes, receipts, and messages relating to the Jungle Prom and the miniyearbook; the box contained pamphlets, posters, and T-shirts donated by Environmental Alert. *If it weren't for all my work, this prom wouldn't be happening,* Elizabeth concluded. *I deserve to get some recognition. I want this title!*

A voice broke into Elizabeth's reverie. "Hi, Liz."

Elizabeth looked up. "Hi, Penny. Hi, Olivia."

The two girls deposited their book bags on a table. "I think we're the only three people who aren't going over to Big Mesa for the track meet," Penny remarked.

"I know." Elizabeth tapped the pages lying in front of her with her pencil. "I'd love to go, but I'm way behind on this week's 'Personal Profile.' The prom is really eating up a lot of my time."

"Well, don't forget it's not just a chore," Olivia reminded her. "It's supposed to be fun!"

Elizabeth smiled. "Don't worry, I haven't forgotten! I'm planning to enjoy myself."

Penny pulled up a chair. "You know, I used to dread these school dances," she confessed. "First there was the mortifying possibility that no one would ask you to go with them and you'd end up sitting home alone while everybody else had the time of their lives. Then, when you *got* to the dance, you had to start worrying all over again. 'Will my date ditch me for the girl he *really* wanted to go with in the first place, the one who turned him down?' 'What if somebody else is wearing the same dress as me?'"

Olivia and Elizabeth burst out laughing. "The trials and tribulations of prom night," Elizabeth joked.

"That dress thing is a serious issue, though," said Olivia. "That's why I'm going to look for something at the vintage-clothing store I always go to, the one with the neat twenties-style dresses and stuff."

"You don't need to worry," Elizabeth told her. Olivia had a very distinctive and unconventional sense of fashion. "Nobody at Sweet Valley High dresses quite like you do."

"What are *you* going to wear?" Penny asked Elizabeth. "Have you started shopping for a prom dress yet?" Elizabeth's smile faded. Against her will, she felt herself transported back to the eerie, terrible moment when she'd stepped out of the dressing room at Lisette's and come face-to-face with Jessica, wearing the dress—the *identity*—that Elizabeth had chosen for herself.

"I did go shopping, yesterday afternoon," Elizabeth answered, "and I found a dress I thought I liked, but . . ."

I wouldn't be caught dead in it now.

Elizabeth shrugged dismissively. "Once I had it on, I realized it was way too flashy," she explained. "Like something my *sister* would buy!"

Bruce nosed the Porsche into a parking space at the Sweet Valley Marina and killed the engine. Locking the car behind him, he strode purposefully down to the dock where his father's sailing yacht was moored.

It was another flawless Southern California day.

The sky was a clear robin's-egg blue, without a cloud in sight. A light but steady wind scudded across the ocean, kicking up small whitecaps. *I can't wait to get out there,* Bruce thought impatiently. It would feel so good to turn his back on land and point the boat out to sea, to feel nothing but the rope in his hands, the salt spray on his face. And best of all, to be alone—absolutely alone.

Thank God I didn't go to that stupid track meet. Bruce picked up a stone and tossed it, startling some seagulls roosting nearby. Maybe Roger would be bummed that his cousin didn't show up to cheer him on as he ran around in circles like a total idiot; Roger made a point of watching all of Bruce's tennis matches.

That brotherly stuff is for the birds, Bruce thought disdainfully, throwing another pebble. It had been a lot cooler being an only child, before Roger's mother died and his aunt and uncle, Bruce's parents, decided to take him in.

Lost in his own thoughts, Bruce practically ran over someone walking up the dock in the opposite direction. "Hey, Bruce!"

Bruce narrowed his eyes, focusing. When he saw who had hailed him, he had a hard time disguising his surprise—and his displeasure. *Of all people to run into . . .*

Tall, black-haired Nicholas Morrow wore a baseball cap embroidered with the name of his boat, the *Seabird*. Under the bill of the cap, his emerald-green eyes crinkled in a friendly smile. "Bruce, good to see you."

Nicholas stuck out his hand. Bruce shook it reluctantly. "Yeah," he mumbled.

"It's been a while," observed Nicholas. "I haven't seen much of you since . . . since Regina's death. How's everything going?"

Bruce flinched. How could Nicholas say those words so casually? How could he speak Regina's name without crying, without cursing?

Bruce swallowed. He knew Nicholas was just trying to be nice; that was Nicholas, always too good to be true, so sincere it made you want to puke. But his throat had tightened; for his life, Bruce couldn't speak.

"I heard you've been seeing Andrea," Nicholas remarked conversationally. "She's a lot of fun to hang out with, isn't she?"

Bruce recovered his voice. "If she's such a blast, why aren't *you* still going out with her?" he asked sarcastically.

If Nicholas thought Bruce's comment was rude, he didn't show it. "I guess I was too old and stodgy for her," he said, his tone light. "She got bored with me."

And I'm getting bored with you, too! thought Bruce.

He remained stubbornly silent. He really didn't want to stand around on the dock making meaningless small talk with his dead girlfriend's older brother. Maybe Nicholas would get the hint and let him alone.

But instead of moving on, Nicholas stepped closer to Bruce. Reaching out, he put a hand on Bruce's shoulder. "It's been tough on all of us," he said, his voice rough. "Mom and Dad and I miss her so much. . . . I know it's hard for you, too, Bruce."

Bruce shrugged off Nicholas's hand as if it had been a red-hot iron. "Look, I'm fine," he snapped. "You've got to get over these things, you know? I've moved on with my life. I'm *fine*."

Nicholas gazed at Bruce for a long moment, a deep sadness in his eyes. "If you say so," he said quietly.

Bruce couldn't bear the look in the older boy's eyes; he couldn't stand his pity. "See ya," he muttered, brushing past Nicholas.

"See ya," Nicholas echoed.

Bruce hurried down the dock. He didn't glance back, but he could tell without looking that Nicholas was still standing there, watching him go. Those sad, pitying eyes pierced him like poison arrows.

* * *

"Wasn't that the greatest?" Jessica gloated, her eyes alight with the joy of successful revenge. "Talk about a beautiful sight. Ten Big Mesa High cheerleaders yelling for all they were worth with bright, broccoli-green teeth!"

"I can't believe they fell for trick gum." Lila bent to pick up a seagull feather. "It's got to be the oldest trick in the book."

"That's why it's so sweet," explained Jessica. "We made them look stupid because they *are* stupid!"

"And not only that, we won the track meet," commented Lila, pretending that she cared.

"And *that* was no trick," Jessica agreed. "We're just faster and stronger and all-around better than they are!"

It had been Jessica's idea to stop by the beach for a stroll on their way home from the meet. Lila had tried to veto the suggestion, but now that they were there, she was glad for a chance to stretch her legs and take deep breaths of salty, fresh air. The late-afternoon sun, dipping low in the sky, bathed the scene in a warm, golden glow. Ahead of them, the sand stretched, endless and empty.

"Don't you love the beach when there's no one else around?" Lila asked Jessica.

"It's OK," Jessica replied. "But I prefer a crowd,

myself. A cookout, a volleyball game with lots of muscular guys in bright-colored swim trunks and no shirts . . ."

A cookout, a volleyball game, guys in bright-colored swim trunks . . . Lila blinked. The cookout and the volleyball game hadn't materialized, but the guy in swim trunks had. He came around the edge of a sand dune, preceded by a big, romping black Labrador dog with a Frisbee in its mouth.

Lila knew that shaggy brown hair—the guy's, that is. And she had heard enough about the stupid dog to recognize it, too.

Talk about the last person on earth I feel like bumping into! Lila did an abrupt about-face and marched rapidly in the opposite direction, dragging Jessica along with her.

"Hey, what's going on?" Jessica cried.

"It's almost dinnertime." Lila picked up the pace. "I really think we should be getting—"

"Lila! Wait up!" a male voice called from behind them.

"Rats," Lila muttered under her breath.

The two girls turned. As Nathan jogged across the sand in their direction, J.D. galloping at his side, Jessica's eyes widened. "Who is *that*?" she murmured, tossing her hair back and getting ready to flash her brightest, most flirtatious smile.

"Hi, Nathan," Lila said flatly.

Jessica stuck out her hand. "Nathan, pleased to meet you," she purred.

"Nathan's my counselor at Project Youth," Lila informed her friend.

Jessica looked surprised. "Oh, *that* Nathan."

Nathan grinned. "I recognize you from school," he told Jessica. "You're one of the Wakefield twins."

Jessica's smile dimmed somewhat. "I'm Jessica. *Jessica* Wakefield."

Nathan turned to Lila. "Great day for a walk on the beach, huh?"

Lila shrugged. "It *was* nice and peaceful."

He laughed. "I get the message. You're not in the mood to toss the Frisbee for J.D."

Lila's lips twitched. She couldn't help smiling. "Maybe some other time."

"Well, not everybody's a dog person," Nathan said amiably. "I understand."

"I'm a dog person," Jessica piped up. "We have a golden retriever named Prince Albert. Sometimes I bring him to the beach for a jog."

"Then maybe J.D. and I will run into you," said Nathan. "See you guys around."

"So long," said Lila.

"Nice talking to you!" called Jessica.

Nathan flipped the Frisbee. J.D. tore after it, his big paws flinging up buckets of sand. With a good-bye wave at the girls, Nathan jogged off.

Jessica and Lila continued walking. "So, *that's* Nathan," remarked Jessica. "What a great guy! Now that I think about it, I do think I've seen him from a distance around school, but I've never talked to him."

"That's because *you're* not messed up, like me," Lila said dryly.

Twisting her neck, Jessica looked over her shoulder. "He's really cute up close, too. I didn't recognize him, wearing a bathing suit!"

"You think he's cute?" Lila asked, surprised.

"Definitely," Jessica asserted. "He's adorable."

Adorable? Lila wrinkled her nose. "I guess I never noticed. I mean, he's my *counselor*. Our relationship is purely professional."

"Well, duh, of course it is," said Jessica. "But at least you could have told me how nice he is. From what you've said, I assumed he was a real meanie."

They turned away from the water, cutting across the sand toward the parking lot. Lila jingled her car keys, pondering. *A real meanie . . . Is that really the impression I gave Jessica? Is that how I talk about Nathan, about the whole counseling thing?*

A minute later, they were in the Triumph, cruising through downtown Sweet Valley. Lila braked at a red light. On the corner was a bicycle shop. Lila gestured at the store. She was still thinking about her counselor. "You know, Nathan has one of those mountain bikes—he rides it to work. Do you think they're any fun?"

"Mountain bikes?" repeated Jessica. She looked at the shop. Then she gasped and slapped her hand over her mouth. "Oh, no! I totally forgot!"

"Forgot what?"

"Sam." Jessica grimaced. "He was going to be in Sweet Valley this afternoon, and I promised to pick him up after the meet and give him a ride home." She checked the clock on the dashboard and groaned. "He would've been looking for me more than an hour ago! Shoot. What was I thinking? I don't even have the Jeep today."

"Sounds like you're losing your mind," Lila said. "Maybe you *do* need counseling!"

"I bet he had to call someone to come and get him." Jessica bit her lip. "I bet he's really mad at me. I'd be mad at *him* if he left *me* stranded like that."

"Well, cheer up." The light changed and Lila gunned the engine. "When you see him, just tell him you had to make an emergency visit to the dentist. And chew a piece of that trick gum first!"

Elizabeth tossed her books behind the seat, then climbed into the Jeep and started the engine. *What a long afternoon,* she thought, glancing at her watch. Long—but productive. She'd finished her newspaper column *and* she'd blocked out the entire prom miniyearbook with Penny! It was almost ready to go to the printer's.

She turned out of the parking lot, heading for home. About a mile along, she spotted a boy in blue jeans and an orange T-shirt walking along the side of the road. She was pretty sure she recognized the blond curly hair. . . .

As she passed the boy, she looked in her rearview mirror. *Yep, it's him. How strange!*

Elizabeth flicked on her right-hand turn signal and hit the brakes. She pulled over to the side of the road, then leaned over and opened the passenger-side door. "Hey, Woodruff," she called. "I don't think I've ever seen you on foot before! What's up?"

Sam stepped up, a wry grin on his face. "Hey, there, Liz. Your sister was supposed to meet me here after the track meet and drive me back to Bridgewater," he explained, "but she never showed. I got a ride over with a friend this afternoon, but he was going over to his girlfriend's house for dinner . . ."

"Say no more," commanded Elizabeth. "Hop in—I'll drive you home."

She pulled back into the street and at the next intersection, took the road to Bridgewater. "Jessica is so spacey. She knew I'd have the Jeep today—Lila drove her to the meet." Elizabeth glanced at Sam, smiling sympathetically. "What were you going to do, *walk* to Bridgewater?"

Sam chuckled. "Actually, I was heading to your house. I figured I'd find somebody there who'd take pity on me. A little walking wouldn't kill me, anyhow. I could use the exercise—I need to get in shape for the big race."

"What big race?" asked Elizabeth.

Sam raised his eyebrows. "Hasn't Jessica said anything about it?"

Elizabeth shook her head. "We . . . we've both been kind of busy lately," she lied, not wanting to let on that she and Jessica were avoiding each other like the plague. "We haven't had a lot of chances to talk. So what's the story?"

"There's a big dirt-bike rally in a couple of weeks, with some serious prize money—which, needless to say, would really come in handy down the road, for college. So, I'm training pretty hard. I can win—if I have the best race of my life."

"You can do it," Elizabeth encouraged him. "You've got determination and that's half the race, right there!"

"Unfortunately, there are going to be some other pretty determined guys," said Sam. "I'm not the only one who wants that prize!"

I'm not the only one who wants that prize. . . . Sam's words seemed to linger in the air. For a moment, they were both silent, contemplative.

"You know, Liz," Sam said after a while, "I hope you don't think I'd ever take sides or anything. I mean, about this Prom Queen business."

Hmm . . . So Jessica told him about that! "Well, it *does* look as if she and I are competing for the crown," Elizabeth remarked. "And *we're* both pretty determined!"

"It doesn't need to get in the way of your friendship, though," said Sam. "It won't get in the way of *our* friendship, anyway—I mean, yours and mine."

Elizabeth glanced at him, touched. "Thanks," she said softly.

"Hey, don't mention it." Sam's gray eyes twinkled. "I figure I have to butter you up—or I'll be hitchhiking again!"

Elizabeth laughed. Sam was really something else. He had a great sense of humor, but more important, he had a kind heart. Elizabeth had always hoped that someday her sister would find a boy as nice as Todd, someone who loved and appreciated her, someone she could count on. And it really seemed to Elizabeth that in Sam Woodruff, her twin had struck gold. The four of them—Elizabeth and Todd, Jessica and Sam—had had a lot of fun together. *And we'll have fun again,* Elizabeth promised herself. *After the prom is over . . .*

Bruce walked quietly through the big empty house. The sun was setting, but he didn't bother turning on any lights. He preferred the dark.

Mom and Dad must have gone out to dinner, he thought, glancing into the shadowy living room. He mounted the wide, curved staircase. Down the hall, he saw that his cousin's bedroom door was ajar. Roger was out, too—either celebrating or mourning, depending on the outcome of the track meet.

Entering his own room, Bruce kicked off his leather boat shoes. He ran a hand through his hair. It was sticky with salt from his long, solitary afternoon on the water; he needed a shower.

But instead of heading for the bathroom, Bruce

sat down on the edge of his wide, four-poster bed and pulled open the drawer of the night table.

Gently, he removed something that he kept hidden at the back of the drawer. It was a silver frame, and in the frame was a photograph of a girl.

A beautiful girl, with long, wavy black hair, eyes the color of sapphires, and a smile like an angel's. Bruce stared at the face in the picture, smiling out at him—so warm, so alive. She was smiling that way because she was in love with the boy who was taking her picture. *She was in love with* me, Bruce remembered.

But he had let her go. And then—and then . . .

Bruce stared at the face in the photograph, stared into the pure, trusting, adoring eyes. No one would ever look at him that way again.

A drop of water fell onto the glass that covered Regina's face, and then another. Her image blurred as Bruce's eyes brimmed and spilled over with anguished, bitter tears.

SVH

Ten

"Do you mind if we stop at the *Oracle* office on the way to lunch?" Elizabeth asked Todd on Friday. "Mr. Collins was going to leave something for me there."

"No problem," said Todd. "As long as you promise you're not going to try to squeeze some work in. You need to take a break now and then."

Elizabeth took his hand, swinging it lightly as they walked down the corridor. "OK, I promise. But I'm not the only one who's overextending myself lately. You spend every spare *minute* shooting baskets—I never see you anymore!"

"The extra practice'll pay off when we wipe the floor with Big Mesa High a week from now," Todd said. "Then I'll make it up to you for this horrible neglect," he added teasingly. "I'll trail around after you like a puppy dog."

Elizabeth laughed. "Down, boy."

The newspaper office was empty—of people, that is. As usual, papers and photographs were scattered everywhere. Elizabeth's desk was relatively uncluttered. Only two things lay on top of it: the file Mr. Collins had dropped off for her, and a manila envelope with the words "The Oracle" scrawled on it.

She tucked the file in her book bag. Then she examined the manila envelope. It didn't have a return address. "I wonder where this came from."

"Open it and find out," Todd suggested.

Elizabeth opened the envelope, sliding out its contents. "It's the mock-up of a newspaper article," she told Todd. "But it's not one of ours."

Glancing at the first sentence of the article, she knew immediately who had sent the mysterious envelope. "It's from Big Mesa High! And it didn't come through the mail. Someone must have delivered it here in person."

"What do they have to say this time?" Todd asked grimly.

Elizabeth unfolded the sheet of paper. As she did, a smaller sheet fluttered to the ground.

She picked it up. It was a handwritten note. "Just thought you might like a sneak preview," she read aloud, "of the front page of the next *Bull's Eye*. Read it and weep."

"Those idiots," Todd scoffed. "If you want my opinion, Liz, you should just toss the whole thing in the garbage can right now. Don't even look at it—don't give them the satisfaction."

Todd was probably right. But Elizabeth's curiosity was too strong. "I have to read it," she said. "I want to know what kind of dirt the *Bull's Eye* staff is dishing out now."

Pulling out a chair, she sat down and started reading. As she read, her face gradually grew flushed with anger. "What?" said Todd, watching her. "What?"

"They're accusing us of cheating at the track meet yesterday," fumed Elizabeth. "They say we hired incompetent and dishonest referees!"

"That's ridiculous," Todd exclaimed.

"They also say our mile relay team intentionally bumped into their guy after the second lap. I heard about the Big Mesa guy Roger was up against, the one who dropped the baton."

"Roger wasn't anywhere *near* that guy!" Todd protested. "Roger was already way out ahead."

"Well, according to *this*, Roger ran right over

him." Elizabeth's eyes dropped to the next paragraph. Its allegations were even more outrageous. "And get this—they say our cheerleaders tried to *poison* their cheerleaders!"

"Poison them? All they did was dye their teeth green with trick gum!" Todd couldn't help laughing. "And if you ask me, some of those girls actually looked better afterward."

"This is unbelievable." Elizabeth shook her head. "It's a deliberate attempt to make their student body feel even more antagonistic toward us and to force this rivalry to get even more out of hand." She quoted the article's conclusion: "'We can't let Sweet Valley High's cheating and aggression go unpunished. We must revenge ourselves—both on and *off* the athletic field!'"

Elizabeth tossed the article onto the desk, disgusted and furious.

"I told you it was garbage," said Todd. "Just throw it away. Forget about it."

"Turn the other cheek, is that what you mean?"

"Yeah."

"Well, we've turned the other cheek already," Elizabeth said angrily. "We're black and blue all over at this point!"

Todd raised his eyebrows. "It's just a stupid newspaper article, Liz. Don't take it so seriously.

Don't take it so *personally.*"

"Don't tell me how to take it," she snapped. "I'm sick of letting them get away with these asinine lies!"

Todd didn't reply. His silence jolted Elizabeth back to her senses. *What was that all about?* she wondered, startled herself by the sudden upsurge of emotion that had momentarily overcome her.

"Sorry," she said remorsefully. "I didn't mean to bite your head off. I guess . . ." For some reason, she thought of Jessica and her stunt at the pep rally. "I guess I'm just getting fed up with people who don't play fair."

"Forget about the rivalry with Big Mesa," Todd advised her. "You've got more important things to think about, like organizing the prom."

"That's right, the prom." Elizabeth retrieved the *Bull's Eye* mock-up. Holding it at arm's length, she tore it in half and then in half again, and allowed the pieces to flutter into the wastebasket. "C'mon. I think I'm just cranky because I'm hungry. Let's go to lunch!"

Todd held the cafeteria door open for Elizabeth. "After you," he said gallantly.

Elizabeth stepped into the lunchroom. As she expected, it was already packed with students and humming with noise. But the crowd seemed especially dense in the middle of the cafeteria. Dozens of students were gathered around a lunch table, on top of which stood . . .

Jessica.

"What on earth . . . ?" Elizabeth exclaimed. What was her sister up to now?

She and Todd hurried forward. As they drew near, Elizabeth could see that Jessica held a small cardboard box. She was taking things from the box and handing them out to people.

A boy standing next to Elizabeth held up an object for a friend to inspect. Elizabeth stared at it.

A button! A big, colorful button printed with a picture of a parrot and the words "Save the Rain Forest—Come to the Jungle Prom."

"Where did those come from?" Elizabeth wondered aloud. "I don't remember ordering any buttons. And Environmental Alert didn't send any. . . ."

Two freshman girls pushed their way past Elizabeth and Todd, pressing up to the table to receive their buttons. "Aren't these cool?" Elizabeth heard them rave.

Another student turned toward the girls. "Jessica bought them with her own money," the student said, "just to encourage people to go the prom and support a worthy cause."

"Wow." The girls gazed adoringly up at Jessica, who was still handing out buttons and waving to people, looking for all the world like a beauty queen on a parade float. "Talk about dedication!"

Elizabeth couldn't believe her ears, *or* her eyes. She stared at Jessica. *Dedication?* she thought. *Her own money, just to support a worthy cause?*

"Sounds like bribery to me," someone mumbled in Elizabeth's ear.

Elizabeth turned. Enid had stepped up beside her. "Bribery," Elizabeth repeated, her eyebrows coming together in a frown. Of course! It was so obvious—to her and to Enid, at least. But were they the only ones able to see through Jessica's saintly masquerade?

Elizabeth couldn't stand to watch her duplicitous sister for a single second longer; she didn't trust herself not to reach up and shove Jessica right off the tabletop. Whirling on her heel, she stalked off to the far corner of the cafeteria, Enid and Todd trailing after her.

Yanking out a chair, she sat down with a thump. "I want that Prom Queen title," she announced, her eyes blazing. "I'm not going to let her steal it from me!"

Enid and Todd both gaped at her. "Take it easy,

Liz," Todd counseled, putting a hand on hers. "It's not worth it to get so worked up over something so trivial."

Elizabeth thought he spoke in the same slightly patronizing "be reasonable" tone he had used on her back in the newspaper office. It was like hot coals under her feet.

"Trivial?" she practically shouted. "How can you say it's trivial?" She gestured to the other end of the cafeteria. "Jessica doesn't think it's trivial. Look at everything she's doing to make sure she wins!"

"She's just handing out some stupid buttons," Todd pointed out. "They say 'Save the Rain Forest,' not 'Vote for Jessica.'"

"It's the same thing," Elizabeth insisted. "It's all part of her campaign." She ticked off Jessica's offenses on her fingers. "First there was that sleazy interview she gave to Caroline Pearce, where she hogged all the credit for the prom. Then she did that cutesy little solo cheerleading routine at the pep rally, after which she basically nominated herself for Prom Queen in front of the entire school. And now this! She actually spent her *own* money on these buttons. Believe me," Elizabeth said with authority, "Jessica's no philanthropist. She only spent that money because she knew there'd be a payback. It's total *self*-promotion, no matter *what* the buttons say!"

Todd nodded reluctantly. "I see what you mean," he acknowledged. "My point was just that maybe it's sort of like those anonymous letters from the Big Mesa *Bull's Eye*. It's not worth taking seriously. So Jessica's hitting the campaign trail pretty hard—so what? It probably won't make that much of a difference, come prom night. Kids'll vote for the person they like best."

"But it shouldn't be a popularity contest," Elizabeth argued. "I deserve the prize. I've *earned* it. Wasn't the prom my idea in the first place?"

"I don't know," said Todd, uncertain. He looked to Enid for confirmation. She shrugged. "The night of the beach party, you and Jess made it sound like you came up with the idea together."

The night of the beach party . . . It seemed like a million years ago now. *Did Jessica and I really hit on the Jungle Prom theme during a sisterly gab session?* Elizabeth thought in disbelief. Given the state of their relationship now, it seemed highly unlikely. And knowing Jessica . . .

No, now that Elizabeth looked back on that conversation, she was one-hundred-percent certain that *she* had come up with the idea, all by herself. Jessica had just jumped on the bandwagon, trying to take credit, as always.

"It was *my* idea," Elizabeth asserted. "And who's doing all the real work for the prom, anyway?"

"The Prom Committee," Todd answered.

"In other words, *me,*" said Elizabeth. "But that's not even the most important factor here. I'd be a much better Jungle Prom Queen than Jessica. She'd only make a mockery of the whole thing—she has no interest in working for Environmental Alert."

"You never know," Todd said mildly. "She could surprise us."

"Why would she take the spokesperson responsibilities seriously when she won't even come to Prom Committee meetings?" Elizabeth countered. She frowned at her boyfriend, suddenly as irritated with him as she was with Jessica. *I can't believe he's making me defend myself this way.* "Whose side are you on, anyway? You're supposed to be my most loyal supporter!"

"I am," Todd protested. "I'm with you all the way, Liz, you know that. I really hope you win the title, and the trip to Brazil, and the spokesperson job. But having said that, now don't get offended, but I wish you'd just *relax* about all of it." He leaned across the table toward her. Taking her hand, he gave it a squeeze. "This is supposed to be *fun*, remember?"

Fun. Elizabeth cracked a smile, but it wasn't a very convincing one. From her point of view, planning the Jungle Prom had stopped being fun a long time ago—and she knew exactly who to blame for that. As for relaxing, no way. There was just too much at stake.

"This was a good choice," Jessica told Sam on Saturday night. "They have great food here and I'm starving."

They were seated at a corner table for two at Oggi, a romantic Italian restaurant on the outskirts of Sweet Valley. "The food is good," Sam agreed, watching as Jessica ate a huge forkful of salad. "But I picked it because I know it's one of your favorites, and it's been a while since we've gone out someplace special on a Saturday night, just the two of us. You haven't had much time for me lately."

He put out a hand, reaching for one of Jessica's. At the same moment, she reached for the bread basket. "I've been so busy," she explained. "Do you know I haven't even had time to eat *lunch* any day this week?" she complained, examining the contents of the basket with interest. Selecting a roll, she tore off a piece, buttered it, and then popped it in her mouth. "For example, yesterday I spent my whole lunch period handing out 'Save the Rain

Forest' buttons just to get people psyched for the Jungle Prom."

"Buttons—that's a good idea," Sam said.

Jessica nodded, happily recalling the enthusiasm of her fellow students . . . and the dirty look she had gotten from Elizabeth. "I figure it doesn't hurt to remind people that this prom is my project too. Everyone just assumes that Elizabeth is doing all the work for it."

"Well, what really matters is that—"

"I still can't believe she wants to be Prom Queen!" Jessica exclaimed, so preoccupied with her own train of thought that she didn't even notice she had cut Sam off in midsentence. "And she's doing it in such an underhanded way. Of course she would never actually *campaign*. Oh, no, she's above all that. But she's not above having her hordes of nerdy friends campaign *for* her! But I don't want to talk about it." Jessica waved a hand dismissively. "Let's talk about something else."

"OK," Sam said agreeably. "Here's something that might interest you—I know you're a big fan of my biceps. Today I started a really high-power weight-training program at the gym so I can get in top form for the big race. I have a hunch I'll need all the help I can—"

"Do you think it's enough, though?" Jessica asked urgently.

"Just working out at the gym? Well, no. I'm also going to—"

"Not the *race*, the *buttons*," she said impatiently. "Do you think I was too subtle, just saying 'Save the Rain Forest, Come to the Jungle Prom'?" She pondered the question. "Or would it have been totally tacky to print up buttons that said 'Jessica Wakefield for Prom Queen'?"

"I thought we were going to change the subject," Sam pointed out dryly.

"What, don't you think this is important?" Jessica demanded.

"Sure, I think it's important. But it's not the *only* thing happening in the world right now."

"It's the only thing *I'm* concerned about," Jessica told him.

"Gee, that makes me feel great," Sam grumbled. He pushed his salad plate aside. "I guess it was pretty lucky I ran into Elizabeth yesterday, since obviously I'm not one of *your* top priorities nowadays."

Jessica's eyebrows shot up. "You *what*?"

"I ran into Liz, or rather she ran into me. When I was hitchhiking. Because *you* forgot to pick me up."

Jessica bristled. "I apologized, didn't I?"

"Yeah, but that doesn't change the fact that I'd have been stranded if Liz hadn't come to my rescue," Sam pointed out. "She went out of her way to drive me home. It was really thoughtful of her."

"Thoughtful." Jessica spat out the word as if it tasted bad. "That's our perfect little Elizabeth, all right—our perfect *sneaky* little Elizabeth. Always everyone's friend, always saving the day . . ."

"It wasn't like she planned it," Sam protested. "She happened to be in the right place at the right time and she did me a favor."

"She's just looking for opportunities to make me look bad," Jessica insisted, her eyes flashing. "And she's got you brainwashed like everybody else. I'm the only one who sees through her anymore!"

Sam shook his head. "Don't you think you're getting a little carried away, Jess, a little paranoid? This is your *sister* we're talking about, not some master spy."

"She's like a spy, though," Jessica muttered. "Everyone thinks she's so angelic, but she's really the Queen of the Sneak Attack. I used to trust her, but now . . . I don't know where she's going to hit me next."

Just then, the waitress served their entrées. Sam picked up his fork. "Let's start this evening over," he suggested, his eyes intent on her face.

"Let's not talk about the prom, or Elizabeth—let's talk about you and me." He smiled teasingly. "By the way, how'd your French exam go today? I'm pretty sure I aced my math test." He nudged her foot with his under the table. "It's going to be a fun bet, for the winner *and* the loser."

Why's he leering at me that way? Jessica thought, distracted. *And what's with the footsie? Doesn't he know we're in a restaurant?*

"What bet?" she asked, meanwhile silently figuring the odds that she would beat out Elizabeth for Queen on the night of the prom, now only one week away.

SVH

Eleven

"Ugh. I hate Monday mornings," Lila groaned as she rolled out of bed.

A long hot shower woke her up a bit, but didn't really improve her mood. She was tempted to dry her hair and crawl right back into bed. *I wouldn't have to go to school,* Lila thought. *I wouldn't have to take that biology test; I wouldn't have to talk about the stupid prom or the stupid basketball game against Big Mesa. I wouldn't have to face people, ever again.*

With a sigh, she dropped her wet towel on the floor and wrapped herself in a plush terry robe. Stomping across her bedroom, she flung open the door to her enormous walk-in closet.

She flipped through her skirts, jackets, and tops, searching for something to wear to school, but she was sick of all her clothes; nothing appealed to her. *I should just show up at Sweet Valley High like this,* she mused, smirking at the thought. *A bathrobe, bare feet, and stringy wet hair. Chrome Dome Cooper would give me detention for life!*

Lila considered a cherry-red tank dress. Nah—she'd worn it two weeks ago. She paused at a baggy black linen shorts-and-jacket set. Hmm . . . a possibility. She squinted at the right sleeve of the jacket, examining it more closely. "Where did that spot come from?" she wondered aloud, flinging the jacket aside.

She wandered to the other end of the closet, where a row of party dresses and ball gowns hung, swathed in plastic bags, waiting for the next special occasion. Lila's heart warmed at the sight of them. She loved the rich fabrics—creamy silk, soft velvet, crisp taffeta; she loved the glittering sequins, the festive colors.

Gently, Lila removed a hunter-green velvet dress from the rack. Slipping it out of the dry cleaner's bag, she held the dress against her body and turned to admire the effect in the full-length mirror on the back of the closet door.

Maybe I should *go to the prom,* she thought. *I*

don't have to have a date—I can just go by myself, like Jessica said. Lila pushed her robe off one shoulder so she could place the velvet against her flawless golden skin. Maybe she wasn't running for Prom Queen, but that didn't mean she couldn't be the prettiest girl at the dance!

For some inexplicable reason, Lila suddenly found herself thinking about bumping into Nathan at the beach the other day. Jessica had been so impressed by him. "He's *so* adorable, he's *so* nice," Lila said out loud, mimicking Jessica's gushing tones.

Lila tilted her head to one side, narrowing her eyes. She pictured Nathan, his warm hazel eyes, his broad shoulders, that mischievous smile that so often forced her to smile, too, no matter how determined she was to remain aloof. *He* is *cute,* she thought. *Jess is right about that. And he* is *nice. I just haven't wanted to admit it to anyone, not even to myself.*

From the start, she hadn't wanted to go to counseling—she had refused to admit how much she needed it. So she had also been unwilling to recognize how much Nathan had actually helped her. When push came to shove, though, Lila couldn't deny it: Nathan had done a lot for her. She fingered the rich green velvet, thinking. *He gave me back some of my courage. If it weren't for him, would I even consider braving the prom scene all by myself?*

Suddenly sentimental, Lila recalled all their counseling sessions, how kind and patient Nathan always was, no matter how nasty a mood she was in. He never lost his cool, he never hit back. *My friends are getting fed up with me,* Lila reflected, *but Nathan's sticking by me. He won't give up on me, and he won't let me give up on myself.*

In fact, now that Lila thought about it, she realized that Nathan was probably the best friend she had. He was the only person who really seemed to care about her these days, the only one who really *listened.*

Who needs parents? Lila thought, buoyed up by a new feeling of independence. Nathan was a hundred times better than any parent could be. He was young and cool; he understood what it was like to be a teenager. And he was cute.

I can't believe I've been taking him so much for granted! Hanging up the velvet gown, Lila reached for a sexy gold-sequined cocktail dress. *I* will *go to the prom,* she determined, the decision now firm. She wouldn't have a date, but she wouldn't be alone, either. Nathan had told her he would be there as a chaperon—she could always hang out with him.

Lila held the dress up to herself. A smile softened her face as she contemplated her reflection. Would Nathan like this dress? Suddenly, Lila couldn't wait until the night of the prom.

Tossing the cocktail dress aside, she returned to the task of choosing an outfit for school. She wanted to make sure she wore something especially cute . . . just in case she ran into Nathan.

"C'mon," Jessica said to Amy, Robin, and Lila. It was the beginning of lunch period on Monday and the three girls had deposited their trays on a table in the cafeteria. "Pick those up. We're going to a Prom Committee meeting."

"I'm not *on* the Prom Committee," Robin pointed out.

"You are now," Jessica informed her briskly. "Let's go. Hup, hup!"

Jessica herded her friends toward the door to the outside eating area. "All right, all right, we're going," Amy muttered. "Stop stepping on my heels! Since when are you so fired up about Prom Committee meetings, anyway?"

"Since I figured out that Elizabeth is trying to take over the whole prom," said Jessica. "She packed the committee with *her* friends; she's trying to make it look like she's the only one with ideas and initiative."

"Well, isn't she?" Lila kidded.

Jessica glared. "Hardly. This prom was my idea too, and I think it's time I reminded my sweet sister of that fact." There certainly didn't seem to be any time to lose. The walls of the cafeteria were plastered with posters advertising the prom—and the contest for Prom King and Queen—which was only a few days away.

With Jessica in the lead, the girls marched across the courtyard to where the Prom Committee sat in a large circle on the grass. Winston, DeeDee, Bill, and the others were talking while Elizabeth studied her clipboard, her head bent.

At the sight of Jessica, the Prom Committee members clammed up. The sudden silence caught Elizabeth's attention and she looked up.

As she focused on Jessica, Elizabeth's eyes widened with surprise. *Hah!* Jessica thought with satisfaction. *You didn't expect this, did you, little Miss Prom Committee Dictator!*

"Jessica!" Elizabeth exclaimed.

"Hi, Liz," Jessica said breezily. She dropped down onto the grass. "Hi, everybody. Did we miss anything?"

"No, you're right on time." Elizabeth smiled stiffly at Amy, Robin, and Lila. "It's great to get some new recruits. There's still plenty of work to go around."

"Well, *I'm* not new," Jessica reminded the group. "I'm co-chair of the committee, as you all know. Oh, by the way." She dug around in her shoulder bag. "Here. Did everybody get a button?"

She tossed out a few "Save the Rain Forest" buttons and the gang grabbed for them eagerly. Elizabeth scowled; Jessica beamed. "So, Liz," she said sweetly. "What's on the agenda today?"

Elizabeth's cheeks were flaming. Jessica was pleased to see that her sister could barely contain her anger. "Well, as *you* know," Elizabeth replied, her tone heavy with sarcasm, "the prom is *this* Saturday, as in five days from now. Most of the arrangements have been taken care of."

"I thought you said there was still plenty of work to go around," Jessica pointed out, unintimidated.

"There is." Elizabeth gripped her pen tightly, tapping it on her clipboard. "We need volunteers to come to the gym during the day on Saturday to set everything up and decorate."

"Let's make a sign-up sheet," Jessica suggested. Ripping a piece of paper from a notebook, she jotted down a schedule. "Here, I'll pass this around. Everybody can pick a shift."

"Aren't *you* going to sign up for one?" Amy prompted as Jessica handed her the sheet.

"That's right." Jessica smiled winningly. "Of course. Let's see . . ." She considered for a moment, then wrote her name down for the last shift. *With any luck, everything will be done by the time I get there!* "OK, Amy. Your turn."

As the sign-up sheet made its way around the circle, Jessica watched her sister. Elizabeth was tapping her pen faster and faster. *This is too easy,* Jessica thought. *She's already off balance, and I haven't even thrown my curveball yet!*

"Well, that's all taken care of," Jessica announced when the sign-up sheet was filled out. "Now what?"

"Winston, Patty, and Andrea were going to tell us about their plan for managing ticket collection, the raffle, and the ballots for Prom King and Queen on Saturday night," said Elizabeth.

"It's pretty straightforward," Patty explained. "We'll have a couple of people at a table by the door, collecting tickets. At the same time, we'll give each person a raffle ticket and a Prom King ballot. Around nine o'clock, we'll collect the Prom King ballots and hand out ballots for Prom Queen. The three of us will tally the votes for King and the emcee—"

"That's me," Winston interjected.

"What a surprise," Amy murmured to Jessica.

"The emcee will announce the winner," Patty continued. "An hour later, we'll collect the ballots for Prom Queen. In the meantime, the King will be drawing raffle winners."

"And handing them to the emcee, who will call out the numbers and present the prizes," Winston added.

"Which are Environmental Alert T-shirts and posters," said Andrea. She smiled shyly. "And my dad donated a bunch of copies of his latest CD—autographed."

"Cool!" Jessica exclaimed.

"I guess that's about it for now," said Elizabeth, checking her list. "We can meet one last time during lunch on Thursday, to organize shopping trips to buy the refreshments and art supplies."

Elizabeth started to put her clipboard back in her book bag. Jessica lifted one hand. "Wait a minute," she requested. "There's one more thing we need to talk about."

Elizabeth raised her eyebrows. "There *is*?"

Jessica nodded. "We still haven't decided a *very* important policy question. What do you think, guys?" She looked around the circle, her eyes flashing a challenge. "Should Big Mesa High students be allowed to come to the dance? I say no." Jessica's gaze flickered to Enid. "Not even as *dates,*" she added.

"But Sweet Valley High has always had an open policy," Elizabeth declared. "We've *always* let kids from other schools buy tickets to our dances."

"Big Mesa High isn't just another school anymore," Jessica rejoined. "They're our archrival!"

"I'm with Jessica," said Tony Esteban, Sweet Valley High's star distance runner. "I've had enough of those jerks on the track—I don't want to have to look at them at the prom, too."

"But what if somebody's girlfriend or boyfriend goes to Big Mesa?" Melanie asked. "Maybe we should make exceptions. It would really ruin the prom for some people if we make a rule like that."

"We're not going to make a rule, period," Elizabeth cut in. "The prom is going to be open to everybody."

"Don't you think that's something the committee as a whole should decide?" Jessica challenged.

The twins stared fiercely at each other for a long, drawn-out moment. No one else dared to speak.

"OK," Elizabeth agreed at last. "Let's get some other opinions. Winston, what do you think?"

Winston looked from Elizabeth to Jessica and back again. "Well, to tell you the truth, Liz . . . I kind of agree with Jess," he confessed. "Not that I think it's fair to punish kids who go out with people from Big Mesa," he hurried to add, glancing apologetically at Enid. "It's more a question of security. Big Mesa High's been out to get us for weeks. I don't think we should give them a chance to trash our dance the way they trashed our beach party."

"Good point," Jessica commended him.

"I disagree," Penny spoke up. "If you're talking security, I think that's one more reason we *should* sell tickets to anyone who wants them. If word gets around that we're closing the dance to kids from Big Mesa, it will only antagonize the troublemakers among them."

"Right," said Roger. "Refusing to let any Big Mesa kids in is like an invitation to disaster. If that gang is really set on trashing the prom, they'll do it. They're not going to bother buying tickets!"

"That's beside the point," Jessica told Roger. "This is a question of school spirit, pure and simple. It's *our* prom." Jessica allowed her voice to tremble with emotion. "We shouldn't have to share it with *anyone,* especially not Big Mesa!"

A few members of the Prom Committee applauded spontaneously. *I've got her now,* Jessica gloated. *She can't argue with that without sounding like a complete traitor!*

But to Jessica's surprise, Elizabeth smiled. "If that's the way you want it. Maybe *no* dates from other schools should be allowed to come."

Elizabeth didn't name names, but it was obvious she was referring to Sam. "No way," Jessica protested. "It's only Big Mesa kids we want to keep out!"

"Either the prom is open or it's closed," Elizabeth insisted.

Everyone started talking at once, their voices rising as they tried to make themselves heard. Finally Jessica clapped her hands. "There's one surefire way to resolve this," she declared. "We'll vote on it—the majority rules. OK, let's see a show of hands. Who thinks no Big Mesa High students should be allowed at our dance?"

The hands shot up. Amy, Robin, Lila, Winston, Tony, Annie, DeeDee, and Bill. Triumphantly, Jessica counted them out loud. "One, two, three, four, five, six, seven, eight. Oh, and of course me. That makes nine! Now, who thinks we should let Big Mesa kids in?"

She counted again. Nine different hands, including Elizabeth's, went up in the air. "It's a tie!" Jessica announced. "Now what do we do?"

"Maybe the whole school should vote on this," Winston suggested. "We could ask Mr. Cooper to bring it up in assembly tomorrow."

"I guess we'll have to." Elizabeth didn't seem

happy at the prospect. "I'll go talk to him about it right now."

She got to her feet; so did Jessica. "Get the word out to vote no to Big Mesa," Jessica urged her fellow committee members as the meeting broke up. "I want to see you guys standing up for our school during assembly!"

Jessica waved to her departing friends, then turned to face her sister. Elizabeth stalked right past without even a good-bye nod. Enid, Penny, and Olivia scurried after her.

Jessica folded her arms across her chest, a satisfied smile wreathing her face. That would teach Elizabeth not to be so high and mighty, not to assume that she was always right, that she had her finger on the pulse of Sweet Valley High!

In five minutes, everyone in school would be talking about what had happened at the meeting and debating whether or not Big Mesa High kids should be allowed to attend the Jungle Prom. *Everyone will be talking about* me, Jessica thought. *Me and my incredible loyalty to Sweet Valley High!*

The word would be out. Elizabeth Wakefield wasn't the only candidate for Prom Queen—she wasn't even the best candidate. For kids who wanted to vote for a Prom Queen who would be true to her school, the choice would be clear: Jessica Wakefield!

Elizabeth slammed her locker door shut. "Ouch," Todd joked. "I'm glad you're not taking that temper out on me!"

Elizabeth didn't crack a smile. "I've had a long day," she said tersely, gritting her teeth as she remembered the Prom Committee meeting during lunch.

Todd put a hand on her shoulder, massaging it lightly. "You're really tense," he observed. "Let's do something to relax those old muscles. How about playing some tennis, or going to the beach for a swim?"

"You have basketball practice," Elizabeth reminded him with a sigh. "And I have a ton of work to do."

"Just wait until the weekend," Todd promised. "We'll make Saturday night special—unforgettable. How about dinner at the Valley Inn before the dance?"

Elizabeth shrugged. She didn't want to hurt Todd's feelings, but only one thing would make Saturday night unforgettable for her: to be chosen Prom Queen.

"Whatever you want," she said. "I really don't care. As long as we get to the dance at eight o'clock on the dot. I don't want to miss a minute of it!"

"Forget it, then," Todd said. "The whole point of going out first would be to relax, and if you won't even try to think of something other than this stupid rivalry with Jessica . . ." He bent, brushing her cheek with a good-bye kiss. "See you later, Liz."

Elizabeth watched him go, feeling a slight pang of guilt. It wasn't fair to use Todd as a punching bag. *Then again, maybe he'd better start getting used to the new me. . . .*

"Hey, Liz!" someone called out behind her.

Elizabeth turned to see Penny making her way through the traffic jam that always followed the final bell.

"Hi, Penny. What's up?"

Penny was about to respond to Elizabeth when she spotted someone in the crowd. "Jessica!" she said, waving an arm. "Just who I was looking for. Can I talk to you for a minute?"

Elizabeth raised her eyebrows. *Jessica* was just who Penny was looking for?

"If you're looking for Jessica, you probably don't need me," Elizabeth said stiffly.

"No, I need to talk to you both," Penny said. "It'll only take a sec, but it's important."

Jessica joined them. "You rang?" she said ironically.

"There was something I completely forgot to mention during the Prom Committee meeting today," Penny began. "I guess I got . . . distracted."

Jessica smirked. "It *was* a pretty exciting meeting."

"It was a totally disorganized meeting," Elizabeth countered.

"Well, whatever," Penny went on. "Just listen to this! A features editor from *Sweet Sixteen* magazine contacted me yesterday—"

"*Sweet Sixteen?*" Jessica squealed. "That's my favorite!"

"It's a lot of people's favorite," said Penny. "Everybody reads it. Anyway, the magazine heard about the Jungle Prom from some P.R. person at Environmental Alert and they want to do a story about it. They want to *interview* the prom organizer!"

The prom organizer—is that her or me? Elizabeth wondered. Who was going to get the interview?

As she and Jessica stared daggers at each other, memories of Caroline Pearce's prom article for *The Oracle* flashed through Elizabeth's head. No two ways about it—if *Sweet Sixteen* interviewed Jessica, Elizabeth wouldn't get a scrap of credit. It would be like she didn't even exist. *I'm not going to let her get away with that again!* Elizabeth vowed.

Penny picked up on the tension crackling between the two girls. "I told the editor that there were two of you," she hurried to explain. "I told them twin sisters came up with the Jungle Prom concept, and they got even more excited about it—they decided right then and there to do a special Jungle Prom fashion pictorial. They want to interview *and* photograph *both* of you tomorrow afternoon!" Penny smiled apologetically. "Sorry about the short notice. They'll meet you in the main lobby at four thirty—I hope you're free."

Jessica tossed her hair back. *"I'm* free," she asserted.

Elizabeth lifted her chin. "Me, too."

Since the Prom Committee meeting during lunch that day, it was more apparent than ever to Elizabeth that Jessica was willing to do anything to discredit her sister and claim the Prom Queen crown for herself. From now on, Elizabeth didn't intend to turn her back on her twin—not for a single minute.

"Me, too," Elizabeth repeated. "I wouldn't miss this interview for the *world."*

SVH

Twelve

Elizabeth pushed through the front door of Sweet Valley High at four thirty on the dot on Tuesday afternoon. "The photographer, Weldon, told me he wants to use the late-afternoon sun," Penny had explained to Elizabeth that morning during assembly. "You know, to get 'that sexy, healthy glow.' I told him it probably wouldn't make a difference, since you and Jessica *always* glow, but he insisted!"

Now Elizabeth smiled to herself, but not because of the "sexy, healthy glow" remark. She was remembering the pleasure of Jessica's resounding defeat during assembly, when the majority of the student body had backed Elizabeth's open-prom policy.

She walked across the school's empty lobby, her heels clattering loudly. The sounds drew the attention of the man and woman standing at the foot of the staircase.

"You must be one of the *twins*!" the woman declared. She held out her hand. "I'm Fran Trafton, from *Sweet Sixteen.*"

"Hi, Fran." Elizabeth shook her hand. "I'm Elizabeth Wakefield."

"I'll be interviewing you," Fran told her.

"Well . . . it'll be fun," Elizabeth said, suddenly feeling shy at the prospect of being the focus of an interview for a change, rather than the person asking the questions.

"And I'll be photographing you." The man stepped forward. To Elizabeth's surprise, he put out a hand and lightly patted her hair. "It's like spun gold, and it's *real,*" Weldon raved. "I know a dye job when I see one. Oh, just look at her, Fran! She's twice as pretty as Penny said."

Fran smiled. "She's a natural-born model. This will be the easiest shoot we've ever done."

"And there are *two* of you. It's simply a dream come true." Weldon looked around, as if perhaps Jessica had snuck up while his back was turned. "Where's our other little Prom Queen?"

Our other little Prom Queen . . . ! *If he only*

knew, Elizabeth thought. "I don't know where my sister is," she answered somewhat stiffly. "She had cheerleading practice right after school, but that would have been over a while ago. She often runs a little late—she doesn't wear a watch," Elizabeth explained.

"Well, while we're waiting, let me show you some of the adorable outfits we're going to photograph you in at the beach," Weldon said. He unzipped a dress bag that was draped over the bannister. "How do you like this?"

"This" was a colorful, jungle-print minidress. Elizabeth's eyes lit up with pleasure. "It's gorgeous," she exclaimed. "Jessica will *love* it."

"Note the tagua-nut buttons, an organic rain-forest product," said Fran. "The fabric is unbleached cotton printed with natural dyes. And of *course* the belt isn't made of *leather*—it's organic Brazilian rubber. All the accessories you'll model are one hundred percent environment-friendly."

"Wow." Elizabeth fingered the long strand of exotic beads Weldon was holding up. "Everything is beautiful."

"It will be a terrific feature," Fran said. She checked her watch. "If your sister ever gets here, that is."

Elizabeth glanced at the clock on the wall. It

was a quarter till five. "I'm sure she'll be here any minute," she assured Fran, meanwhile thinking, *Jess, where are you? Why couldn't you be punctual for once in your life?* "I'm really excited about this interview," Elizabeth babbled, hoping to distract Fran and Weldon from the ticking of the clock. "I mean, not just because the clothes are cool, but because it'll be great P.R. for Environmental Alert."

"And great P.R. for your Jungle Prom," said Fran. "I bet a lot of high schools will follow your lead and do the same sort of thing."

"That's the best thing I could hope for," Elizabeth confided. "To get other kids interested in the environment—to inspire them to get active."

"Speaking of getting active," Weldon interjected, "I think *we* should get active and get out of here. If we don't, we're going to miss the best light. Is your sister coming or not?"

Fran looked at the clock. It was five minutes before five; clearly, she was growing impatient too. "Weldon and I both have other things to do tonight—we need to get back to L.A. at a reasonable hour. Maybe we should just go ahead and do the interview without her."

Elizabeth bit her lip. "Do the interview without her?"

Fran shrugged. "Why not?"

She's right—why not? So . . . just say it, Elizabeth counseled herself. *Just do it.* It would serve Jessica right. It wasn't Elizabeth's fault Jessica was late—Elizabeth shouldn't always have to make excuses for her!

Suddenly, a new angle presented itself. If Jessica *didn't* come on the shoot, then the *Sweet Sixteen* article would be all about Elizabeth. The photographs, the interview . . . for once, it would be *her* story.

She'd do it to me in a second, Elizabeth guessed, her blood starting to boil. *She wouldn't think twice about elbowing* me *out of the way so she could have the spotlight all to herself!*

Just as quickly as she'd started to heat up, though, Elizabeth cooled off. It was tempting to grab the interview and run—to get even with Jessica for all the publicity-grabbing stunts *she'd* pulled lately. But even though Elizabeth had vowed to be more self-assertive, she realized she couldn't do it at the cost of being dishonest and deceptive. She wouldn't let her anger at Jessica warp her better instincts.

"Let me just check the girls' locker room down the hall," Elizabeth said to Weldon and Fran in a last-ditch attempt to stall for time. "Maybe she's touching up her makeup. I'll be right back!"

She sprinted off before they could protest. There really was a distinct possibility that Jessica was dawdling in the locker room, idly brushing her hair, completely oblivious to the fact that she was half an hour late for the appointment.

Elizabeth pushed open the door, half expecting to find Jessica standing in front of the long row of mirrors. But the locker room was empty.

At a slower pace, she walked back to rejoin Fran and Weldon. "Any luck?" asked Fran.

Elizabeth shook her head. "I'm afraid not."

Weldon bent over and hoisted his big leather camera bag. "Well, *I'm* afraid I'm tired of standing around," he announced irritably. "Either we shoot you now, or we shoot nobody."

"It's up to you," Fran told Elizabeth. "We'd love to do the story, but we really can't wait any longer for Jessica."

It was a very straightforward choice: go ahead with the interview on her own, or give up the interview altogether. Give up the interview, and keep waiting for Jessica.

Elizabeth wavered, but only for an instant. Once she made her decision, it was firm.

I won't give it up, she thought. *I've been waiting all my life—and I'm sick of it.*

"Let's go take some pictures!" she declared.

* * *

Jessica sauntered through the main door of the high school and paused for a moment just inside the entrance, to give the photographer and interviewer from *Sweet Sixteen* a chance to appreciate how stunning she looked in her teal-green sand-washed silk shorts and tank top. She tossed her hair back dramatically . . . then noticed that nobody was watching. *I can't believe I'm the first one here!* she thought, crossing to the foot of the staircase.

She looked around. It was pretty odd that Elizabeth hadn't shown up yet, especially seeing as how, according to the clock, it was five fifteen. *Oops! Well, at least I'm not the only one who's late.*

The door to the front office was ajar; someone was still working. Jessica trotted over and knocked. "Anybody home?" she called out. She peeked around the door. Lois Waller, a classmate of Jessica's and the daughter of the school nutritionist, was typing at a computer. "Oh, hi, Lois. What's up?"

Lois squinted at Jessica through her oversize glasses. "I'm typing up a report for my mother," she explained. "A nutritional analysis of the cafeteria's lunch menu." Lois smiled. "You'll be happy to know Sweet Valley High serves the healthiest institutional food in Southern California!"

Jessica wasn't particularly interested. "Have you seen Elizabeth, by any chance?"

Lois nodded. "Yeah, she was standing out in the lobby for a while with two other people, but they left."

"They left!" Jessica cried.

"Yep," confirmed Lois. "About ten or fifteen minutes ago."

"I can't believe it. I can't believe they didn't wait for me!" Jessica glared at the other girl, as if it were all Lois's fault. "Where'd they go?"

Lois lifted her shoulders in a helpless shrug. "I really couldn't tell you. They said something about an interview, and a shoot—"

"A photo shoot and an interview for a famous magazine," Jessica informed Lois. "Yeah, yeah, and what else?"

"Well, they had a whole bunch of outfits, some pretty wild stuff," Lois volunteered. "I guess they were going to take pictures of Elizabeth wearing them."

Jessica stamped her foot. "They were supposed to take pictures of Liz and *me*! C'mon, Lois, they must have said *something* about where they were going. Think, think!" she urged.

"Somebody might have mentioned a beach. . . ."

"What beach?" demanded Jessica.

"I don't know." Lois wrinkled her nose. "Or maybe it was a park. . . ."

"A beach or a park. Well, that narrows it down to only about a thousand places," Jessica said sarcastically. She fought back the urge to give Lois a hard shake. How could anybody be so slow and stupid? "Thanks, Lois. Thanks a lot."

Jessica flounced out of the office. *So, they want to shoot Elizabeth.* I *want to shoot Elizabeth!* she thought, fuming.

It was only too obvious what had happened. Elizabeth showed up early and lied to the people from *Sweet Sixteen* so she could steal the interview and photo opportunity all for herself. Maybe she said Jessica was sick and couldn't come. Or maybe she told them Penny made a mistake, there was no twin sister in the first place!

Jessica clenched her fists, tears of disappointment and rage springing to her eyes. In the past, she would never have believed that Elizabeth would do such a cruel, heartless, selfish thing. But Elizabeth had changed.

"Hi, Nathan," Lila sang out as she strolled into her counselor's office. "How are you this afternoon?"

Tossing aside the book he was reading, Nathan

jumped up from his chair. "Disorganized, as usual. Here, let me clear off the sofa."

"Don't worry about it," Lila told him. She shoved a pile of magazines aside and plopped herself down. "This is fine."

Nathan cocked his head to one side. "You're in a good mood today," he observed.

Lila smiled at him. "I am," she confirmed. "Isn't it a nice change of pace?"

Nathan grinned. "No comment."

"You can be straight with me," Lila said teasingly. "I know I've been a complete drip. But I'm just feeling so much *better* all of a sudden!"

"I'm glad," Nathan said sincerely. "Let's zero in on this good feeling, Lila, so we can hold on to it. Why do you think you're so up today? What's been happening lately?"

"Oh, nothing's *happened*. I guess I'm just getting my positive outlook back." She laughed. "Pretty miraculous, huh? I bet you thought I'd *never* come around."

"I had faith," Nathan assured her. "But I'll confess you're surprising me today."

Lila smiled coyly. "Good."

Nathan contemplated her for a moment. "So, you can't point to an event—something you did, someone you talked to—as being a catalyst for this change in outlook?" he asked. "Think about it, Li."

Lila laughed again, brushing off his psychobabble terminology about events and catalysts. "I don't *want* to think. I feel better—does it really matter why?"

"It always pays off to investigate changes like this," Nathan responded, "to try to locate the source of your feelings. The more you understand yourself, the more in charge you'll be."

"Oh, who cares?" Lila waved one elegantly manicured hand. "I'm tired of all this self-examination. I'm tired of talking about me, me, me." She flashed him her most dazzling smile. "Let's talk about *you* for once."

"Me?"

"Yes, you." Lila crossed her legs and bent forward, her elbows propped on her knees and her chin resting on her clasped hands. "What's new in *your* life?"

"Not a lot." Nathan smiled. "I switched J.D. to a new all-natural dog food. He hated it—he'd rather have fast food, Big Macs and fries."

"You and J.D.," Lila said, amused. "Is he going to be your date on prom night?"

Joking aside, she *was* wondering if Nathan would bring someone to the prom. Did he have a girlfriend?

But Nathan answered the question in the same jesting tone. "Maybe," he said. "He looks pretty hot in a tux."

Lila sat back in her chair. She had never felt so relaxed during a counseling session. Before she knew what she was saying, she had spoken her thought out loud. "You know, I used to be so *tense* during these sessions," she confided. "Is that crazy or what? You've got to be the easiest person in the world to talk to!"

Nathan smiled. "So, you're going to stick with it?"

Lila smiled back. She was pretty sure she didn't *need* counseling anymore. Her depression had basically disappeared overnight. She was cured.

But she wasn't about to tell him that. She didn't want to stop coming to Project Youth. She didn't want to stop seeing Nathan. "I'm going to stick with it," she affirmed.

"Yo, Bruce." Roger knocked on his cousin's door, then pushed it open before Bruce had a chance to respond. "Mind if I come in?"

"You're already in," Bruce remarked dryly.

Bruce was sitting on his bed reading *A Tale of Two Cities* for English. Roger collapsed into the easy chair under the window. "I just wanted to share my triumph with someone," he explained. His gray eyes twinkled happily. "I called Rosa Jameson just now. She said she'd go to the prom with me!"

Roger's goofy grin got on Bruce's nerves. "Congratulations, old chap," he said in a sarcastic mock British accent. "I hope the two of you have a *grand* time."

Roger's grin didn't fade. "She's such a terrific girl," he enthused. "Smart, fun, gorgeous . . . I can't believe she said yes."

Bruce yawned widely. *I can't believe that talking to you is actually more boring than reading Charles Dickens!* Bruce waved his book at his cousin. "Do you mind? I've got a quiz tomorrow."

"Sure. I'll get out of your hair." Roger put his hands on the arms of the chair, preparing to push himself up. "Hey, who are you taking to the dance?" he asked.

"No one," Bruce drawled. "I'm going stag. I've had everyone at Sweet Valley High I wanted to have—and the others aren't worth bothering with."

Roger opened his mouth, as if he were about to say something. *Another sales pitch for Andrea,* Bruce bet, getting ready to shoot his cousin down.

But instead of speaking, Roger just shook his

head. Rising to his feet, he walked out of the room, closing Bruce's door quietly behind him.

Bruce reopened his book with an impatient gesture and stared down at the page. But for some reason, he couldn't read. His temples throbbed; the words just melted together in a meaningless black smear.

Throwing the book aside, Bruce dropped his head in his hands and pressed his fists against his burning eyes.

Jessica sat in the dark kitchen, drumming her fingers on the butcher-block table. Her eyes smoldered like embers about to explode into a raging forest fire; with every minute that passed, her anger grew.

Six o'clock, seven o'clock, seven thirty . . . Her parents were out for the evening, and she had been sitting in the kitchen since she'd gotten home, watching the hands move around the clock, not even bothering to eat dinner. She didn't have an appetite for food; the only thing she was hungry for was a fight.

I can't believe she did this to me, Jessica fumed. *I can't* believe *she did this to me!* She pictured Elizabeth posing for the photographer, strutting around on the beach, smiling and tossing her hair like a fashion model. *Who does she think she is?* Jessica wondered. *I'm the one who likes to pose. I'm the one who's good at that sort of thing!*

Jessica just didn't understand it. Elizabeth had never been interested in things like Prom Queen crowns. "Wasn't *I* the one who entered the Miss Teen Sweet Valley pageant?" Jessica asked out loud. "Wasn't it *my* idea to audition for 'The Young and the Beautiful' soap opera? Sure, she ended up getting a part, too, but she never would've gone for it on her own!"

Jessica drummed her fingers faster. She had never really thought about it, but now it occurred to her that being a twin was a delicate balancing act. On the one hand, you looked alike physically, and emotionally you were incredibly close. But despite that, or maybe *because* of that, you *had* to create some distance, maintain some differences. If you styled your hair the exact same way and wore all the same clothes, people wouldn't be able to tell you apart. If you set all the same goals, the competition would destroy you. You'd never get a chance to be your own person.

We used to harmonize, me and Liz, Jessica reflected. *But now we just clash.* Instead of music, there was chaos and noise. And it was all Elizabeth's fault. Not only was she intent on stealing the

Prom Queen crown away from Jessica, she was attacking Jessica's whole identity!

Suddenly, over the sound of her own tumultuous thoughts, Jessica heard the rumble of an engine. The Jeep was pulling into the garage—Elizabeth was home.

A key rattled in the door. Through the gloom, Jessica saw the knob turn. The door swung open.

Elizabeth stepped into the kitchen and hit the light switch. When she saw Jessica, she jumped.

"Oh!" Elizabeth squeaked. "Geez, Jess, you scared me! What are you doing sitting in the dark?"

Jessica lit right into her sister, not even pausing to take a breath. "Did you have a nice time, Liz? Do you feel good about sabotaging my chance to be interviewed and photographed for *Sweet Sixteen*?"

"Sabotage?" Elizabeth stared at Jessica. "You were the one who was late—you blew it, not me."

"How long did you wait for me?" Jessica demanded. "Five minutes? Ten?"

"A lot longer than that!" Elizabeth retorted.

"Yeah, right," scoffed Jessica. She jumped to her feet; her voice rose too. "Admit it, Liz. You wanted that interview all to yourself and you made sure you got it!"

"I did no such thing!" Elizabeth protested,

dropping her purse and putting her hands on her hips. "I showed up—on time. You didn't show up, period. We had no choice—we had to leave without you. You goofed, Jessica. Don't blame *me* for your mistakes."

"You're so good at this, aren't you, Liz?" said Jessica, her eyes narrowing to angry slits. "You're so good at playing the high-and-mighty, holier-than-thou role. *You're* always right and *I'm* always wrong. Well, acting superior doesn't make you superior. You sabotaged the photo shoot—you know it, and I know it!"

"I know that you're acting like a complete jerk." Elizabeth turned sharply on her heel and headed toward the door to the hallway. "I don't have to listen to this garbage!"

"Yes, you do." Jessica dashed across the kitchen, blocking her sister's path. "I'm onto you, Liz. You sabotaged this interview—you purposely stole it away from me. You want to be Prom Queen, but you won't compete fairly. You're sneaking around campaigning for support behind my back, and telling who knows what lies about me to everybody you see!"

"You're the sneak!" Elizabeth cried hotly. "You're the one who doesn't fight fair. What about the interview with Caroline, the one you *stole*? What about the lies *you've* told? You're the one who's causing trouble!"

"I'm just going about my business," Jessica countered. "I haven't made any secret about the fact that I'm campaigning for Prom Queen."

"And you'll do anything to get the crown, won't you?" Elizabeth accused.

"I intend to win, but not by stooping to back-stabbing treachery. That's *your* technique."

Jessica's voice dropped ominously and her eyes flickered, like the distant threat of lightning on a hot summer night. Elizabeth stood her ground, her own eyes as cold and angry as a storm at sea.

"But I'm telling you something, Liz. It's not going to work," Jessica warned. "Sooner or later, everyone at Sweet Valley High will wise up to your act. They'll figure you out. So, go ahead," she challenged. "Lie and cheat and sneak around all you want to. We'll see who comes out on top!"

SVH

Thirteen

As Elizabeth stepped through the door of the cafeteria on Wednesday, the reality hit home and a surge of adrenaline coursed through her body. The lunchroom was festooned with banners, some touting the Jungle Prom and others urging the Sweet Valley High athletic teams to victory. It was only two days until the big basketball rematch against Big Mesa . . . and only three days until the prom!

Winston and Andrea were selling prom tickets at a table by the door; when they spotted Elizabeth, they both waved. "How's business?" Elizabeth called.

"Booming!" Winston replied cheerfully.

She gave them the thumbs-up signal, then made her way among the crowded tables to where Todd was sitting with a bunch of his basketball teammates.

"Hi, you guys," she greeted them. "You all getting psyched for Friday's game?"

"Psyched isn't the word," the team's forward, Keith Webster, declared. "Try pumped to the max."

"Driven with a capital *D*," contributed Tom Hackett, the Gladiators' stellar point guard.

"We're going to pound them," Jim Daly predicted.

"We're going to pummel and pulverize them," said Jason Mann.

"Yep, we're going to win, all right," A.J. Morgan concluded. "The only question is by how much!"

Todd grinned at Elizabeth. "As you can see, we've got our confidence level back up."

Elizabeth smiled. "It's off the charts. I think that's great. Here, I want you to read something." She pulled a computer printout from her shoulder bag and handed it to Todd. "It's an editorial I wrote for *The Oracle*; it'll be in Friday's special Prom Weekend issue."

Todd glanced at the title and his eyebrows shot up in surprise. "'Back Off, Big Mesa!' What . . . ?"

"Go on," Elizabeth urged. "Just read it."

She watched him closely as he started reading. She was gratified to see that the more he read, the more shocked he looked. That was exactly the effect she had hoped to achieve through her scathing attack on Big Mesa High School, from their basketball team to their newspaper staff.

"I really gave it to them, huh?" she said when Todd was finished.

Todd shook his head. "I'd say. This is harsh. I can't believe you wrote this, Liz. I can't believe you're *printing* this!"

Elizabeth's smile turned into a frown. "Why? What's wrong with it?"

"Nothing . . . I guess. It's just not like you to go on the offensive like this. I thought you'd made up your mind to stay out of the fray, to stay clean."

"Well, I changed my mind," Elizabeth declared. "I'm sick of just sitting back and taking it all the time. I decided I needed to learn how to hit back. And you know what?" Her eyes glittered. "It feels good. It feels *really* good."

Todd tapped the piece of paper. "But you're not just hitting back at the kids who wrote that trash in the *Bull's Eye*," he pointed out. "You're taking a shot at the entire school."

"What's wrong with that?" Elizabeth wanted to know.

"Those Big Mesa kids are the worst—all of them. They think they're so hot, but they don't even have the guts to fight fair. They've been beating us because we let them—we let them intimidate us. It's all in the attitude."

"So—you're changing your attitude," Todd said.

"You bet," Elizabeth confirmed. "And you'd better change yours, too, if you want to win on Friday night!"

Todd stared at Elizabeth. "What's *really* going on here, Liz?" he asked, lowering his voice so the guys, who were absorbed in an animated conversation about basketball, wouldn't overhear him.

Elizabeth folded her arms across her chest. "What do you mean?"

At that moment, Jessica and a couple of her friends walked by the table with their lunch trays. Elizabeth didn't so much as glance in her sister's direction.

Todd looked from Elizabeth to Jessica, and then down at Elizabeth's anti–Big–Mesa editorial. "What's this article really about?" he pressed his girlfriend. "Who are you really mad at, Liz? Big Mesa or your—"

"I'm standing up for myself and for my school," Elizabeth cut in. "What's wrong with that? How come it's OK for you and the basketball team to be supercompetitive, but not for me?"

"But this editorial isn't competitive," Todd pointed out. "It's mean. It's hostile."

Elizabeth snatched the sheet of paper away from him. "Thanks for your support," she said sarcastically. She shoved her chair back.

"Wait a minute, Liz." Todd grasped her hand gently to stop her. "I'm sorry. I didn't mean to be critical. I'm just concerned about the problems you and Jessica are having."

"*I* don't have a problem," Elizabeth informed him coolly. "Jessica's the one with the problem."

She pushed back her chair again, and this time Todd let her. "Does this have anything to do with the vow you made—you know, the vow to develop all your talents and explore all your desires?" Todd asked abruptly.

Elizabeth stood still and silent for a moment before answering. "Yes, Todd," she said finally. "It does. I guess I'm becoming a different person."

Todd smiled a bit sadly. "You're becoming a different person, all right," he said softly. "But is it someone you're not meant to be?"

"Well, it looks like no one else is going to show up," Elizabeth observed on Thursday. "We might as well get started."

The Jungle Prom Committee had gathered for their final lunchtime meeting. Elizabeth had waited, tensed for a confrontation, until ten past twelve. By now it looked as if Jessica and her cronies were boycotting the meeting.

For Elizabeth, it was a relief—and a victory. *It just goes to show how much Jessica cares about this prom!* she thought.

"So." She looked at the friends circled around her on the grass, a fierce glow in her usually mild blue-green eyes. "It's finally here, the weekend of the prom! Everyone's done a great job so far—thanks."

"We couldn't have done it without you," said Enid.

"Let's give her a hand," Roger suggested.

Everyone clapped and cheered. Elizabeth lifted a hand for quiet. "It's too soon to start congratulating each other," she pointed out. "We haven't pulled it off yet."

"Everything's pretty much in place, though, isn't it?" asked Andrea.

"We have a plan, but we still have to put it into action," Elizabeth reminded Andrea. "This is the most crucial stage—we can't relax yet."

"Hey, are we getting ready for a prom or a military battle?" joked Winston.

"Yeah, isn't this where we're supposed to start having fun?" DeeDee teased.

"We're in great shape," Penny assured Elizabeth. "We can afford to take it a little easy."

"I don't happen to think we can," Elizabeth said curtly. "I've invested a lot in this prom, and I intend to see that every last detail is absolutely perfect."

"It will be," Enid promised.

"We're just kidding around, Liz," Winston said. "You don't have to worry; we're not going to drop the ball."

"C'mon, Liz, smile," Olivia cajoled her. "The Prom Queen's going to need a happier face than that!"

Elizabeth tried to smile, but she couldn't quite manage it. "I'll smile on Saturday night," she promised dryly, "when the prom's a huge success." *And I'm wearing the Queen's crown. . . .*

There really wasn't all that much to go over. Elizabeth checked her reminder list. "Bill, did you confirm with the band?"

He nodded. "Yep. We're all set."

"Is everybody else clear on what they need to do between now and Saturday?" she asked.

"Yes, but that reminds me," said Olivia. "The decoration stuff needs to be picked up at the art-supply store this afternoon, but I can't make it over there—I have a painting class. Any volunteers to go for me?"

"Sorry, I've got swim team," said Bill.

"Track practice," said Roger.

"Dance class," said Patty.

There were more excuses and apologies; everybody was already booked. "I'd do it, but I'm meeting with the printer—the prom miniyearbooks are ready," said Elizabeth.

"Maybe Jessica's free," Andrea suggested. "Why don't you check with her, Liz?"

Elizabeth's jaw tightened. She hadn't said a word to Jessica since their fight Tuesday night—and if Elizabeth had her way, she wouldn't speak to her sister ever again.

An awkward silence settled over the group as they waited for Elizabeth to respond to the question. Olivia looked at Enid and then at Penny. Penny lifted her shoulders, puzzled. "Tell you what," Olivia said hurriedly, "I see Jessica in my next class. I'll ask her then."

Elizabeth sat frozen, still unable to speak.

Enid came to her rescue. "I guess that's it for now, then," she said, rising to her feet. "See you later, guys."

The meeting broke up. As the others moved

off, Enid hung back with Elizabeth. "Liz, are you OK?" she asked, her eyes warm with concern.

Elizabeth shrugged. "I'm fine. Why?"

"I don't know. You just seem kind of . . . wound up. Maybe you shouldn't take this so seriously; it's just another dance, after all."

"It's *not* just another dance," Elizabeth disagreed.

"Yes, it is, when all is said and done," Enid argued. "The whole point is to have fun, not to get stressed out. If you ask me, this Prom Queen thing has totally—"

She broke off when she saw Elizabeth's frown.

"I really don't need a lecture," Elizabeth told her.

Enid bit her lip. "I wasn't going to lecture you. I just wanted . . ." Suddenly she threw up her hands in frustration. "I really can't wait until the basketball game against Big Mesa and the prom are over," she exclaimed, "and things finally get back to normal!"

Back to normal . . . Elizabeth couldn't help wondering. Would they ever? *Could* they ever?

"I can't believe I got railroaded into schlepping over to the stupid art store," Jessica grumbled to Lila, whom she'd talked into coming with her. "Like I don't have better things to do."

She swung the Jeep into a parking space in

front of the store. The two girls hopped out. "Miss School Spirit seems a bit reluctant to actually roll up her sleeves and get dirty, doesn't she?" Lila chirped teasingly.

Jessica glared at Lila, who for some reason was being annoyingly cheerful lately. "Oh, shut up, Lila," she snapped. "I'm doing it, aren't I?"

Lila nodded. "Sure. And you're doing it for the votes. You don't fool me for a minute, Jessica Wakefield. You never have."

Jessica grinned despite herself. "But you're not one of the ones I *wanted* to fool!"

Lila laughed. "Good point."

"Not that I'm worried," Jessica said a minute later as they lugged cardboard boxes full of streamers, construction paper, uninflated balloons, and fat, colorful Magic Markers out to the Jeep. "Contrary to what *some* people might think, I'm still the natural choice for Prom Queen. *Some* people have simply been wasting their time campaigning—or rather, pretending *not* to campaign while kissing up to people left and right."

"What makes you so sure more people are going to vote for you rather than for Elizabeth?" asked Lila.

Jessica heaved the box into the back of the Jeep. "Picture this," she said, painting the scene for

Lila. "It's tomorrow night, the big basketball rematch with Big Mesa. The gym is packed—everybody is there, and I mean *everybody,* even the kids who don't usually watch sports. This is big—really big. Our school pride is on the line."

Lila nodded. "Yeah, so?"

"You're sitting up in the bleachers, you're Joe Average Sweet Valley High student."

"Or Josephine Average," Lila contributed.

"Right. You look down at the court and what do you see?"

"Ten tall, sweaty guys running around bouncing a ball," Lila guessed.

"Well, yeah, but you also see . . ." Jessica struck a pose. "The gorgeous, gifted Sweet Valley High cheerleaders! Strutting their stuff and showing their school spirit. And who's leading the cheers? Who's captain of the squad? Who has more spirit than anyone?"

"Robin Wilson," Lila said slyly.

Jessica put her hands on her hips. "The *other* captain, silly."

"Oh." Lila smiled. "Jessica Wakefield, of course."

"Of course!" Jessica said serenely. "*C'est moi,* yours truly. Take my word for it, Li—this will clinch it." Her eyes glittered with confident anticipation. "It'll be the final reminder of who's who and what's what, the last big impression before the ballots are handed out."

"I hope you're right," Lila told her.

"I hope I'm right, too," said Jessica. "No, scratch that. I *know* I'm right!"

On Friday night, the Sweet Valley High boys' basketball team jogged out onto the basketball court to the sound of deafening cheers, mingled with faint boos and hisses from the Big Mesa High students gathered in one corner of the Sweet Valley High gymnasium. Elizabeth, Penny, Neil, Enid, and Olivia leaped to their feet. "Yay, Sweet Valley High!" Elizabeth screamed. "Go get 'em, Todd!"

The cheerleaders bounced up and down on the sidelines. Elizabeth saw her sister raise her megaphone to her mouth. "Give me a *G*," Jessica shouted up to the bleachers.

"G!" the crowd yelled back.

"Give me an *L*."

"L!"

"Give me an *A*."

"A!"

Jessica spelled out the word and the enthusiastic crowd spelled it with her. "What does it spell?" she demanded.

"Gladiators!" the crowd boomed.

"Gladiators!" the cheerleaders echoed. "Go, team!"

Elizabeth clapped a little less wildly than before. *Jessica couldn't do much more to put herself forward,* she thought, disgruntled. *Why doesn't she just spell out the words "Prom Queen"?!*

But Elizabeth had anticipated that, as head cheerleader, her twin would be very visible during the big game. She had made sure that in her own way, *she'd* be equally prominent. Directly above where she sat with her friends, a huge banner fluttered. On the old white bedsheet, Elizabeth had painted the words in bold red and blue letters: "Go Gladiators, Bulldoze Big Mesa!"

Olivia leaned over to talk to Enid. "Where's Hugh tonight? I thought we were going to have to share our bleacher seat with the enemy!"

"He stayed home," Enid replied. She gestured to the rowdy contingent of Big Mesa students. "He knew it was going to be a crazy scene here. Anything could happen after the game, and he didn't want to get caught up in a brawl."

"I can understand that," Olivia said sympathetically.

"I can't," Elizabeth interjected. "It's bad enough that he goes to Big Mesa. At least he could have the guts to support his rotten school!"

Her friends looked shocked. "Liz!" Olivia exclaimed.

Deep inside, Elizabeth knew the instant the words came out of her mouth that they were unforgivable. The hurt on Enid's face confirmed it. But for some reason, she couldn't stop herself. She didn't even try.

"I mean, face it," she continued. "It was a wimpy move."

An angry flush stained Enid's cheeks. "Hugh is not a wimp! He was only thinking about me. He didn't want to put me in a bad situation."

"Fine." Elizabeth raised her hands in mock surrender. "Hugh's a hero." She directed a pointed glance at the basketball court, where Todd was in the process of stealing the ball from his Big Mesa High counterpart. She paused just long enough for him to find an opening and shoot.

"Two points!" she exulted loudly, feeling a surge of pride and self-satisfaction that *her* boyfriend was the star of the avenging Sweet Valley team. "All I can say is, I'm glad Todd's not *that* kind of hero."

"You're way out of line, Elizabeth," Enid snapped. "Say what you like about me any day of the week, but leave Hugh alone."

"OK, I'll say what I like about you," Elizabeth said cheerfully. "*You* should be more grateful,

Enid. If it weren't for me—if it had been up to Jessica and *her* friends—you wouldn't be taking your darling Hugh to the prom tomorrow night!"

Enid opened her mouth to reply. At that moment, Sweet Valley High's Keith Webster sunk a shot, nearly from midcourt. The crowd roared, drowning out Enid's sharp comeback.

"Three points!" Neil hollered.

As the game progressed, Elizabeth had to admit—to herself, anyway—that Hugh had been right. The Sweet Valley and Big Mesa teams were closely matched, and the game was a hot one. The players seemed to be keeping themselves under control; there was very little elbowing and shoving. But in the bleachers, it was another story.

The noise never let up; it just increased in volume as time went on. By the fourth quarter, it didn't seem to matter whether points were being scored or not—people were just yelling for the sake of yelling.

Elizabeth found herself completely caught up in the intense excitement. She had always been Todd's biggest fan, but ordinarily she maintained a fairly mellow attitude. Tonight, though, she wanted to see the basketball team win more than she'd ever wanted anything. The spirit of competition had seized control of her soul.

Suddenly, Elizabeth glimpsed something sailing through the air. There was a volley of tiny explosions as a bunch of water balloons burst on the court near the Big Mesa team's bench. "Did you see that?" she cried out to her friends.

A time-out was quickly called so they could mop up the water. "It was Bruce," Neil said, pointing. "They've been wild all night."

Bruce and some of his tennis teammates, in a rowdy and jubilant mood following their own victory over Big Mesa earlier that day, were sitting on the other side of the gym. "They'd better watch out," remarked Penny. "They're right smack in the middle of enemy territory."

"I'm sure they planned it that way," Neil said. "Bruce is looking for a fight."

Elizabeth squinted, focusing on Bruce. From across the gym, she could see the gleam of buttery black leather. "He's wearing his Club X jacket!" she exclaimed.

"It's' going to get him in trouble," Olivia predicted.

The seconds raced by on the official time clock. The score remained incredibly close; first Big Mesa would lead by a point or two, then Sweet Valley would rally, intercepting a pass and dashing forward for the dunk to claim the upper hand. Back and forth and back and forth . . .

"I can't stand it," Elizabeth groaned, clapping her hands over her eyes. Only thirty seconds remained in the fourth quarter and Sweet Valley trailed by three points. "Tell me when it's over!"

A huge hoorah reverberated around the gym. She dropped her hands in time to see Todd sprinting down the court with the ball. He dribbled with his right hand and then his left, and then shot. Two points!

"They can do it," Olivia shouted. "There's still time!"

But Big Mesa had the ball now, and they were just as determined to walk out of the gym winners. Elizabeth held her breath. The seconds ticked down. Ten, nine, eight, seven, six . . .

A.J. Morgan stole the ball just as the Big Mesa player was about to go in for a lay-up. Pivoting, A.J. pulled the ball into his chest, then thrust it outward in a hard, direct pass to Jim Daly. Jim ran, dribbling. Another pass, this time to Todd, who had put himself in position to score. Todd leaped skyward and the ball spun from his fingertips, rotating through the air. To Elizabeth, the ball seemed to hang suspended for hours. Then, *swish*; it dropped in, for two points, just as the buzzer sounded. The game was over. Sweet Valley High had won by just one point!

With a triumphant roar, the Sweet Valley fans surged to their feet. Down on the court, the Gladiators high-fived one another jubilantly. Elizabeth and her friends jumped up and down, grabbing each other in victory hugs.

"We did it!" Elizabeth cried. "We got them back!"

Just then, she was shoved from behind. From both sides of the gym, kids were flooding down from the bleachers onto the court.

"Uh-oh," Neil yelled. "Here comes the rumble!"

In the tradition of good sportsmanship, Todd had lined up his squad to shake hands with their opponents. But exuberant fans rushed the court, breaking into the ranks of athletes.

Elizabeth watched in astonishment as the Big Mesa team hightailed it for the locker room, barely escaping with their shirts. At the same time, shaking their fists at the mob of Sweet Valley High students pressing after them, the contingent of Big Mesa spectators raced toward the exit at the other end of the gym.

"They're not sticking around," Penny observed. "They know they're outnumbered."

"But they'll be back," Neil predicted. "We won tonight, but this wasn't the final showdown between our schools—not by a long shot."

Jessica entered the Dairi Burger riding on Sam's shoulders and waving her pom-poms. She was greeted with cheers by the students already gathered to celebrate the basketball team's thrilling win over their Big Mesa archrivals.

"Yes!" Jessica shouted in response. "We're the best!" Sam carried her through the crowd, depositing her at a big table in the middle of the restaurant.

"Hi, everybody," Jessica chirped, flashing a bright smile at Ken, Terri, Winston, and Maria. Then her smile faded. Todd and Elizabeth were also sitting at the table.

"Hi, Todd," Jessica said. Folding her arms and lifting her chin, she turned her head away from Elizabeth, refusing to recognize her sister's presence.

Elizabeth also raised her chin in haughty disdain. Shifting her chair, she turned her back to Jessica.

Jessica saw this; she also saw Todd raise his eyebrows at Sam. "What's with these two?" Todd mouthed.

Sam shrugged helplessly. "I have no idea," he mimed back.

Jessica dropped into a seat; she was just going to have to make the best of the situation. "What a game, huh?" she remarked brightly, figuring it didn't hurt to remind everybody within earshot that she had played a starring role that night too. "It's great to be a cheerleader, isn't it, Maria? The action on the court was so hot tonight, I almost got burned!"

"It was outrageous," agreed Maria. She turned to Todd. "You were absolutely awesome."

"Here's to Sweet Valley High's high scorer!" Winston boomed, raising his milk shake in salute.

A bunch of people who had been milling about the restaurant now crowded around the table to slap Todd on the back and rumple his hair. "Way to go, Whizzer!" Bill said.

"Nice job, Todd," said DeeDee, bending to brush his cheek with a congratulatory kiss.

Elizabeth smiled smugly as Todd was showered with adulation. Jessica frowned.

"You were great," Roger praised Todd. "And not just because you were high scorer, either. You helped the team keep their cool, and with all the harassment we've been getting from Big Mesa lately, that was no mean feat."

"I just wanted to play clean," Todd said modestly. He grinned. "And win. Those were my goals."

"Well, it'll go on the record as the best game you guys have ever played," Ken predicted. "It was a great night for the team."

"And a great night for the school," said Jessica

in an effort to steer the conversation away from the subject of Todd's heroism. When people focused on Todd, they focused on Elizabeth, too; and that, in Jessica's opinion, was *not* good. "We put Big Mesa in their place, once and for all!"

"I wish I believed that," said Todd. "But the last thing the captain of the Big Mesa team shouted—"

"As he ran like a rabbit into the locker room," put in Winston.

Todd grinned. "His last words were, 'We'll be back.'"

"But not on the court," Sam pointed out. "That's the last time you guys play them for a while."

Todd nodded. "Right. Not on the court."

"So, what do you think they have in mind?" asked Maria. "You don't think . . ." Her dark eyes widened. "You don't think they'll try to trash the prom, do you?"

"They'd better not," Elizabeth declared fiercely. "Not after all the work we've put into it!"

"I hope they don't, but . . ." Winston nodded toward a nearby table. "I get the distinct impression *some* people are getting ready for action."

Jessica turned to look. She saw Bruce sitting with some of his friends—some of the more aggressive tennis players, and a few former members of the disbanded Club X. The boys had their heads together; it looked like a strategy session, all right.

"Getting ready for action? Getting ready for *trouble,* you mean," said Terri.

"They're not just *ready* for it—they're looking for it," Ken stated.

Elizabeth bit her lip, looking anxious. "Don't worry," Todd said to her. "Nothing'll happen to ruin the dance. The chaperons'll keep an eye on things."

"*You* can keep an eye on things." Terri smiled at Todd, her eyes twinkling. "From your Prom King throne. You'll have a good view from there!"

Everybody laughed, including Todd. Only Jessica didn't join in the mirth.

A terrible realization had just come over her. *Todd . . . Prom King . . . of course! Why didn't that occur to me before?*

She had been so absorbed in her campaign for Prom *Queen,* Jessica hadn't given a single moment's thought to the question of who might be elected *King.* And now the natural choice for King of the Sweet Valley High Jungle Prom was sitting right across from her: Todd Wilkins, her twin sister's boyfriend.

The blood drained from Jessica's face, leaving her pale as a mushroom. Todd had always been one of the most well-liked boys at school—that was no secret. But after tonight's game, it was clear his popularity was greater than ever. The timing couldn't have been more perfect; he had been the star of the decisive basketball victory over Big Mesa, and now he was a shoo-in for the title of Jungle Prom King.

And if Todd's chosen King . . . Jessica gulped. If Todd was chosen King at nine o'clock, Elizabeth was sure to be chosen Queen at ten o'clock.

Jessica groaned inwardly. *Why didn't I think of that? No wonder Elizabeth looks so darned smug!* Meanwhile, *she* was stuck with a nobody boyfriend who didn't help her campaign in the least—a dumb dirt biker, of all things, from stupid old Bridgewater.

As the talk swirled around her, Jessica did her best to disguise her anxiety. She couldn't take the crown for granted—not anymore. It was going to be a close contest, a race to the wire.

Jessica eyed her twin, her expression as hard as nails. In less than twenty-four hours, the ballots for Prom Queen would be tallied up. *I'd better be ready to play rough,* Jessica thought, *to throw out an elbow or stick out a foot to trip her up.*

No doubt about it; she had to be on the lookout—she had to watch for *any* opportunity to knock her sister out of the way and snatch the crown for herself.

SVH

Fourteen

Midafternoon on Saturday, Elizabeth paced to the middle of the Sweet Valley High gymnasium. She closed her eyes for a moment, then opened them and looked around, pretending it was that night, that she'd just arrived at the prom and was seeing the decorated gym for the first time.

She caught her breath, her eyes lighting up with pleasure. Thanks to a hard day's work on the part of the Prom Committee, the cavernous, unromantic gym had been transformed into a veritable tropical paradise. Glossy green paper leaves and vines covered the walls; real potted palm trees scattered here and there lent the artificial jungle depth and realism. Life-sized cardboard cutouts of wild animals loomed from the foliage: lions, monkeys, giraffes, and elephants. A smattering of colorful Environmental Alert posters completed the backdrop.

It's beautiful—it's perfect, Elizabeth thought with a sigh of satisfaction. *This is going to be the best prom ever!*

Her eyes roamed the length of the gym, settling on the low stage that had been erected at the far end. The band would set up at the opposite end; this stage was where the Prom King and Queen would be crowned, and to prepare for the coronation, Olivia, DeeDee, and David had constructed two thrones wound with real vines and fresh flowers.

Elizabeth gazed at the thrones, trying to imagine herself seated in one. For weeks she had been obsessed with such fantasies. But for some reason, this afternoon, the picture didn't come. Her mind remained blank.

With another, heavier sigh, Elizabeth sank down into a folding chair at one of the little tables set up next to the dance floor. It looked as though every element of the prom was going to turn out just right; her hard work had paid off. Still, something was missing . . . and Elizabeth knew what it was.

I can't share my joy and pride with the person I'm closest to, she reflected bitterly. *The person who was with me when the Jungle Prom was just a brand-new idea.*

She and Jessica had had a lot of fights over the years; they were sisters, after all! But most of their spats had been minor. Elizabeth got mad at Jessica for borrowing her new sundress without asking; Jessica was peeved because Elizabeth wouldn't swap kitchen duties with her. They usually didn't stay mad at each other for long; sooner or later, one of them would do or say something that would make the other person laugh. Neither of them was very good at holding a grudge. But *this* fight . . . !

A sharp pain stabbed Elizabeth's heart. *Maybe I made a mistake,* she thought, staring hard at a brightly painted cutout of a tiger preparing to pounce. *Maybe I've been wrong to want the Prom Queen title so badly—and in thinking I'd be so much better at the job than Jessica—and in wanting to become a different person. If it costs me my friendship with my sister . . .*

A solitary tear rolled down Elizabeth's cheek. Her vision blurred; she blinked, but she still couldn't see clearly. *What will the night bring?* she wondered, wiping her eyes. *Only one of us can win the crown. If it's me, if I beat Jessica . . . will it even feel like winning? And if she beats me, after all this feuding, will I even care?*

A voice broke into Elizabeth's glum reverie. "Hey, Liz!" DeeDee shouted from behind the stage. "Stop daydreaming and get back here to help us. We still have a hundred balloons to blow up!"

This reminder of her friends' presence was like sun on the morning mist; Elizabeth's feeling of foreboding was instantly dispelled. "Coming," she called, the smile returning to her face.

What a smart move, signing up for the last shift! Jessica commended herself as she entered the deserted gymnasium late Saturday afternoon. In a glance, she could see that the work was done; everyone had long since gone home to get ready for the prom.

She lingered a moment, wandering around the gym to admire the extravagant decorations. Everything looked exactly as she'd imagined it would: the greenery, the animals, the two thrones. . . . The Jungle Prom had been transformed from dream to reality.

It will be a perfect evening, Jessica anticipated as she climbed the stairs to the stage. *And the most perfect moment of all will be when the crown is placed on the head of the Prom Queen . . . me!*

She approached the Queen's throne with measured, reverent steps. Then she turned, smiling to an imaginary crowd of adoring fans.

In an instant, all her doubt and anxiety disappeared like rain clouds retreating before a dry, clearing wind. *I might as well get used to the view,* Jessica thought, her heart beginning to pound with excitement as she lowered herself onto the throne. *It's going to be me tonight. I just know it!*

It didn't matter that Todd was the obvious choice for Prom King, Jessica decided. When push came to shove, when people actually sat down to fill out their ballots, they were going to think of Jessica, glamorous head cheerleader and school idol; not Elizabeth, who, no matter how much work she put into the prom, was still a boring old bookworm. *Elizabeth Wakefield, Queen of the Jungle Prom?* Jessica laughed out loud. *Hardly!*

After reveling in her fantasies for a few minutes longer, Jessica got to her feet and jumped down from the stage. As she did, she glimpsed something on the floor, half hidden by a potted palm tree.

She bent to see what it was. It was a small leather book, and it looked vaguely familiar.

Jessica picked up the book. As she got a closer look, she realized why it looked familiar: because she'd seen it in her sister's hand on about a million occasions.

Liz keeps track of everything in here! Jessica reflected as she opened the book to confirm that it was actually her sister's. Homework assignments, meetings, newspaper deadlines . . . Sure enough, it was all there—Elizabeth's whole life was mapped out on the little pages.

Jessica read a few of the neatly printed entries. "Baby-sit for Teddy Collins, eight P.M." "French Club meeting, Tuesday after school." "Take Jeep for tune-up." "Beach Disco with Todd!!"

Jessica's conscience flickered to life and she felt a sharp pang of guilt. This appointment book was so important to Elizabeth; she would never have left it behind if she hadn't been terribly preoccupied and busy.

She really has gone all out for this prom, Jessica realized. She looked around at the beautifully decorated gym, a wry smile on her face. She herself had paid money out of her own pocket to have some "Save the Rain Forest" buttons made—big deal. *If it had been up to me to decorate the gym,* Jessica thought, *I would've thrown around a bunch of streamers and opened some bags of potato chips! Maybe . . . maybe she* does *deserve to be named—*

Somewhere nearby, a door slammed; its heavy, echoing thud cut off her thought like a sharp blade. Jessica shivered, suddenly feeling cold and alone. The sound was so desolate, so final. . . .

The big house was empty and as quiet as a tomb, but for once Lila didn't mind. She didn't feel compelled to turn on a TV in every room, or to blast the stereo to try to fill the space with distracting noise.

At five o'clock, the powder-blue princess phone in her bedroom rang. Lila picked it up, slipping off her chunky gold earring before placing the receiver against her ear. "Hello?"

"Hi, Li. It's Daddy."

"Oh, hi, Daddy!" she said cheerfully. "What's up?"

"Nothing terribly fun," Mr. Fowler told his daughter. "MacMillan and I just wrapped up a long day of meetings with some clients and now we have to let them take us out to dinner."

Lila clucked her tongue in sympathy. "Poor Daddy. What a yawn."

"I'm on my way to squeeze in an hour on the fitness machines at the hotel," her father said, "but first I wanted to check in with you and see how your weekend was going. What have you got planned for tonight?"

"It's the Jungle Prom, didn't I tell you about it?" Lila couldn't believe she had neglected to mention such an important social event to her father. "It's a big, all-school dance with a jungle theme. All the proceeds go to save the rain forests."

An ironic chuckle came over the line. "How philanthropic."

Lila smiled. "Isn't it, though? The do-good angle aside, it should be a pretty fun party."

"And that's what matters. Well, it sounds like I don't have to worry about you being bored and lonely while I'm out of town," he joked.

"You never do," Lila replied. "I'm just fine."

"That's my girl," Mr. Fowler said. "See you for dinner tomorrow night."

"So long, Daddy." There was a click; the connection between her and her father went dead.

In the past, Lila had often dreaded this moment—the silence that followed, the feeling of distance and abandonment. But this time after she hung up the phone, instead of sagging dejectedly onto her bed, she danced across the room to the closet, energized by high spirits. She had lied a lot to her father lately, pretending to be happy when she wasn't. Tonight, though, she hadn't needed to lie. She *was* looking forward to the dance; it *was* going to be a fun night.

Lila was ready to take on the prom—and the world. She felt like her confident, beautiful, smart, sexy old self again. And all because of Nathan. . . .

* * *

As the sun set in a blaze of purple and orange outside her bedroom window, Elizabeth gently removed her prom dress from her closet. As she slipped the dress from its hanger, for a split-second she pictured another dress—the daring, midnight-blue taffeta gown she'd tried on that day at Lisette's. *I wish I'd bought that one. . . .*

No, I like this dress much *better,* she told herself firmly. The simple, flowing lines of the silk allowed her natural beauty to shine through; her eyes reflected the ice-blue shade, sparkling like gems. The other dress would have been wrong—all wrong.

Dropping her robe on the back of a chair, Elizabeth pulled the dress over her head. Reaching around to her back, she tugged at the zipper, but she could get it only halfway up. Instinctively, she opened her mouth to shout, "Jess! Get in here, I need help!"

She caught herself just in time. *That's right—we're not talking to each other.* Gritting her teeth, Elizabeth stretched her arms the other way, over her shoulders. Wriggling and straining, she finally managed to get the dress zipped.

She looked at herself in the mirror on the back of her bedroom door and smiled with spontaneous pleasure. The dress *was* beautiful. Elizabeth twirled, watching the skirt spin around her. A little makeup, her new dangly pearl earrings, a special hairstyle . . . *And I'll be drop-dead gorgeous,* she thought with satisfaction. *Sweet Valley High's going to get an eyeful. Jessica's not the only one around here with style!*

The shower had been running in the bathroom. Now Elizabeth heard the tap turn off. Then for a second or two the music blasting from Jessica's bedroom increased a few decibels. When it returned to its previous level, Elizabeth figured it was safe to open the bathroom door.

No such luck. Wrapped in a fluffy pink bathsheet, Jessica was standing in front of the sink, leaning toward the mirror with a mascara wand in her hand.

Elizabeth started to back up, then stopped. *I need to get ready too. If I wait for her to finish, I'll miss the whole dance!* Without a word to Jessica, Elizabeth took up her own position in front of the mirror and started to brush her hair.

Upon her sister's entry, Jessica had frozen, the mascara brush halfway to her right eye. Now, her face stony, she resumed attending to her lashes.

Elizabeth gathered a handful of her silky hair, pulling it up and back. It was an elegant, pretty look—just what she was aiming for. With her free hand, she reached for the drawer where she kept her hair accessories.

The silver hair comb she was looking for wasn't there. *Is it in my room?* Elizabeth visualized the top of her dresser. No, it wasn't there. *Maybe Jessica borrowed it. I bet anything it found its way into* her *drawer somehow!*

She had no choice; words had to be exchanged. Elizabeth cleared her throat. "Excuse me," she said, her tone stiff and formal. "Did you by any chance borrow my silver hair comb?"

Jessica didn't bother speaking or even looking at Elizabeth. By way of reply, she just nodded curtly toward the drawer on her side of the bathroom. Elizabeth stepped around her sister, careful not to brush against her, and retrieved the comb from the drawer.

She had intended to put on a little makeup—some lip gloss, a touch of mascara. But as she fixed the comb in her hair, Elizabeth realized that her hands had started to shake. She was tense from head to toe, her nerves stretched as taut as a bow about to fire off an arrow. And Elizabeth knew her sister almost as well as she knew herself; Jessica was tense too. The bathroom fairly crackled with electricity.

With an abrupt gesture, Elizabeth snatched a

few items off the counter and fled the bathroom, slamming the door shut behind her.

Safe in her room again, she dropped the make-up with a clatter on top of her dresser. As she did, she noticed that her leather appointment book was lying next to her jewelry box, half hidden by a silk scarf. *So that's where I left my date book,* she thought, relieved. *I've been looking all over for it!*

Fumbling in her jewelry box, Elizabeth located and put on her earrings, large, luminous pearls hanging delicately from gold settings. When she was done she looked at herself in the mirror.

Gazing at the face she saw reflected there, Elizabeth felt a sudden wave of wistful regret. She couldn't help remembering that at about this time of evening just a few weeks ago on the Saturday night that started it all, she and Jessica had been getting ready for the fateful beach party. They had talked and laughed, run in and out of each other's rooms. . . .

Elizabeth shoved the recollection from her mind; she refused to allow herself to succumb to sentimental nostalgia. *That was then and this is now,* she reminded herself sternly. There was no point crying over spilled milk, no point sighing over a broken bond.

Because the battle wasn't over yet. *I've worked hard for this and I'm not going to crumble now,*

Elizabeth determined, her eyes flashing with cold, hard light. *I'm going to wear the Prom Queen's crown. This is going to be* my *night!*

Jessica gazed at herself in the mirror over the bathroom sink, her eyes glittering with satisfaction. *I look twice as good as Elizabeth,* she thought happily. *Make that ten times as good!*

She couldn't believe Elizabeth had settled for that boring old light-blue dress. It didn't do *anything* for her; it certainly didn't scream out "Prom Queen." Not like this dress! Jessica smoothed her hands down her sides from her waist to her hips, admiring the way the ruby-red, strapless dress clung to every curve. Yep, this was the kind of dress that stopped people in their tracks; this dress was fun, flashy, and fancy enough to go with a tiara. *I'm going to knock 'em dead,* Jessica anticipated gleefully. *Elizabeth doesn't have a prayer!*

Bending over, she ran a brush quickly through her hair. Then she stood up, tossing her hair back and fluffing it with her fingers. As she spritzed some jasmine cologne behind her ears, Jessica smiled at herself in the mirror. Her wild, sexy look was complete. She was ready for her big night—the night she had been waiting for and working for.

As she stepped back into her bedroom, Jessica

heard the doorbell ring. Prince Albert, the family's golden retriever, started barking.

For a moment, she frowned, wondering. Who could be stopping by the house at this hour on a Saturday night? Then she put a hand over her mouth, stifling a giggle. She had completely forgotten about Sam and Todd. Either her date or Elizabeth's had arrived.

Jessica slipped on her high heels and grabbed her black beaded purse. She darted into the hallway and almost collided with Elizabeth, who had burst out of her room at the exact same moment.

"Excuse me," Elizabeth grumbled.

"Hmph," Jessica grunted.

Elizabeth stepped aside, extending one arm in a mocking gesture. "After you," she said, her voice heavy with sarcasm.

"No, after *you,*" Jessica insisted, equally snide.

There was a momentary standoff. Then Elizabeth preceded Jessica down the staircase.

Sam and Todd, both dressed in tuxedos and holding corsage boxes, stood in the front hall. When he saw Elizabeth, Todd's face lit up like a sunrise. "Liz, you look fabulous," he exclaimed, sweeping her into his arms for a kiss.

Jessica frowned. Now that she took another look, she saw that Elizabeth *did* look fabulous. The dress was plain—Jessica herself wouldn't be caught dead in it—but she had to admit, somehow it suited Elizabeth. Elizabeth looked like a princess. *Or maybe even a Queen . . .*

"Jess, you're a goddess," Sam declared.

Tearing her eyes away from Elizabeth, Jessica looked at Sam as she descended the rest of the stairs. His eyes were glowing with love and admiration; like the mirror upstairs, they confirmed her own sense of her superior beauty. *A goddess—that's better than a princess any day!* Jessica decided, once again confident that she had a definite edge over her twin.

Stepping to Jessica's side, Sam bent his head to hers for a kiss. Jessica turned her face away, presenting him with her cheek so he wouldn't smudge her lipstick. "You look nice too," she said mechanically.

"Hey, kids!" Jessica looked up to see her father waving at them from the living room, a camera in his hand. "Come in here for a picture!"

Jessica rolled her eyes. "Do we have to, Dad?"

"This is a very special occasion. You'll be glad later that you have photos to remember it by," said Mrs. Wakefield, stepping into the hall from the kitchen. She held up two small florist's boxes and smiled. "Besides, you have to pin these on. It's not a prom without corsages and boutonnieres!"

Elizabeth and Todd marched into the living room; Jessica and Sam followed suit. Jessica grabbed one of the boxes from her mother. "Here," she said, pinning the carnation unceremoniously to Sam's lapel.

From the box he had brought, Sam now removed a beautiful red rose set in ferns and baby's breath, attached to a slender elastic bracelet. "It's a wrist corsage," he explained. "I knew you were going to wear something bare, so there wouldn't be anyplace to pin it."

"That's fine," said Jessica. She held out her arm so he could slide the corsage onto her wrist, meanwhile scowling at Elizabeth out of the corner of her eye. *These wrist corsages are so tacky,* she thought jealously as she watched Todd pin a beautiful white orchid to her sister's dress. *Elizabeth's is much prettier—and twice as big!*

Mr. Wakefield aimed the camera at Jessica and Sam, clicking a picture. "I love these candid shots," he said enthusiastically. "Isn't this fun?"

"It's a riot," Jessica muttered. "OK, Dad. We're ready. Can we get on with it?"

"Sure," he said amiably. "Why don't you and Sam stand in front of the window?"

Obediently, Sam and Jessica adjusted their

position. "Great—that's perfect," Mr. Wakefield declared. "Say cheese!"

Sam put his arm around Jessica's waist and pulled her close to his side. She forced a big, artificial smile. *Click.*

"Now, let's get an official Jungle Prom portrait of Elizabeth and Todd," Mr. Wakefield said. "How about in front of the fireplace, you two?"

"Whatever," said Elizabeth.

She and Todd struck a classic pre-prom pose, standing face-to-face with their arms around each other. Mrs. Wakefield clasped her hands together, her eyes misty. Jessica wanted to gag. *Click.*

Jessica tugged at Sam's hand. Thank goodness the photo session was over; she couldn't wait to get out of the house. "C'mon, let's get out of here!" she urged.

"Whoa, hold on," her father commanded. He smiled broadly. "I've got to get one of the four of you together, don't I?"

Jessica and Elizabeth glared at one another. "Do you?" Elizabeth asked.

Mr. Wakefield chuckled. "Of course I do," he said. "Your brother will want to see a picture of his lovely sisters, and you two will want to look back on tonight. Trust me. Now, c'mon, kids, line up."

Elizabeth, Todd, Jessica, and Sam lined up, facing Mr. Wakefield and the camera. Jessica smiled another big, fake smile. Out of the corner of her eye, she could see Elizabeth doing the same. *Click.*

"Is that it?" Jessica asked, tapping her foot impatiently.

"That's it," Mr. Wakefield told her.

Mrs. Wakefield stepped forward to kiss each of her daughters on the cheek. "Have a wonderful time, Elizabeth. You, too, honey," she said to Jessica.

"Thanks, Mom," Jessica replied. She shot a meaningful glance at her sister. "I plan to!"

The two couples headed for the door. "Good night, kids," Mr. Wakefield called after them. "Have a night to remember!"

One way or another, it will be, Jessica thought as she stepped through the door and out into the dark, cool evening. *A night to remember . . .*

SVH

Fifteen

A thrill of excitement chased up Elizabeth's spine as Todd opened the door for her and she stepped out of the BMW. A steady stream of students all dressed up for the dance flowed from the parking lot toward the gymnasium, following a trail of softly flickering Japanese lanterns—another of DeeDee and Olivia's inspirations. It was a magical sight . . . and Elizabeth knew that even more magic awaited them inside.

"What a night," Todd said, taking a deep breath of the fragrant evening air. "I'm in the mood to dance, aren't you?"

Elizabeth smiled up at him. "I can't wait."

The pulse of reggae music wrapped around

them as they entered the gym. Elizabeth heard the students near her gasp in surprise and delight as they caught their first glimpse of the decorated gym. Todd was one of them. "It's wild," he raved, giving her a hug. "Terrific job, Elizabeth."

"Liz! Todd!" boomed Winston, whose formal black tuxedo was livened up by a bright floral cummerbund and bow tie. "Welcome to the Jungle Prom!"

Todd handed two prom tickets to Winston, who stuck them in a cash box. "This job'll keep you out of trouble," Todd joked.

"You're not kidding." Winston put his arm around Andrea, his ticket-table partner. "Business is booming. We're thinking of opening up franchises."

"Here are your raffle tickets and prom mini-yearbooks," Andrea said. She winked at Todd. "*And* your Prom King ballots. We'll be collecting them in an hour, at nine o'clock."

Winston leaned confidentially toward Elizabeth and Todd. "Here's my plan, folks. This guy, Wilkins, have you heard of him? He's expected to win the King's crown by a landslide. But I figure if we rally people to vote for *me*"—Winston poked himself in the chest with a forefinger—"we have a good chance at an upset. What d'you say?"

Todd laughed. "You've got my vote, pal."

He steered Elizabeth toward the dance floor. "Have a good time," Andrea called after them.

The prom was already in full swing. "It didn't take long for this party to get started," Todd remarked to Elizabeth.

"No." A broad smile wreathed her face as she looked around. "It sure didn't!"

The jungle decorations were even more impressive by night. The breeze created by moving bodies caused the paper leaves to flutter; the wildly painted animals seemed to leap out from the wall. But even more brilliant and exotic than the decorations were the Sweet Valley High students themselves.

Elizabeth had never seen so many stunning dresses. Cheryl Thomas wore bright lemon-yellow; Terri's dress was peacock-blue; Dana Larson looked feline in a black and orange tiger-striped minidress; Maria glittered in gold sequins; Amy Sutton could have passed for a model in a silver sheath. A lot of the guys had gone all-out on the fashion front too. There were bright bow ties and tropical-print shirts aplenty. All around the gym, people talked and laughed and danced in a kaleidoscope of colors, pausing only to collect autographs in their prom yearbooks. With the music of Island Sunsplash completing the exotic atmosphere, it was a breathtaking spectacle.

"Great job, Elizabeth," Rosa raved, coming up to give Elizabeth a quick hug. "You really made it happen. It's the perfect prom!"

"Thanks," said Elizabeth. "I love your dress, Rosa."

Rosa looked down at her slim, emerald-green dress. "It's camouflage," she said, casting a teasing glance at her date. "In case Roger and I decide to hide out among the palm trees."

Roger grinned. "Don't get my hopes up."

As Rosa and Roger whirled off into the crowd, more people approached Todd and Elizabeth, showering Elizabeth with compliments on the work she had done to make the evening possible.

"Thanks, you guys," Elizabeth said to April Dawson and Michael Harris. "I'm glad you're having fun!" she told Claire Middleton and Danny Porter.

After a few minutes of greeting people, Todd took Elizabeth's hand and drew her away from the press of admiring friends. "I'm stealing Rosa's idea," he explained as they ducked behind a palm tree and wrapped their arms around each other. "I can see I'll have to go to extremes tonight if I want a moment alone with you. You're really the woman of the hour!"

Elizabeth beamed. "Do you think so?"

Todd stroked her hair. "It looks like you're already wearing the Queen's crown," he teased.

"You can relax now. Your dream is coming true."

Elizabeth hugged him tightly. "Oh, I hope so!" she exclaimed. Now that the moment was at hand, the doubt and regret that had nagged her earlier in the day melted away. *There's nothing wrong with wanting it all,* she thought, *with enjoying my moment in the limelight. I've earned it!*

"C'mon," she said to Todd, pulling him back toward the crowd. "Let's dance!"

"This is terrible," Jessica grumbled to Sam. "Just terrible."

"What are you talking about?" he asked her. "The prom is a huge success. Everyone's having a blast!"

"That's just the problem. The prom is a huge success, but everybody's giving *her* all the credit." Jessica pointed to where Elizabeth stood, surrounded by congratulatory friends. "Not a single person's come up to *me* to thank *me* for doing such a great job," she complained.

Sam ran a hand through his thick, curly blond hair. "Well, she *did* work awfully hard on this," he ventured.

Jessica put her hands on her hips. "What! I can't believe you!" she cried, astounded by his betrayal. Maybe Elizabeth *had* worked hard—Jessica herself was willing to admit this, *off* the record—but that didn't mean Sam of all people should be singing her praises. "Why don't you just carry a sign, 'Elizabeth Wakefield for Prom Queen'?"

"Don't get your nose out of joint," Sam said somewhat impatiently. "All I meant was—"

"I really don't want to hear it," Jessica declared. "Obviously I can't count on you to help me win votes, so I hope you don't mind fending for yourself for a while. You know lots of people here—go ask someone to dance."

Turning on her heel, she stomped off. "Jess, wait!" Sam shouted after her.

Jessica pretended not to hear. *I don't feel like dealing with him right now,* she thought irritably. He was just going to get in the way, and she really didn't have any time to waste. She needed to talk to and dance with as many people as possible over the next hour and a half if she wanted to scrape together enough votes to beat Elizabeth in the Prom Queen balloting.

The refreshment table—that looks like a good place to corner people, Jessica decided.

She headed in that direction, on the lookout for people who might not have made up their minds yet about whom to vote for for Prom Queen. "Hi, Sally, Mark," she said brightly. "*Hot* dress, Sally."

"It's one of Dana's," Sally Larson confided.

Like I couldn't have guessed that, thought Jessica. *You usually dress like someone who works at a morgue.* "Are you two having a good time?"

Sally's boyfriend, Mark Riley, nodded. "We've already worked up a thirst on the dance floor." He handed Sally a cup of tropical punch. "The band is awesome."

"Aren't they?" said Jessica, figuring it didn't hurt to pretend she had had something to do with booking them. "We listened to a lot of demo tapes and they were by *far* the best."

"It must've taken a hundred people to decorate this place," Sally commented.

"It was a long day," Jessica confirmed. "But we had fun. All the work was definitely worth it, in my point of view. I was ready to do *anything* to make this prom happen."

I have to remember that one, she told herself as she wandered off in search of more converts. *"I was ready to do anything to make this prom happen"—just the right note of selfless dedication!*

Jessica zeroed in on Julie Porter and Josh Bowen, who were standing by a giant bowl filled with popcorn. Just then, the band paused between songs.

In the momentary lull, Jessica became aware of a murmur going around the room. "Big Mesa," she heard someone say. "They just showed up, nine or ten of them. . . ."

Jessica's heart somersaulted and a shot of adrenaline flooded through her veins. Big Mesa kids, at the Jungle Prom!

Her mission temporarily forgotten, Jessica pushed toward the gym entrance to see what was going on. As she neared the ticket table, she saw that a number of people had gotten there before her . . . including Elizabeth and Todd.

"Look, we're not trying to pull anything," a tall, good-looking boy in a tuxedo was saying to Winston. "We bought tickets earlier in the week from someone on the Prom Committee. We just want to dance."

"Well . . ." Winston glanced at Elizabeth, who nodded. "OK. Hand 'em over." The boy handed Winston two tickets. Winston stuck them in the cash box. "Oh, what the heck," he said, tearing a couple of raffle tickets from the roll. "Here. Maybe you'll win a T-shirt."

"Thanks, man." The boy took his date's arm. "C'mon, Angie."

Jessica watched in astonishment as Winston allowed two more well-dressed Big Mesa High couples and four single guys to enter. Then she bolted up to the ticket table. "I can't believe you let them in!" she cried. "Do you want the prom to end up like our beach party a few weeks ago?"

Winston lifted his shoulders. "Hey, they'd paid for tickets. And they looked legit—they weren't exactly dressed for a fight. Plus," he grinned before continuing, "they had *girls* with them."

"There were some girls along the night they raided our party, too," Jessica reminded him.

"I say we throw them out."

Jessica turned. She wasn't the least bit surprised to see Bruce swagger up, with Ronnie and Charlie at his heels. "Those losers don't belong here," Bruce pronounced. "You need some bouncers, Egbert? You've got 'em."

"I think everything's under control, Bruce," Winston said. "I'm not thrilled either about them showing up, but our policy is to let in anybody who bought a ticket."

"Policy's one thing—practice is another. And I say they're out. C'mon, guys," Bruce said to his companions. "Let's take care of this!"

"Hold it," a deep voice commanded.

Jessica held her breath as Todd intercepted Bruce, blocking his path. "They're not causing any trouble, Patman. I think you'd better leave them alone."

"Who died and made you ruler of the universe?" Bruce asked sarcastically. "You're not Prom

King *yet,* Wilkins. Why don't you keep your opinions to yourself?"

A crowd of students had gathered around, curious to witness the outcome of this showdown. Bruce looked as tense and angry as a snake, coiled and ready to strike. But Todd didn't flinch. "Because they're not just *my* opinions," he said calmly. "If you want to pick a fight, that's fine with me. But do it someplace else. Don't ruin the prom for everybody else."

"Don't ruin the prom for everybody else," Bruce mimicked. Ronnie and Charlie guffawed loudly.

Now Ken Matthews stepped up. "I don't know, Todd," he said, his jaw clenching in a tight line. "I'm with Patman on this one. I think we should toss those Big Mesa kids out of here. That's the best way to make sure nothing gets started."

What's he going to say to that? Jessica wondered, breathless from the suspense. *He won't listen to Bruce, but what about Ken?*

But Todd stood his ground. "It would be stupid to antagonize them. Let's just leave them alone. I bet they won't stick around long; they just came to make a point." He looked meaningfully at Terri and Elizabeth and a few other girls standing nearby. "This *isn't* the place for a fight," he insisted.

Ken nodded slowly. "You're right," he conceded. "OK, Patman. Let's back off."

A collective sigh of relief arose from the onlookers as Bruce and his cronies disappeared grumbling into the crowd. "Nice going," Winston told Todd.

Todd shrugged his shoulders. "We just don't need a scene like that," he said simply. "The Big Mesa kids seem to be acting OK. We're their hosts; we should try to do the same."

Jessica shook her head in reluctant admiration. *I've got to hand it to the guy. He sure knows how to work a crowd!* Once again, a crisis had come up, and once again, Todd had seized the opportunity to look like a leader and a hero. *They shouldn't even bother counting the ballots for Prom King,* Jessica thought. *He's got it all sewn up.*

She watched unhappily as Todd put his arm protectively around Elizabeth. The image printed itself on Jessica's brain . . . and on everyone else's brain too, she bet. The crucial question still remained: would Elizabeth ride to victory on Todd's coattails?

Lila stood at the edge of the dance floor, half hidden by the fronds of a potted palm. She felt alone and different, as if she were the only person in the whole room who was standing still and quiet, who wasn't moving, laughing, talking, kissing.

I shouldn't have come, she thought, tugging at

the hem of her short black and fuchsia flowered dress. It was a pain, dodging the hopeful boys who asked her to dance. There was really only one person she felt like talking to, and so far she hadn't seen him anywhere. . . .

"Hi, there."

Lila whirled, her cheeks turning as pink as her dress. She knew that voice—it was the one she had been dying to hear.

But now that Nathan stood in front of her, a friendly smile on his face, she was completely tongue-tied. Except for that one brief encounter at the beach, they had never really had a conversation outside of their counseling sessions. What was she supposed to say to him?

"Uh, hi, yourself," Lila mumbled, ducking her head.

"How's it going?"

Nathan looked nautical, and cute, Lila thought, in a navy-blue sports coat, white oxford shirt, and slightly rumpled khakis. Now he tugged at his rainbow-striped tie. "I'll tell you, Li, this isn't really my scene," he confided. "I was never good at high-school dances."

"Because you hate to iron?" she guessed, eyeing his wrinkled trousers.

Nathan laughed. "Yeah, that's one reason. But

mostly because I could never get up the nerve to ask girls to dance."

"You're kidding." Lila couldn't believe it. Nathan must've been the most adorable boy at Sweet Valley High, back in his day! "How come?"

"It's the approach," he explained. "That's the hard part, getting your opening line right. I never knew exactly what to say."

"Did you ever try 'Would you like to dance?'" she teased.

Nathan grinned. "I didn't want to sound like all the other guys. I wanted to be original."

"Well, it's too bad," Lila commented, a flirtatious lilt in her voice. "There were probably a lot of disappointed girls, a lot of broken hearts."

"Oh, I don't know about that," he said lightly. "Hey, it's good to see you here, Li. I'm glad you stuck to your decision to come. Are you having a good time?"

His tone had become purely professional; he was expressing a counselor's concern. *Was I just imagining it?* Lila wondered. *Were we talking differently before, like real people, like friends . . . like a guy and a girl?* "Yeah, I'm having a good time," she answered.

"I'm glad," Nathan said sincerely. Narrowing his eyes, he looked around the gym. "Well, it's time for me to get back on the beat," he told Lila. "We're not expecting trouble from the Big Mesa kids, but I'm going to keep an eye on them, to be on the safe side."

"Right," she said, disappointed. "You're a chaperon; you're on duty."

"Save a dance for me later, though, OK?"

Her expression brightened. "Only if you come up with a really original line," she kidded.

Nathan laughed. "I'll be working on it."

Walking purposefully, he disappeared into the crowd. Lila watched him go, a bright flush on her cheeks. She couldn't wait for Nathan to claim his dance.

"It's nine o'clock," Winston boomed into the microphone. "And you know what that means, Sweet Valley High. It's time to find out who we've elected King of the Jungle Prom!"

His words were met with enthusiastic cheers and piercing whistles. From the back of the gym, somebody booed. *One of the Big Mesa kids,* Elizabeth guessed, frowning. *Maybe we shouldn't have let them in after all!*

Winston lifted a hand for silence. "Even as we speak," he continued, "my two lovely assistants, Patty Gilbert and Andrea Slade, are circulating among you, collecting the Prom King ballots that we gave out at the door. So if you haven't already turned in your ballot, do it now!"

Elizabeth had already turned in her ballot, with the name "TODD WILKINS" printed in big capital letters. Now she squeezed her boyfriend's hand. "Are you nervous?" she whispered.

Todd smiled. "The only reason I'd want to be Prom King would be so I could keep you company onstage," he whispered back.

All around the gym, voices buzzed excitedly as Winston, Andrea, and Patty counted up the votes. It didn't take them long. Within minutes, Winston was stepping back up to the microphone. Behind him, Olivia stood holding a crown woven of ivy leaves.

"Ahem." Winston cleared his throat to signal the importance of the moment. Elizabeth bit her lip, so nervous she could scream. "We have a winner," Winston announced. "The King of the Jungle Prom—who, by the way, received ten times as many votes as the runner-up—is a guy who brings a lot of honor to Sweet Valley High, on and off the basketball court. He's the best we have to offer . . . Todd Wilkins!"

A collective roar of approval resounded through the gym. "All right, Todd!" his schoolmates shouted. "Way to go!"

Elizabeth threw her arms around Todd, hugging him tightly. In that moment, she forgot all about her own desire to be crowned Prom Queen. Nothing mattered but Todd and this well-deserved recognition of all he gave to his school, day in and day out.

"I'm so proud of you," Elizabeth whispered, her eyes bright with tears.

Todd held her close. "You know, those words mean more to me than any crown or title," he told her.

Their lips met in a warm kiss. The people standing near them clapped wildly.

"Stop smooching and get up here on the stage, Wilkins!" Winston ordered.

Elizabeth and Todd pulled apart, smiling sheepishly. Todd squeezed Elizabeth's hand one more time, then jumped onto the stage. He lifted a hand in a triumphant wave. To the sound of deafening applause, Olivia placed the crown on his head.

Todd started to step off the stage. "Whoa, where are you going?" Winston asked him. "You think you can just grab your crown and run?"

Todd nodded; the audience laughed. "No, sir," Winston said sternly. "The Prom King has *responsibilities*; this isn't a glamour job. Todd will be drawing raffle winners," Winston informed the crowd, "fifteen in all between now and ten o'clock when we'll collect the ballots for Prom Queen. Andrea and Patty are handing those out now. Don't forget to vote!"

With a roll of steel drums, the band kicked off their next set of songs. Elizabeth looked around for someone to talk to. She needed to distract herself, to burn up some of her nervous energy on the dance floor, maybe. Somehow, she had to get through the next hour. . . .

While everyone around her clapped and hollered for Todd, Jessica stood with her mouth pursed and her arms tightly crossed. Todd's victory had probably been inevitable; still, Jessica had hoped against hope that someone else—Ken, Aaron, A.J., even Winston—would be named Prom King.

But now Todd stood on stage, with the crown on his head and a big grin on his face. Only one thing was needed to complete the perfect picture: Elizabeth, the King's girlfriend, standing by his side as Queen.

It's not fair, Jessica thought bitterly. *Everyone's going to pick her just because she goes out with Todd, not because she deserves it. Unless . . .* Jessica narrowed her eyes, racking her brain. *Unless I do something . . . fast.*

But what? With a sigh, she turned away from the depressing sight of Todd posing for photographs on his throne. Who was she kidding? It was too late—too late to choreograph another special cheerleading routine, too late to print up another batch of buttons. People were probably already scribbling Elizabeth's name on their ballots. Jessica might as well start getting used to the idea: Elizabeth was going to be the Queen of the Jungle Prom; Elizabeth would win the trip to Brazil.

And what did Jessica have to show for all her trouble? Her own boyfriend was mad at her and nowhere to be seen. Jessica sighed again. *What a fun night this is turning out to be!*

"Hey, why the long face, babe?"

Jessica turned. A boy she had never seen before had sidled up next to her. Or maybe she *had* seen him—wasn't he one of the Big Mesa High kids? *Yuck, I can't believe we let these guys in!* "My name *isn't* babe," she said frostily, taking a step away from him.

The boy grinned, amused rather than discouraged by her coolness. "So, what is it?" he asked, staying close to her side.

Jessica rolled her eyes. "Guess."

"Hmm . . ." The boy studied her through sly,

blue eyes. "You look like a . . . Tiffany."

Jessica snorted. "Hardly."

He snapped his fingers. "I've got it. It's Ashley."

"Nope."

Jessica glanced toward the dance floor, contemplating potential escape routes. *This guy is really a drone—I'm getting out of here. . . .*

Before she could make a move, she saw something that stopped her dead in her tracks. Elizabeth, dancing with . . . Sam!

Jessica stared at her boyfriend and her sister. The song was lively, and they were really going wild. *Elizabeth doesn't usually shake it like that,* Jessica thought, suddenly suspicious. *And why does Sam have that foolish smile on his face?*

The Big Mesa guy was still trying to guess Jessica's name, but she barely listened to him. She couldn't tear her eyes away from the sight of Elizabeth and Sam. *It's not enough for her, is it?* Jessica thought, paralyzed with anger and confusion. *It's not enough to steal my crown—she has to steal my boyfriend, too!*

". . . Elizabeth."

Jessica turned to the boy from Big Mesa. "*What* did you say?" she demanded.

"Elizabeth. I bet your name is Elizabeth," he repeated, slurring his words slightly.

"My name is *not* Elizabeth," she stated, glaring at him. "It's . . ."

For the first time, Jessica actually took a good look at the boy who had approached her. She discovered that he was actually kind of cute, with wavy auburn hair, chiseled features, and extremely blue eyes. But she noticed something else about him too. The reason his eyes looked so bright, practically jumping out of his tanned face, was that the whites of his eyes were bloodshot.

Jessica's gaze shifted to the large paper cup he was holding. *Aha . . .*

"It's . . . what?" The boy swayed nearer to Jessica.

Jessica looked at Elizabeth, still dancing with Sam, and then back at the guy from Big Mesa. "Jessica," she said, giving him an encouraging smile. "It's Jessica."

"That was going to be my next guess," the guy declared. He raised his paper cup. "Here's to you, Jessica. And here's to getting out of here. Sweet Valley High throws a lousy prom. What d'you say?"

"I'll think about it," she promised. The boy stepped closer, brushing against her. A shiver of repulsion ran down Jessica's spine, but she resisted the urge to jump away from him. "So, what's in the cup?" she asked playfully. "Can I have some?"

"I don't know if you can or not," he responded with a leering smile. "Are you old enough to drink the hard stuff, Jessica?"

"Are you?" she countered.

He guffawed. "Good point. Sure, you can have some. See, mixed with the punch, you can't tell it's there. Go ahead."

He held the cup out to her and waited for her to take a sip. "Umm . . . I should drink out of my own cup. I have a cold," Jessica fibbed. Reaching over, she grabbed an empty cup from the refreshment table.

The boy reached into the inside pocket of his jacket and pulled out a large silver flask. He poured some of the liquid into her cup. "Oh, c'mon," Jessica wheedled, batting her eyelashes. "Can't I have a little more than that?"

He raised his eyebrows. "For my friends," Jessica told him. "My girlfriends. I bet I can talk a bunch of them into leaving the dance too. We can all go someplace and party together."

The Big Mesa guy clearly liked this idea. He sloshed the remainder of the clear liquid into Jessica's cup.

Jessica looked toward the dance floor, a cold, speculative glint in her eye. "Thanks. I'll be right back," she promised.

SVH

Sixteen

Pushing her way through the crush of students, Jessica stepped nearer to the dance floor, the cup clutched tightly in her hand. It was really unbelievable, she thought. Todd was still on stage fulfilling his Prom King duties . . . and taking shameless advantage of that fact, Elizabeth was still dancing with Sam! *How many songs has it been now?* Jessica wondered, her expression as dark and threatening as a thundercloud.

She stared hard at her sister and Sam, as if by sheer force of will she could force them apart. Instead, as Jessica looked on in complete outrage, Elizabeth shimmied closer to Sam in order to tell him something that made him throw back his head and laugh.

Jessica was sure that she herself was the subject of the joke. Were they laughing about the foolishness of her ambition to become Prom Queen, at the hopelessness of her soon-to-be-shattered dream?

Spurred by her anger, Jessica made her way purposefully to the table where Elizabeth and Sam had left their things. She double-checked to make sure she had the right one. Sure enough, there was Sam's jacket, Elizabeth's purse, prom miniyearbooks . . . and two cups of Jungle Prom tropical punch.

Jessica looked down into the contents of her own cup. The liquid was as clear as water. *Is it true what they say?* she wondered. *That you can't even taste it when it's mixed in with other stuff?*

She focused on the two cups on the table. One was almost empty and one was half full. Whose was whose? Bending, Jessica peered more closely at them. She noticed a slight smudge of pink lip gloss on the cup to the left, the one with more punch in it. *That's the one!*

Quickly, she glanced around to make sure no one was watching. She was safe; everyone was too busy talking and laughing and dancing to pay attention to her.

With an abrupt flick of her wrist, Jessica tipped her own cup, pouring some of the alcohol into Elizabeth's cup. She hesitated, and then flicked her wrist again, emptying her entire cup into Elizabeth's. *Why not?* she thought recklessly. *I might as well get rid of the evidence!*

The deed done, she scurried away from the scene of the crime. Just then the song ended. Fanning herself with one hand, Elizabeth said something to Sam and the two left the dance area to return to their table.

Watching, Jessica held her breath, her heart pounding with suspense. *Will she drink it?*

As if on cue, Elizabeth reached for the cup and put it to her lips. She took a small sip; then a longer, deeper one.

A wicked smile spread slowly across Jessica's face. *What an idiot—she can't even tell it's spiked!* It was really a hoot, Jessica decided: Elizabeth Wakefield, the most upstanding, self-righteous person at Sweet Valley High, breaking the cardinal rule against drinking!

So, Elizabeth wants to have it all, even what doesn't belong to her. Well, this'll show her! Jessica thought, a satisfied smirk on her face. She moved away in order to put a little more distance between herself and the spiked punch . . . just as Elizabeth poured half of her drink into Sam's empty cup.

"You're a great dancer," Lila shouted to

Nathan over the sound of the music.

"You've got to be kidding," he shouted back. "I stink. I have absolutely no rhythm."

"Well, then you fake it really well!" she replied with a teasing smile.

Nathan returned her smile, his eyes warm. *What is he feeling right now?* Lila wondered, her face flushed from dancing, and from her pleasure in Nathan's company. *Is he just being polite? Or does he like being with me as much as I like being with him?*

When the song ended, Nathan put up his hands to indicate he was ready to quit. "No more," he told Lila. "I need a breather."

"So do I," she said. "Let's get some punch."

They walked together to the refreshment table. As Nathan ladled out two cups of punch, Lila eavesdropped on the conversation of a cluster of girls standing nearby. ". . . Stinking drunk," one girl declared as the others gaped at her in utter shock.

Lila's ears perked up. *Stinking drunk? Who?* she wondered. *Where?*

". . . Her own sister's boyfriend, Sam what's-his-name from Bridgewater," another girl contributed.

Sam what's-his-name from Bridgewater . . . her own sister's boyfriend . . . *No,* Lila thought in disbelief. *They can't be talking about Elizabeth!*

She glanced at Nathan, who had stepped away from her in order to hold an urgent, whispered conference with Ms. Frankel, the music teacher. Together, the two chaperons turned to look at the dance floor. Lila followed the direction of their gaze, eager to see what was going on.

And there was the sight that suddenly had everyone buzzing and pointing—not just the bunch of girls and the two chaperons, but dozens of other people as well, Lila realized.

And what a sight it was! Elizabeth Wakefield and Sam Woodruff were dancing as though they were in some kind of contest. They twirled each other around in crazy circles; Sam dipped Elizabeth down to the floor, then flung her high in the air while he spun around on his heel. Both of them were laughing like hyenas.

Lila's jaw dropped. She had never seen Elizabeth act like this—never, in all the years she had known and despised her. *Those girls must be right. Elizabeth* is *stinking drunk—and so is Sam!*

Or were they? Lila wasn't so sure about Sam, but Elizabeth had to be the last person she would ever expect would be caught drinking at a school dance. What was going on?

Lila trotted back to Nathan's side, eager to get the dirt. "What's the story?" she asked as soon as

Ms. Frankel was out of the way. "Is something the matter?"

Nathan wrinkled his forehead. "I'm not sure. I guess you know the rumor that's going around . . ."

"Elizabeth and Sam are plastered!"

Nathan smiled grimly. "Well, they do seem to be having an exceptionally good time. I'd approach them, if it were anybody else . . . if it weren't Elizabeth Wakefield. . . ."

Lila waved a hand dismissively. "Look, I've known her since we were *infants* and there's absolutely no way Elizabeth Wakefield would ever touch a drop, or associate with anyone who did," she assured Nathan. "I mean, I personally think it would be hilarious if she *were* drunk, but it's just not possible! She's probably just excited because her boyfriend got picked Prom King."

Nathan's brow cleared. "You know, Li, I think you're right." He looked over at Elizabeth and Sam again. The frown returned. "I hope you're right," he added.

"Let's not worry about them," Lila suggested. "Why don't we—"

"Hey, Mr. Pritchard!" someone yelled.

Lila and Nathan both turned. Winston was hurrying toward them, a panicked look on his face. "Mr. Pritchard, I need some help," Winston said.

He ran a hand nervously through his unruly hair. "There's a whole bunch of Big Mesa kids—twenty or thirty of them—and they want to get into the dance. They didn't buy tickets in advance, but they have money and they're dressed OK. I really don't want to let them in, though—I just don't like the looks of this. . . ."

Nathan patted Winston on the shoulder. "I'm right behind you, Winston," he said, calm and reassuring. "Let's go check it out." As he headed off, he turned to flash Lila an apologetic smile. "Duty calls again," he explained. "I'll talk to you later, Lila."

"Good luck," she called. Her eyes grew soft as she watched Nathan stride through the crowd, his shoulders square and strong. Forget all the Sweet Valley High guys, Lila thought with a dreamy sigh, even Todd, Mr. Prom King. They were just *boys*; no wonder she had gotten so fed up with them. Whereas Nathan Pritchard was a *man*. . . .

Elizabeth squealed with laughter as Sam, one arm crooked around her waist, dipped her so far backward that her hair swept the floor. "Do that again!" she begged. "That was fun!"

Sam dipped her again. This time, they were both laughing so hard he almost dropped her.

They rocked back to an upright position,

Elizabeth hanging on to Sam's neck so as not to lose her balance. "Oh, Sam!" She hiccupped. "I had no idea you were such a good dancer."

"You're pretty hot yourself," Sam said, steering her into a tango.

"You know, everyone thinks *Jessica's* the only one in the family who can dance," Elizabeth confided. "But I'm not so bad, am I? When I'm in the mood, anyway. And for some reason, I'm really in the mood tonight!"

They reversed direction abruptly in classic tango fashion, and collided head-on with Ken and Terri.

"'Scuse us," Sam said solemnly. "We're tangoing."

Elizabeth burst out laughing. "Is that a word?"

"Sure, it's a word. We're *doing* it, aren't we?"

This witty response made Elizabeth laugh even harder. Terri and Ken stared at her, then moved out of the way, shaking their heads.

"How 'bout the Charleston?" Elizabeth said to Sam. "Do you know how to do that?"

"Sure, like in that movie where the kids are dancing in the gym and the floor opens up and they fall into a swimming pool."

"Yeah, like that!" Elizabeth started doing the Charleston, or what she thought was a fair imitation of it, anyway. She got going so fast, she started to feel dizzy. "Uh-oh!" she cried to Sam. "Watch out. I think the floor's opening!"

Sam grabbed her to pull her aside to safety. "Phew, that was close," he declared.

Elizabeth noticed that a group of kids standing near the edge of the dance floor were staring at her and Sam. "The floor was opening," she explained to them. "We almost fell into the swimming pool!"

Just then, someone tapped Elizabeth on the shoulder. Elizabeth whirled around, tripping over her own feet in the process. Sam caught her just in time to keep her from falling flat on her face.

Enid peered at Elizabeth, her brow furrowed. "Liz, are you all right?" she asked.

"Sure!" Elizabeth giggled. "I'm just clumsy. Aren't I, Sam?"

"You're clumsy," he agreed amiably. "You're a good dancer, but you're *awfully* clumsy."

Enid glanced at Hugh. He shrugged. "So, you don't need any . . . help?" Enid asked.

Elizabeth shook her head. "No, but I'm glad I ran into you. I want to apologize." Sentimental tears leaped to Elizabeth's eyes as she recalled how mean she had been to Enid, her very best friend. "I'm sorry, Enid." She gripped Enid's arm, gazing earnestly into her eyes. "I didn't mean to say bad things about Hugh." Elizabeth turned to Hugh. "Really, Hugh. I don't have anything against you because you're from Big Mesa."

"Er, thanks, Elizabeth," mumbled Hugh.

Elizabeth sniffled. "So we're friends again?" she asked Enid hopefully.

"Of course. We were always friends," Enid assured her. "But, Elizabeth . . ."

"We can talk later," Elizabeth promised. "Right now, Sam and I have to dance. Don't we, Sam?"

"Yes, we have to dance," he confirmed.

He swept her back onto the dance floor. "I'm having a *fabulous* time," Elizabeth told him. "I wasn't when I first got here, you know."

"How come?" wondered Sam.

"Because all I could think about was whether or not I'd get to be Prom Queen—whether I'd beat Jessica. And you know what else?"

"What?"

"I don't care anymore!" Elizabeth proclaimed. "It's so stupid, all this competition. Who needs it? It isn't *me.*"

"It's not?"

"No. It's Jessica." Elizabeth pointed. "I mean, look at her! She's good at this sort of thing. She was *born* to be Prom Queen."

Sam craned his neck to look at Jessica, who was apparently in the middle of telling a very funny story to Amy, Barry, Jean, and Scott. All five were laughing uproariously. "She *was* born to be Prom Queen," Sam agreed wistfully.

"I don't *really* want the title," Elizabeth continued. "I don't know why I let myself get so carried away! I don't need to change—I don't need to compete with Jessica. I like myself just the way I am!"

Sam stopped dancing so he could rest his hands on Elizabeth's shoulders. "You're terrific just the way you are," he told her, putting his face close to hers. "I mean, *Jessica* is wonderful." He cast a mournful look in his girlfriend's direction. "I love her."

Elizabeth sniffled. "I know."

"But you're . . . you're . . ." Sam searched for the word. "You're *you*. Don't change, Liz."

"Oh, Sam!" Elizabeth flung her arms around his neck. "I'm not going to. C'mon."

Grabbing his hand, she dragged him toward the ticket table. "Andrea, Patty!" she yelled.

The two girls looked up in surprise.

"I have an announcement." Elizabeth licked her lips, which suddenly felt as dry as sandpaper. "As of this moment, I am wif—wif—" She stopped. *Why can't I say this stupid word?*

"Wif*drawing* from the race for Prom Queen."

"You're *what*?" said Andrea.

"Dropping out," Elizabeth translated. She talked extra loud so Andrea and Patty would be sure to understand her. "So, tell people not to vote for me. I won't accept the crown." She turned to Sam. "Let Jessica have it, right?"

"Let Jessica have it," he agreed enthusiastically.

"It doesn't matter to me that she'll get to go to Brazil. And so what if she screws up as smokes—*spokes*person for the rain forest. So what!"

"So what!" Sam echoed.

"Got that, girls?" Elizabeth asked Andrea and Patty.

Andrea and Patty exchanged an uncertain glance. "Yeah . . . we got it," said Patty.

"Good." Elizabeth felt as if a huge weight had been lifted from her shoulders. *What a relief!* She grabbed Sam's hand again, hauling him back toward the dance floor. "C'mon. Now we can *really* start having fun!"

At ten o'clock, Winston took center stage again. The Queen of the Jungle Prom was about to be chosen!

Jessica, standing with Amy, Lila, and Robin, covered her ears with her hands and squeezed her eyes shut. "I can't stand to listen," she wailed. "Tell me when it's over!"

A hush fell over the crowd of students in the gymnasium. Then, as if from a long distance, Jessica heard Winston mumble something into the microphone.

Suddenly, she was almost knocked off her feet. Her friends were jumping up and down and trying to hug her. Jessica dropped her hands and opened her eyes.

"You won!" Robin squealed. "You're the Prom Queen!"

"Me?" squeaked Jessica.

"You!" cried Amy. "Congratulations, Jess!"

All around her, her schoolmates were clapping, yelling, and whistling. *For me,* Jessica thought, a sob of joy escaping her. *They picked me!*

It was the moment she had been waiting for for weeks, and now that it had arrived, she was too stunned to move. Her friends had to push her toward the stage.

As Winston reached down a hand to help her up, the murmurs of some girls standing nearby penetrated Jessica's happy haze.

"She might have won anyway," one of the girls hissed to her companions, "but it sure didn't hurt that Elizabeth dropped out at the last minute!"

Dropped out? Jessica stood on the stage, facing the crowd of cheering, rowdy students. She forced a wide, bright smile and waved at her fans in mechanical Miss America style. But the heart had been carved out of her triumph.

Elizabeth dropped out! But why? Jessica wondered. She searched the crowd, trying to find her sister. Had Elizabeth withdrawn because she was drunk and knew she couldn't walk a straight line, let alone keep a crown on her head? Or did she have another reason?

A stiff smile on her face, Olivia approached Jessica, carrying a crown made of fragrant, tropical flowers. To the sound of ever more deafening cheers, Olivia placed the crown on Jessica's head.

Her dream had come true; the Prom Queen's crown, and the trip to Brazil, was hers. Jessica waited for the rush of joyous emotion, for the electric charge of victory. But instead she felt . . . nothing.

What am I doing up here? she asked herself. *Why don't I feel as thrilled about this as I thought I would?*

The answer was obvious; she couldn't hide from it. In her mind, she saw again the bloodshot eyes of the guy from Big Mesa; she saw him pour the liquor into her cup. And then she saw herself spiking Elizabeth's punch. She had done it on purpose; she had gotten her sister drunk.

I sabotaged my sister's chance to become Queen, Jessica realized. And not only that; in doing so, she had probably also destroyed the fragile remnants of their battle-scarred relationship.

Suddenly, the crown of flowers on her hair felt heavy; its sweetness smothered her. *Was it really worth it?* Jessica wondered.

Todd had been a little surprised when Elizabeth took off for the dance floor with Sam, instead of hanging around near the stage where he was stuck posing for pictures and drawing raffle winners. *At least she's loosening up,* he supposed; that was better than standing around, chewing her fingernails.

But maybe loosening up wasn't the word for it. As he'd handed out a couple of Environmental Alert T-shirts with bright silk-screened rain-forest designs, Todd had looked over at the dance floor . . . just in time to see Sam grab Elizabeth by the waist and flip her head over heels. Miraculously, she landed on her feet and they went on dancing three times as fast as anybody else. *Boy, the adrenaline must really be pumping!* Todd thought, amazed. He had never seen Elizabeth put on a show like that.

Now, as the walls of the gym echoed with applause and Jessica joined him on the stage, Todd tried hard to disguise his disappointment that Elizabeth hadn't been chosen Queen. "Congratulations, Jess," he said with false heartiness as they sat down side by side on their jungle thrones. "You must be pretty psyched!"

"Yeah," she mumbled.

Someone pointed a camera at him. Todd grinned obligingly. "I have to admit," he said to Jessica through his teeth, "I'm just a *little* surprised that Elizabeth wasn't . . . I mean, from the way people have been talking at school . . . Don't get me wrong, Jess. I think you're a great Prom Queen. But I really thought Elizabeth would get picked."

Jessica glanced quickly at Todd. "Well, actually, as it turns out, she—"

"Hey, Jessica, over here!" shouted Allen Walters, a photographer for *The Oracle*.

Jessica turned to face Allen, tipping her head coquettishly and flashing her most dazzling smile. As the flashbulbs popped, Todd scanned the room, searching for Elizabeth. It wasn't the end of the world, not being named Prom Queen, but she'd really had her heart set on it. After all the hard work, all the anticipation and anxiety, this had to be a huge letdown for her. *I hope she's not too upset,* Todd worried.

At that moment, he spotted Elizabeth, standing at the edge of the dance floor with Sam. They weren't even facing the stage; it looked as if neither of them could care less that Jessica had just been crowned Prom Queen. No, they weren't facing the stage—they were facing each other.

As Todd watched in astonishment, Elizabeth flung both her arms around Sam's neck. At the same time, Sam wrapped both of *his* arms around her waist. Todd blinked. Was he seeing things?

No; Elizabeth and Sam were locked in a tight embrace.

Todd's heart dropped like a stone to his feet. He wanted to jump up, to run to them and wrench them apart, but the shock weighed him down, pinning him to the throne. *What's going on?* he thought, baffled and pained. *How could she do this to me?*

"These'll be great," Allen said as he clicked a few more shots. "You're going to be on the front page, Jessica!"

Jessica continued to smile, but for some reason the prospect of getting her picture in the paper didn't gratify her the way it usually did. As soon as Allen used up his roll of film, she faced forward again, looking down from her throne into the crowd.

People had started dancing again; the prom went on as before. With one exception, Jessica realized: Elizabeth and Sam were no longer dancing like maniacs. Their arms wrapped around each other, they stumbled across the floor, charting an erratic path toward the table where they had left their things.

She can barely walk, Jessica observed, biting her lip. *She can barely* stand*!*

What on earth had Jessica done to Elizabeth?

Seventeen

"This Prom King and Queen stuff is really lame," Bruce grumbled to Ronnie and Charlie as they paced the floor of the gymnasium. He shot a disdainful look at Todd; he was still steaming over Todd's bossiness earlier in the evening. "You couldn't *pay* me to sit up there like a bozo on that stupid throne."

"You've just got a case of sour grapes, Bruce," interjected Lila, who was passing by and overheard the remark. "Because you probably got only one vote for Prom King—your own!"

"I don't see *you* wearing a crown," Bruce countered.

Lila extended one slender arm, glittering with

bracelets and rings. "I have plenty of jewelry already," she told him.

"But money can't buy you love, eh, Lila?" sneered Bruce. "What, was Rent-A-Date all out of your usual brand of boy toy?"

"For your information, I *chose* to come to the dance alone," Lila said haughtily. "What's *your* excuse, Bruce? Andrea finally get fed up with your macho behavior? Or did your inflatable doll pop when you pinned on her corsage?"

Charlie snickered. Bruce silenced him with a glare, then turned back to Lila. "Just watch out," Bruce advised her. "There are a lot of single guys roaming around here tonight, and they're not all as chivalrous as me. I bet some of these Big Mesa guys would make our friend John Pfeifer look tame."

Gotcha, Bruce thought with satisfaction as he saw the flicker of apprehension in Lila's eyes. What a pleasure to put a cork in her big mouth, for once!

Bruce, Ronnie, and Charlie resumed stalking among the dancers, their eyes darting from student to student, on the lookout for Big Mesa troublemakers. They had spent the whole evening patrolling, and even though there had been no problems so far, Bruce had no intention of letting down his guard.

That's what sunk us that night at the beach, he remembered. *We looked the other way and they blew us out of the water.* Nope, since the bunch of idiots known as the Prom Committee were allowing Big Mesa kids into the dance, somebody had to stay on the alert—*somebody* had to be ready to take the law into his own hands.

Suddenly, a commotion at the other end of the gym caught Bruce's attention. "Look, guys." He pointed toward the sea of bobbing heads and waving arms. "What's going on down there?"

Ronnie shrugged. "It's just people dancing."

"The party's getting pretty wild," Charlie agreed.

Bruce frowned, his shoulders tensing and his fingers tightening into fists at his side. "I don't think so," he said. "Something's up."

Just then, angry shouts rose up above the sounds of revelry. Like a tidal wave gaining momentum as it tore through the ocean, a surge of bodies powered through the crowd, splintering it. Bruce recognized the boys running toward him, some of them wearing red and black striped school ties. The blood heated in Bruce's veins and he shouted as loud as he could. "Big Mesa!"

The Big Mesa boys raced through the center of the gym, hurling taunts and throwing random punches as they went. Immediately, Bruce guessed where they were heading. "They're going outside, to the football field!" he yelled to Ronnie and Charlie. "C'mon, start rounding people up. We're going to need reinforcements!"

Bruce sprinted into the ranks of confused and excited Sweet Valley High students. Putting his fingers to his mouth, he gave a piercing wolf whistle. "Ken, Michael, Tad—let's go!" he commanded.

Abandoning their dates, a dozen boys rushed to Bruce's side, with dozens more following on their heels.

His heart pounding like a jackhammer from an enormous burst of adrenaline, Bruce led the stampede toward the door, and toward the fight that was sure to follow when they met their foes on the field. All the dark, inexplicable anger, all the frustration that he had been bottling up inside himself for weeks—for months—was ready to burst out. It was time for the showdown.

Jessica jumped down from the stage and started to make her way through the frenzied crowd, aiming for the spot where she had last glimpsed Elizabeth.

"Jessica, congratulations!" shrieked Caroline Pearce, grabbing Jessica's arm. "I just *knew* you'd win. I'm so happy for you!"

Jessica shook herself free of Caroline's clawlike fingernails, not even bothering to reply. *I've got to get to Elizabeth,* she thought fiercely. *I've got to make sure she's all right.*

"Way to go, Jessica," somebody shouted. "Hey, Prom Queen, congratulations!" another voice called out.

Jessica ignored them all. Twisting like an eel, she made her way forward. But her progress was slow. The gym was packed, and for some reason, everyone seemed to be heading in the other direction; Jessica felt like a salmon swimming upstream. But she had to keep going; she had to find Elizabeth.

"Excuse me. Excuse me, will you please *move*?" Jessica cried. *What a stupid thing to do!* she berated herself as she shoved her way through a knot of people. She really wasn't sure who was more of an idiot: herself for spiking Elizabeth's punch, or Elizabeth for not even realizing she was drunk.

It had been an impulsive move; Jessica hadn't really thought through the consequences. As a result, Elizabeth was trashed and the whole school knew it. Now another distressing possibility occurred to Jessica. *Uh-oh. What if Mom and Dad find out?*

It'll be OK, though, Jessica told herself. *I'll*

make it up to her. I'll take care of her; I'll sit her down and get her a cup of black coffee. She'll sober up; she'll be all right.

Finally, there was a break in the crowd. Jessica darted forward just in time to see her sister leave the gym, wobbling through the door with Sam in tow. *Where on earth are they going?* Jessica wondered, looking around now for Todd.

Todd wasn't far behind her; he must have ditched the stage around the same time she did. And for the same reason, Jessica guessed—he was tracking Elizabeth too. As Jessica caught his eye, Todd nodded curtly in the direction of the exit, indicating that he had also seen Elizabeth and Sam leave. Pantomiming a question, he lifted his hands and shouted something, and though Jessica couldn't hear his words over the clamor of the crowd, she could read his lips. "What's going on?"

Todd looked angry, upset, and very confused. *He doesn't know she's drunk,* Jessica realized. Of course; he'd been busy on the stage, with no opportunity to hear the rumors racing around on the gym floor.

She had to communicate the urgency of the situation; she was going to need Todd's help. Jessica put her hands to her mouth, forming a miniature megaphone. "Trouble!" she yelled at the top of her lungs.

Todd cocked his head. He hadn't quite gotten it.

Jessica formed a capital "T" with the forefinger of each hand. She opened her mouth to shout again. But just as she thought she was starting to get the message across, a mob of revelers propelled her back toward the stage, while another irresistible current swept Todd in the other direction.

What a zoo! Lila thought, flattening herself against the wall so she wouldn't be trampled. No one was dancing or having a good time anymore. Instead, people were shouting and running, some toward the exit that led out to the football field and others toward the doorway that connected the gymnasium to the rest of the high school. Some of the students looked angry and eager, others looked panicked and frightened. The Jungle Prom had turned into an even worse disaster than the beach party a few weeks earlier.

It's as good a time as any for me to leave, Lila decided, assessing the situation. She really didn't want to stick around if there was going to be some kind of brawl, and it definitely looked like one was brewing. Bruce had talked about a gang of Big Mesa guys, just waiting for a chance to go on a rampage. . . .

Taking a deep breath, Lila plunged into the stream of bodies. She figured she would go wherever the current took her; she could make her way out to the parking lot through either door.

Clutching her purse tightly under her arm, she went as fast as her high heels would allow her. On all sides, people pressed against her, jostling her. "Ouch!" Lila yelped as someone elbowed her in the ribs. "Hey, watch it, creep!"

She tried to create some more space for herself by sticking her own elbows out at right angles. But it was no use. People pressed closer and closer. . . .

Suddenly, Lila was swamped by a wave of claustrophobia. She breathed faster, trying to suck in some air, trying to quiet her heart, which had jumped into her throat, threatening to choke her.

A body brushed hard against hers . . . a boy's body. Lila's eyes leaped to his face. The boy was a total stranger . . . someone from Big Mesa? Was it an accident, or had he done it on purpose?

I've really got to get out of here, Lila realized, her annoyance starting to verge on desperation. Glancing anxiously over her shoulder, she quickened her pace.

Jessica strained to keep sight of Todd for as long as she could, but in only a matter of seconds he was swallowed up by the boisterous, frenetic crowd. *Shoot, I'll never find him now!*

This could get dangerous, Jessica speculated as once again she tried to wrestle her way through the sea of bodies that blocked her path to the door. She had heard about people getting trampled to death at huge, overcrowded rock concerts or sporting events. Who would've expected the Jungle Prom to turn into such a fiasco?

But she had to keep fighting—there was no time to lose. *Elizabeth is trashed and making a total fool of herself,* Jessica thought, *and she's doing it with my boyfriend!* Jessica couldn't afford to lose sight of them for long. In the messed-up state they were in, and with the prom getting so out of hand, absolutely anything could happen to them.

Suddenly, the crowd started moving with Jessica instead of against her. The shift in momentum knocked her forward; the crown of flowers slipped from her head. Reaching out, she managed to catch it just as it was about to be crushed under somebody's heel. Clutching the crown, Jessica raced for the door. At last—she was outside!

After the heat and confusion in the gymnasium, the cool night air was soothing and refreshing. Jessica paused to catch her breath. Then she looked around her. Where had Elizabeth and Sam gone?

Most of the crowd pouring from the gym was aiming for the football field. Jessica squinted into the dark. She could see flashes of white—the shirts of guys who had stripped off their tuxedo jackets in preparation for a fight. Angry shouts echoed back to her. It could mean only one thing, Jessica knew. The tension had exploded and the long-expected clash with Big Mesa High was at hand.

I told you so, Jessica said silently to her sister. *I knew we shouldn't have let those thugs come to our prom!* But the fight didn't really concern her . . . unless, of course, Elizabeth and Sam had gone off in that direction.

Jessica whirled, looking all around her. "Elizabeth!" she shouted. "Sam! Where are you?"

A smaller stream of students diverged from the main crowd; they were heading to the parking lot. Calling it a night, Jessica guessed. She focused on a couple of people a hundred yards down the sidewalk, a boy and a girl just entering the parking lot. The moonlight shimmered on their hair—both were blond. The boy was tall, an athlete probably, with broad shoulders. And against the dark fabric of the night, the girl's dress seemed to float, a ghostly paler-than-pale blue. . . .

"Liz! Sam!" Jessica shrieked. "Wait up!"

Arm in arm, Elizabeth and Sam weaved on.

They didn't hear her; they didn't stop. Jessica had no choice but to sprint after them as fast as her high heels would allow her.

She and Sam had parked the Jeep under a tree near the entrance to the parking lot; Elizabeth and Todd had driven over in Todd's BMW. But apparently Elizabeth was carrying her set of Jeep keys with her. As Jessica watched in horror, her sister headed straight for the vehicle . . . and climbed into the driver's seat.

"Ohmigod," Jessica gasped. "Elizabeth can't drive in this condition!"

As Sam hopped into the passenger's side, the Jeep's engine rumbled to life. "Elizabeth!" Jessica shouted at the top of her lungs. "Sam! Stop!"

She hurried forward, waving her arms in a desperate attempt to get their attention. But if they heard her or saw her, they didn't heed her. Elizabeth backed out of the parking space, much too fast. Jessica had nearly reached the Jeep when she tripped, catching her heel in a crack in the pavement. She stumbled and fell forward onto her hands. In that instant, Elizabeth stepped on the gas and the Jeep roared off.

Standing up, Jessica waved frantically after them. But it was too late. They were gone.

Jessica turned, brushing the gravel from her

hands, her eyes stinging with tears from the pain. Angrily kicking off the shoes that had slowed her down, Jessica retrieved her bedraggled Queen's crown and ran back toward the gym in her stocking feet. Now more than ever, she needed Todd's help—she needed Todd's *car*.

Just as she reached the door, Todd emerged from it. "Jess!" he shouted. "What's happening?"

"They took off," Jessica panted. "In the Jeep. We have to go after them, Todd. Elizabeth is—" The word died on her lips. She couldn't bring herself to say it, to confess to Todd what she had done to her own twin sister. "She's . . . not herself. She doesn't know what she's doing. We have to catch up with her before—before—"

Jessica stopped, choked by tears. Todd stared at her. There was no mistaking her urgency, even if he didn't understand the reason behind it.

"OK," he said gruffly, reaching into his pocket for his keys. "Let's go!"

The excitement and confusion in the gymnasium had grown into a frenzy. "There's a huge fight," Lila heard one Sweet Valley boy say to another. "Out on the football field. About fifty guys from Big Mesa, supposedly. C'mon, Bruce could probably use some help!"

Lila stared after the boys as they charged toward the exit. If there was a huge fight going on outside, she really didn't want to get caught up in the middle of it.

She tried to change her course, unsuccessfully; she was hemmed in on all sides. A hulky guy stood in front of her like a wall, cutting off her escape route. "Can I get by you?" Lila asked him. But her voice was lost in the din.

This'll make him move, she thought grimly, jabbing down on the top of his foot with her spike heel. With a yelp, the boy grabbed his foot and hopped sideways.

Lila shoved by him, only to be blocked by another immovable mass of bodies. Four girls she didn't know stood shoulder to shoulder in a face-off with four other girls whom Lila recognized as Sweet Valley High seniors. Lila stared at the odd sight in fascination.

"What, are you too chicken to go out to the field?" taunted one of the strange girls, a statuesque platinum blond.

Bad dye job, Lila thought, disdainfully eyeing the girl's dark roots.

"Yeah, are you scared to see your wimpy boyfriends get beaten to a pulp?" another Big Mesa girl chimed in.

"We're not scared of anything," one of the Sweet Valley girls retorted. "But we *are* sick to our stomachs from having to look at your ugly faces. Don't you think you'd better run back to Big Mesa and crawl into your coffins before the sun rises? Or are those plastic fangs?"

"Ooh, you . . . !" The first Big Mesa girl lunged at the girl from Sweet Valley, her friends struggling to restrain her.

I do not *want to get caught in the middle of a catfight,* Lila thought, quickly backing away from them. But was there anywhere she could go to be safe? The tension in the gymnasium was palpable—and building. It had entered everyone, male and female. A force beyond anyone's control seemed to have taken over the night . . . and Lila didn't like it one bit.

As she turned to run in a different direction, someone gripped her shoulders. Lila emitted a strangled squeak.

Then she saw who it was. "Oh," she gasped, going limp with relief. "Nathan, it's you!"

"Lila, are you all right?" Nathan's forehead wrinkled with concern. "Things are really getting out of hand. We had to call the police, and they're on their way. In the meantime, I'm telling everyone I see just to leave the gym as quickly and quietly as possible."

"That's what I'm trying to do!" Lila explained. "But it's like a riot or something. There are so many people, and everyone's pushing and shoving . . ."

Lila stopped as she realized her voice was shaking. In fact, her whole body was shaking.

Nathan peered into her face. "C'mon," he said, his tone firm and reassuring. "Let's get you out of here, OK?"

Taking Lila's arm, Nathan led her quickly toward the door, using his own body to shield her from the increasingly rough crowd. Lila trailed after him, feeling light-headed with relief and gratitude. *Thank goodness for Nathan,* she thought. *He's the only sane, grown-up, responsible person in this whole place.* She could count on him to look out for her, just as he always did. She should have known that sooner or later he would come to her rescue!

Finally, they reached the door that opened into the rest of the school building. Nathan pushed through it, and Lila scurried after him into the corridor. Dozens of students had preceded them into the hallway and more pressed close behind them. Was there any way to escape the crush? Lila wondered.

Apparently, Nathan had the same thought. He looked around, then focused on the half-open door of a nearby classroom. "In here," he commanded, steering her into the empty room.

Lila stumbled into the room, panting from the exertion. Nathan stepped in after her and closed the door, shutting out the noise and commotion in the hallway.

They were alone in the hushed, dimly lit classroom. Suddenly, Lila could hear the rapid, ragged sound of her own breathing; she could hear her heart hammering against her chest.

Nathan turned his back to the closed door. "It's nice and quiet in here, isn't it?" he said softly, taking a step toward her.

Lila's tear-filled eyes widened. As she stared, blinking, Nathan's face seemed to blur and the image of another face flashed across her consciousness. John Pfeifer, a boy she had liked and trusted; John Pfeifer, the night he took her up to Miller's Point, the night he tried to . . .

Why did Nathan bring me here? she wondered, fear sweeping over her like a tidal wave. *What's he going to do to me?*

He could only have one motive, Lila realized. He wasn't trying to protect her at all! He wasn't the kind, trustworthy man he seemed to be; he'd only been pretending to care about her so that he could take advantage of her vulnerability. He'd been waiting for a moment like this, all these weeks. . . .

"Lila?" Nathan asked questioningly.

Lila clapped her hand to her mouth, suppressing a scream.

"Lila, what is it?" A worried frown shadowed Nathan's face. "You're safe now—it's OK." He took another step toward her, his hand extended as if to touch her arm.

Lila leaped backward, the bloodcurdling scream ripping from her throat.

SVH

Eighteen

Bruce sprinted onto the football field, his lean, muscular legs pumping like pistons. He tore off his tuxedo jacket and bow tie as he ran, flinging them carelessly aside. Then he stopped for a second to kick off his tight, creaky dress shoes and yank off his socks. Now he could feel the grass and dirt between his toes; he pushed up his sleeves, baring his arms.

On the field, the guys from Big Mesa were waiting, also having shed their jackets and ties in anticipation of a fight. They stood, tense, tough, and silent, a wall of bodies ready to explode into violent action.

This is what I want, Bruce thought as he raced toward them, his eyes burning. His pace didn't falter for an instant; he wasn't afraid in the least. He'd never been much into down-and-dirty physical brawling; his deadly wit and sharp tongue were his preferred weapons. But tonight he felt as if after months of blind, fruitless searching, of banging his head against the wall, he was finally pointed in the right direction. *This is what I've been looking for.*

"C'mon," Bruce yelled over his shoulder to the Sweet Valley boys who were hot on his heels. "Let's show 'em what we're made of!"

With shouts and grunts, the two groups clashed. Bruce was first into the fray, his fists flying. *Thud*—he landed a punch in a Big Mesa guy's gut, then followed it up with a left to the jaw. Bruce felt something warm and sticky run between his tightly clenched fingers: blood. It didn't matter; he only knew he wanted more of it. It blotted out the dry emptiness that had tormented him for so long.

Bruce fought on, fueled by a sense of pride, purpose, and camaraderie. He was battling side by side with his friends. Out of the corners of his eyes, he could see Ronnie and Charlie, Michael and Jim, Ken and Tad, all pummeling their Big Mesa opponents. Bruce decked one boy, then leaped onto another, delivering a rain of sharp, well-aimed blows. The boy's knees buckled; he started to crumple to the ground.

Bruce drew back his right leg, ready to finish

the bum off with a kick to the shins. But at that moment, he felt his own knees turn to jelly. An excruciating pain exploded across his shoulders and flooded through his whole body. Bruce pitched face-forward onto the grass. He'd been hit!

For a second, he was stunned by the blow. Then he managed to roll over, instinctively preparing himself to ward off another one.

And the second blow was sure to come. Looking up, Bruce saw a huge guy looming over him, his massive form blocking out the star-speckled night sky. The guy raised his arms and with them a wooden baseball bat.

He could kill me! Bruce realized, lifting his arms to his face, hoping to deflect at least a measure of the weapon's deadly force.

He didn't even have time to scramble out of the way, but at the same time, the moment that the bat hung suspended over his head seemed to last forever. Bruce waited for the blow to fall—for the crunch of wood against bone—the pain. And then . . .

A voice. "No, stop!" someone cried.

Bruce glimpsed slender pale arms reaching out to grab the Big Mesa guy from behind. "Craig, don't," the girl pleaded. "He's down already—he's hurt. Please, just leave him alone."

Bruce dropped his arms. He didn't care that he

was leaving himself wide open to attack; he had to see the owner of that sweet, otherworldly voice.

The girl gazed down at him, her midnight-blue eyes glowing with pity and concern. With her pale face and swirling dark hair, she was like a vision, an angel. . . .

Regina? Bruce thought, his brain foggy and confused. No, it wasn't Regina. It was someone else, someone even more beautiful and rare.

The boy with the baseball bat had lowered his arms, momentarily dissuaded from continuing his assault on Bruce's prostrate form. The girl pushed past him and bent forward, stretching out a hand toward Bruce.

Her eyes met his, and even in the dark, they seemed to shine with an inner light and purity. He sensed that she wanted to comfort him, to touch him. Instinctively, he rose to meet her, fumbling to his knees, his own hand extended, his own eyes naked with need and hope.

He was almost there—their fingers nearly brushed. . . .

In the instant that followed, Bruce was aware of three things. A shout: "It's the cops! Let's get out of here!" A flashing shadow, as someone aimed a foot to kick him in the head. A sorrow as the girl, his savior, fell back, out of sight, out of reach. . . .

The vicious kick connected with Bruce's skull and he plunged into blackness.

Todd fumbled with his car keys, his fingers clumsy with panic.

"Hurry!" Jessica cried, hopping up and down next to the BMW. "Oh, Todd, hurry!"

Finally Todd succeeded in unlocking the car doors and he and Jessica tumbled into their seats. Not bothering to fasten his safety belt, Todd backed the car out of the parking space, its tires squealing a protest. Gunning the engine, he roared to the exit. "Which way did they go?" he asked tersely.

"That way," Jessica told him, pointing to the right. "Away from town. Oh, hurry, Todd. We've got to catch them!"

As he stepped on the gas, Todd glanced at Jessica out of the corner of his eye. She sat staring straight ahead with desperate eyes—unaware of her tangled hair, her torn dress, her bare feet, and the crumpled Prom Queen's crown she held on her lap. *There's something really wrong here,* Todd thought. It wasn't just a case of Elizabeth running off for a fling with Sam, as horrible as that would be. Jessica wasn't angry or jealous; she was scared.

"What's going on?" Todd asked her. "Tell me, Jessica?"

Jessica turned toward him, tears streaming down her face. "Oh, it's terrible," she said, sobbing. "Elizabeth is *drunk*, Todd. She shouldn't be driving. Oh, why didn't I stop her?"

"Drunk?" Todd exclaimed.

"Yes. She was drinking, and I think Sam may have been, too."

"Why on earth would she do such a thing?" Todd demanded, shocked and unbelieving. "Where did she get the booze? *Why?*" he repeated.

"I . . . I don't know," Jessica said, choking back another sob. "I don't know where they got it from. But that's why we have to catch up to them. We have to get them off the road. We have to stop them before—"

Five minutes from school, Todd hit a straight, open stretch of road in a woodsy, undeveloped part of town near the Secca Lake recreational area. They had a clear view ahead.

Jessica broke off her sentence. "There's someone up there!" she cried. "See the cars, Todd? I bet one of them's Elizabeth and Sam!"

Todd saw the cars, all right . . . and he also saw the flashing red and white lights. Wailing sirens pierced the still of the night. "They're police cars," he told Jessica. "There's been an accident!"

"Oh, God," Jessica said, her voice low.

The police had already cordoned off the site of the wreck with orange cones and torches. A number of passing cars had pulled over to the side of the road to look. *It's morbid, but they can't help themselves,* Todd thought. *They just have to see. . . .*

Todd braked, yanking the steering wheel in order to bring the BMW to a screeching halt on the gravel shoulder. He had to see too.

It won't be them—it can't be them, he prayed even as Jessica leaned forward in her seat, her eyes seeking a glimpse of the wrecked vehicle.

The vehicle had tumbled down the embankment. Now it lay still, its wheels to the sky, its big, dark body crumpled.

Todd's heart stopped beating.

"The Jeep!" Jessica screamed.

The hallways of the high school echoed with shouts and the thunder of running feet. "Everybody, stop where you are," a uniformed Sweet Valley police officer barked through a megaphone. "Settle down, before more of you get hurt."

But the panicked teenagers kept running, dashing up and down the corridor in a crazed attempt to escape both the brawling students and the police themselves, who were rounding up everyone they could.

Suddenly, above the general tumult, a single

high-pitched scream was heard—a long, drawn-out note of pure and absolute terror.

"It came from in there—that classroom!" one of the officers shouted to a colleague. "C'mon. I may need some help!"

Lunging, he kicked the door open. The two policemen burst into the classroom.

Lila, her face streaked with tears, was twisting away from Nathan's outstretched hands. "Help!" she shrieked desperately when she saw the police. "Get him away from me!"

"OK, buddy, back off," the first officer commanded Nathan.

Nathan stepped away from Lila, his face a mask of distress. "She's upset by the riot," he told the officers. "I'm her counselor—I'm chaperoning the dance. I was just trying to help—"

"No," Lila cried. "He didn't help me. He attacked me!"

"Lila!" Nathan gasped. "What . . . ?"

"Now, what happened?" the first officer asked Lila, his expression grim. "Take a deep breath."

Lila did as she was told, but she was still nearly incoherent. "He—he brought me in here to . . . He—he *attacked* me."

The words poured out in a breathless, sobbing

rush, but one of them came across loud and clear. *Attacked . . .*

The seriousness of her accusation galvanized the policemen. One strode to Nathan's side, and with a rapid gesture whipped both of Nathan's arms behind his back, pinning them securely. The other officer joined Lila, sheltering her from the sight.

"No," Nathan whispered, his face ashen. "No, Lila. That's not the way it happened at all. Tell them it wasn't like that."

"That's enough from you, pal," the officer snapped. "If you want to tell us your side of the story, you can do it down at the station. Now get moving."

The officer dragged Nathan toward the door. "My God, I'm her *counselor,*" Nathan proclaimed hoarsely. "I would never—"

The cop shoved Nathan forward roughly. "I said that's enough!"

Lila stared after Nathan, her entire body numb with shock. When the other police officer touched her arm to guide her from the room, she went passively.

"Do you feel strong enough to come to the station with me to register a formal complaint against your attacker?" he asked.

My attacker . . .

Lila gave a jerky, puppet's nod. "Yes," she said flatly.

The BMW came to a stop in a cloud of dust. Still clutching her crown, Jessica swung open the door and practically fell from the car. Together, coughing from the grit, she and Todd raced toward the crash site.

"Hold it right there," a police officer commanded, obstructing Jessica's path. "Don't you see the tape? Nobody's allowed beyond this point."

"But my sister!" Jessica shouted, struggling to get by him. "My boyfriend!"

Todd clutched the officer's arm. "What happened?" he demanded hoarsely. "Please, Officer. Those are our friends."

Compassion softened the cop's grim features. He turned to Todd, gripping the boy's shoulder with a large, strong hand. "Now, take it easy, son. . . ."

In the moment that the officer turned toward Todd, Jessica pushed past him and ran in the direction of the wrecked Jeep. The flashing lights made her dizzy; the sound of sirens was deafening. She stumbled, but regained her feet and hurried on, closer, closer. . . .

The ground sparkled all around her. *Snow?* Jessica wondered, confused. No—it was shattered glass. From the Jeep's windows, the windshield . . . And those dark spots on some of the fragments . . . was it blood?

A voice nearby stopped Jessica in her tracks.

"It's a darned shame," the man said to another onlooker. "No one could have made it through that crash alive. And so young. It's a darned shame," he repeated sadly.

No one could have made it through that crash alive. . . . No one . . .

The blood froze in Jessica's veins; the earth seemed to drop away beneath her feet.

"No!" she wailed, feeling herself crumple under the weight of an unbearable anguish.

Her hand went limp; the crown of bruised and broken flowers slipped from her fingers. *They were dead . . . they were both dead. . . .*

Jessica fell to her knees. "Elizabeth!" she sobbed into the unforgiving night. "Sam! *No!*"